DEVIL'S CHIMNEY

Eden Grey Mysteries
Book Three

Kim Fleet

SAPERE
BOOKS

DEVIL'S CHIMNEY

Published by Sapere Books.

20 Windermere Drive, Leeds, England, LS17 7UZ,
United Kingdom

saperebooks.com

ISBN: 978-1-913518-87-5

ACKNOWLEDGEMENTS

Writing a book is always a team effort, so huge thanks to Kelly, Sara-Jane and the RABSes, who read and commented on early drafts of the book; to my agent Jane for her help and support.

Thank you to the people who kindly allowed me to 'borrow' their names — you know who you are.

Big love to my cheerleading gang — Mike, Harriet, Wimsey and the Pink Panthers.

And last but not least, thank you to all my readers — I hope you enjoyed Eden's latest adventure.

PROLOGUE

Monday 7th March, 2016

Kate kicked the back of the pushchair, earning herself a disgruntled "Mummy!" from Jessica and a scowl. Both pleased her. Serve her right. Jessica had been a little sod all morning. Breakfast was punctuated by shrieking and ended with Weetabix hurled at the wall. There hadn't been time to mop it up before they had to hurry out the door to meet the other mums. Jessica had resisted being put in the pushchair, arching her back and holding her breath until she was purple in the face and snot bubbled from her nose.

Kate shoved the pushchair into Waitrose and headed for the café. The other mums were already there, clustered round a table of large lattes and babycinos, their off-road prams blocking the entrance. Her birth group, as she thought of them, women who'd been in the same prenatal classes and occupied the maternity ward together. Jessica drummed her feet until she was released from the pushchair, then made the most of her freedom, hurtling round and making that screeching noise that went right through your skull. Above the screech came a scream. Investigation revealed a red mark that was definitely a bite on another child's arm.

Kate lost it. She grabbed her bag and shoved into it the snacks, a bottle of water, a packet of wet wipes, her purse, and a plastic troll doll with purple hair, apologising over and over. Biting! Her child biting! Mortification drenched every cell in her body.

"It's all right," the child's mother said, her lips tight with hatred, and Kate knew that when she came in tomorrow the other mums would shun her, and point out Jessica to their brood, instructing in a stage whisper, "See that little girl? She *bites*."

Jessica, little madam, was nowhere to be seen. Kate stood, her gaze roving the café, until she was alerted by a kerfuffle at the drinks counter.

"Out you go, sweetie." A matronly woman shooed Jessica away from the cappuccino machine, where she'd evidently been trying to twist the lever on the steam frother. "Dangerous back here for little children."

Her eyes met Kate's and shame crawled over her. Bad mother.

"Come on! That's enough!" Kate grabbed Jessica's hand and hustled her to the pushchair. Jessica's limbs went stiff; she wouldn't be folded into the straps; she struggled and spat as Kate tried to fasten her in. "Stop it!"

A full-on tantrum was only seconds away. Desperate, Kate pushed out of the supermarket, and was clear by seconds when Armageddon erupted. Jessica paused for breath, gathering her resources for a fresh onslaught. Before she could unleash it, Kate shoved her face close to hers. "Shut up! Shut up! Shut up!"

Jessica blinked. That showed her, Kate thought with a stab of satisfaction, delirious at being off-script. Normally tantrums were met with sweet bribes, but she was in no mood for it today. Biting! A howl rose in her throat. She swallowed it down hard, tasting blood where her teeth nipped her tongue. Once she started, she'd howl forever.

For a long moment she considered abandoning Jessica and the pushchair and walking away, out of this life and back into her old life. The life where she wore a business suit instead of cargo pants crusted with masticated banana, and where people listened to her opinion; where she conducted employee appraisals and regularly drove to the Swindon office to kick people's arses.

There was a bench nearby. Behind it, a school playground full of kids in grey jumpers running round. All of them nice, polite children who never spat or bit. Kate sank onto the bench, planted her elbows on her knees and her face in her hands, and burst into tears. She wept until she was spent, then pulled out the wet wipes and mopped her face. A corner of wet wipe sliced her eyeball, making it sting. Wonderful, now to cap it all she'd have bloodshot eyes all day.

She glanced at Jessica. She'd rumbled down into sorry sobs, her face white with misery. Kate wiped her daughter's cheeks, crushed by a sudden pang of love.

"Tell you what, why don't we go and look at the fish?" she said. "Cheer us both up."

The fish was a large wooden model that hung at the far end of a shopping arcade in the centre of town. It was powered by a water clock: as the water fell, figures emerged from the clock, and the fish pirouetted gently, twenty feet above shoppers' heads. Every half hour, the model burst into action with a fanfare of 'I'm forever blowing bubbles' and bubbles streamed from the fish's mouth.

When Kate and Jessica got to the arcade, it was almost half past and there was already a cluster of about twenty mums and pre-schoolers waiting. She nodded to the faces she'd seen here before. The bubble fish was regular, free, and endlessly entertaining if you were under five.

Kate inched to the front and squatted beside the pushchair. "Watch the fish, Jessie," she said.

The minute hand moved on a pace, and there was a tinny spurt of 'I'm forever blowing bubbles'. The fish spun, and a gust came out of its mouth.

Kate's eyes streamed instantly. Another gush from the fish and her throat was on fire. Around her, children and mums coughed and roared, their eyes flooding.

Grabbing the pushchair, she wheeled it round and hurtled back down the arcade. Her eyes burned and she could barely see. Dimly she was aware of others running, too. The arcade echoed with screams.

Kate rammed into a shop, grabbed the bottle of water from her bag and splashed it over Jessica's face. Jessica shrieked and ground her fists in her eyes.

"Don't! You'll make it worse!" Kate fought to keep Jessica's hands from her face, sluicing water into her eyes, then her own.

"What's happened?" A shop assistant approached.

"Something in our eyes," Kate said. "Get some water."

Others crowded into the shop, crying and choking. Bottles of water appeared and suddenly everyone was dousing their eyes and gulping water down burning throats.

"Jessica? Jessica!" Kate's fingers scrabbled to unstrap her. Jessica's lips were turning blue. Twisting aside, she shouted, "Get an ambulance!"

Jessica flopped in her arms, her eyes half-closed, her chest motionless. Kate put her cheek to her daughter's lips: no breath stirred her skin.

"She's not breathing!" she screamed.

A woman muscled her way through the chaos. "I'm a first aider."

Together they laid Jessica on the floor and the woman pressed her fingers into her neck. Kate's hands fluttered uselessly over her daughter.

"Jessie! Wake up!"

"She needs CPR." The woman hesitated. "I've never done a child before."

"Help her!"

The woman knelt close to Jessica, linked her fingers above her breast bone, and started chest compressions. Then breaths. Compressions. Breaths.

Oh God, let her be all right. Kate bargained with the universe for an eternity until the paramedics marched in, saviours in green. But by then it was too late.

This time, she didn't hold back the howl.

PART ONE: 2016

CHAPTER ONE

So it had come to this, Eden thought with a pang. So much for her firearms training, fluency in Russian, and passing her high speed driving with flying colours; she was now one step away from hunting down allotment saboteurs and tracking stolen garden gnomes. She looked out across the cemetery and gathered the remains of her patience.

"Tell me again why you're worried," she asked Mrs Wakefield, her putative new client.

At a full head shorter, Susan Wakefield had to tip her head back to look into Eden's face. "It started so suddenly," she said. "Nothing for years, then this." She pointed to a headstone.

Ye gods, Eden thought, brought in to track down someone leaving flowers on a grave. Whatever next, finding out who farted in a curry house?

"Mrs Wakefield," she started, carefully, "you know that if you engage me to investigate this, I will have to charge you my usual rate, and you could end up spending a lot of money for nothing."

"I've only myself to please," Susan said. She pressed her hand against the headstone. "It's the last thing I can do for my boy." Her eyes were suddenly fierce with tears. "Someone knows something, Eden, that's why they're leaving these notes. They want to confess. I have to know why."

"All right," Eden said. She pulled a camera out of her backpack and rattled off a series of shots of the grave and that day's offering. The grave was a simple one, dwarfed by its marble monstrosity neighbours: angels with eight foot wing spans, praying cherubs, and huge obelisks at unlikely angles. The headstone that was causing Mrs Wakefield such angst read simply, 'Philip Jonathan Wakefield. 12th December, 1968 — 25th August, 1981. A life cut short.'

On the grave mound lay a bunch of orange roses swaddled in cellophane, with a hand-written tag that said, 'Sorry.' Beside them were the bedraggled remains of a dozen pink carnations, again with a card that said merely, 'Sorry.' Eden zoomed in on the flowers and photographed the wrappings and the message. The carnations still bore their supermarket price ticket; the roses were from a local florist.

"Do you want to leave the flowers here?" Eden asked.

"Yes," Susan Wakefield said, with a defiant thrust of her jaw. "I don't want them to suspect we're onto them."

Despite her irritation at this bullshit commission, Eden hid a smile. TV crime dramas had fostered many a client for her over the years, and if they wanted to talk the talk, who was she to stop them.

"Do you want some time alone?" she asked, slotting the camera back in her bag. Mrs Wakefield simply shook her head in response and Eden led the way back to the car park and drove her home. "I'll take some details and get cracking," she said, as they pulled up outside Mrs Wakefield's house.

It was a neat Edwardian terraced house behind the Bath Road area of Cheltenham. A short path lined with lavender led to the front door. The rest of the front garden was filled with evergreen hebes. Mrs Wakefield showed her into a small sitting room dominated by a dark brown leather settee. The fireplace held a coal effect gas fire, surrounded by the original tiles in deep greens and reds.

Eden took a seat and opened her notebook, pulling the cap off her pen with her teeth. "Let's start at the beginning," she said.

"It was Philip's birthday," Susan said. "I always go on his birthday, sometimes at New Year. And I go in July, that was his dad's birthday." A spasm crossed her face and she hunted in her sleeve for a tissue — a square of kitchen roll — and blew her nose. "Maybe I should go more often, but it's been so long. Just because I don't visit his grave doesn't mean I've forgotten him. I'll never forget him."

"Of course you won't," Eden said, gently. Her mind flicked back to the dates on the headstone. "So that would have been the twelfth of December?"

"As soon as I got to the grave I could see someone else had been there. There were dead flowers in the vase, and a bunch of roses, fresh ones, wrapped up lying on the grave, and there was a card."

"Message?"

"'Sorry'. That's what they've all said. 'Sorry'."

"What did you think at the time?"

"I wondered who it was. Thirty-five years I've been visiting Philip's grave and I've never seen any other flowers on it. But as it was Philip's birthday I assumed it was someone who remembered him."

"Family?"

"All gone now. And those that are left wouldn't remember, not after this time."

"Philip's father?"

"Died two years ago."

"I'm sorry," Eden said. The words always sounded hollow, however sincerely she felt them. "And when did you go next?"

Susan tugged her cardigan over her fingers. "I went the next week. Curious, I suppose. And I sort of hoped that whoever left the flowers was there. They weren't, but there were more flowers, and another card. I was curious about who it was, so I went the next week, and the next, going on different days, hoping to catch them, but I never did."

"And why did you call me?"

The kitchen roll hanky was deployed again. "I think someone knows something about how he died."

"How *did* he die?"

"It was suicide. He hanged himself."

"That must've been awful for you," Eden said. She gave Susan a few moments to compose herself before she asked, "But you don't think it was suicide?"

"I don't know what to think any more."

Susan got up and left the room, and Eden heard her climb the stairs and rattle about upstairs. She returned a few minutes later with two albums. One was a scrapbook of newspaper cuttings about Philip's death, the other was a photo album recording Philip from red faced baby to gangly twelve year old.

Eden turned the pages of the scrapbook. Ancient newsprint crackled beneath her fingers. Headlines screamed 'Tragedy'. Black and white photographs showed a forest clearing and a swarm of police officers. Later stories covered the coroner's inquest and the verdict of suicide. She picked up the photo album. Photos of Philip in orange shorts, a gap in his teeth.

"Where did he...?"

"Up in the woods. He and his friends had a camp up there."

"He used to go up there by himself?"

Susan shook her head. "No, he always went with his friends. One of them had an uncle who used to take them all up there

16

and teach them how to light fires and make shelters and things."

Eden turned a page and studied a photograph of Philip and a rotund boy. Underneath was a line-up of Philip and three other boys about the same age. "His friends?"

Susan pressed her finger to the top photo. "That's Philip and Simon. They weren't really friends. I think Simon wanted to be part of the group but the others didn't like him. Called him 'Fat Simon'." She paused. "Philip started spending more time with him. I think it was because Simon's family had a video recorder. We didn't even have a washing machine!"

"Who are the other boys?"

Susan touched each one in turn. "Adam Jones, Lance Cotter, that's my Philip in his new jumper, and that's Dave Thompson. They always called him Tommo."

"Where are they now?"

"I'm not sure about Lance and Dave," Susan said, "but Adam Jones disappeared a couple of days before my Philip died."

"Disappeared?"

"The police thought he'd been murdered." Susan swallowed. "I think Philip knew what really happened to Adam. Only now with these messages on his grave, I wonder if someone else knows, too."

"Have any messages been left on Adam's grave?"

"Adam doesn't have a grave," Susan said. "They never found his body."

Her mind whirling, Eden went back to the cemetery. It perched on a hill side, overlooking Cheltenham, behind it the curving sward of limestone escarpment that hulked over the town. The cemetery was divided into smaller landscaped gardens, puddles of tranquillity separated by narrow tarmacked paths.

The wrapped flowers were still on Philip's grave, and no further offerings had materialised in the time she'd been away. Eden picked them up and shook off the raindrops that had gathered in the folds of the cellophane wrapping. She knew the florist: it was a smart shop in the Bath Road area of Cheltenham; sage paintwork and bright blooms in silver buckets. By contrast, the bedraggled carnations were from a supermarket, and as she studied the label, Eden noticed something she hadn't before, when she thought that this was just a wild goose chase and not a case with a whiff of intrigue about it.

There was a supermarket close to the cemetery, but the carnations weren't bought there. They were bought from Asda, on the opposite side of town. A long way from the Bath Road, too, she mused. Already a pattern of life was emerging. Her training taught her that people were creatures of habit: no matter how much they tried to break free or disguise where they were from, they were still drawn to places that were familiar to them. These flowers told her that whoever was leaving them regularly visited both the Bath Road and the area around Asda. And if he or she did their weekly shopping at Asda, then they possibly lived in the area nearby.

She tore the labels from the flowers and slotted them into her notebook, put the flowers in a bin, and headed for the cemetery offices.

"Help you?" asked a round-shouldered man in an emerald sweater. Hunched behind the counter, he looked like a gnome on work experience.

"Can you tell me what happens about old flowers left on graves?" Eden said. "Does someone clean them away?"

The man harrumphed. "The rules are no plastic flowers, and all flowers must be put in the urns provided."

"What if someone leaves flowers wrapped in plastic?"

"They're not allowed to. It's the rules. All flowers in vases. There are taps to fill them up with water."

"But if someone *did* leave flowers wrapped in plastic?"

The gnome huffed; she was a pain in the arse. "We expect whoever owns the grave to keep it clean and tidy, so they should clear the flowers away. But —" he tapped on the desk with a pencil — "sometimes they don't visit all that much, so if our groundsmen find them, they clean them up."

"How often would they do that?"

"Depends. Might be a couple of weeks before anyone notices and takes them away." He fired a look at her. "Why you asking, anyway?"

"Someone's been leaving flowers with cryptic messages, and I'm trying to work out how long it's been going on." Based on what he'd just told her, it could be years, the flowers being cleared away without Susan ever knowing they were there, but instinct told her that wasn't the case, that the flowers were a relatively new phenomenon. Time to check her theory. "I presume that if any grave was a repeat offender then you'd contact the owner?"

"Too right we would! Every now and then we can turn a blind eye to, but if people take the mick then we send a letter."

As she thought. Susan hadn't received a letter from the cemetery, complaining about the flowers littering the grave. Whoever the mystery sender was, they'd started in the past few months.

"And do you have CCTV?" Eden asked.

The gnome stiffened. "Why?"

"Just wondering what the security is like." It was a long shot, and she didn't fancy wading through hours of footage in the hope of seeing someone visiting Philip Wakefield's grave.

"Security is our business, not yours." He stared at her for a long moment. "Anything else?"

"Not right now. Thanks for your help."

She scouted round the exterior of the building, clocking where cameras were positioned and what they overlooked. As she anticipated, security focussed on the buildings, entrance and carpark, not on the cemetery gardens. You could rob any number of graves but the office computer and coffee machine were covered.

Eden climbed back in her car, made a note of her conversation with the gnome and called it a day. Hanging round graveyards was making her depressed. As she made her way down the road to the cemetery gates, she peered out over the ranks of graves, yew trees and statues, and wondered about her own grave. She'd never dared ask where her old self was buried, afraid that if she knew, she wouldn't be able to resist the temptation to visit it and read the memorial to herself. Did she have a headstone, carved with her old name, Sara White, her dates, and a sentence conjuring up what her life meant? Or was there merely a metal square nailed to the base of a tree, marking where her ashes had been scattered? Did anyone still mourn at her grave, or had grief finished with them? Like Susan, did her parents pilgrimage to her grave only on her birthday, or were they regular communicants at her earthly remains?

Eden was unsure which picture she preferred: that of her parents swaddled with grief, clinging to her memory and spending their days haunting a churchyard; or of grief ebbing to a faint bruise, sore when pressed, but no longer an ache that curtailed every day.

At the end of the cemetery drive she indicated left, and waited for a break in the traffic. On the way back home she passed the supermarket where the flowers on Philip's grave hadn't been bought, and she thought again about which area of Cheltenham the flower giver lived in. Not round here, she'd put money on it.

The traffic was slow, stop-starting with people leaving work and heading home, and it was thirty minutes before she pulled up outside the Art Deco block that contained her flat. A police car was parked in front of the building, and when she went up to her flat, she found police officers outside her door, ringing the bell.

"Is there a problem, officers?" she asked, praying there hadn't been a break-in.

"Are you Eden Grey?" one asked.

"Yes. What's the matter?"

"You need to come with us, madam."

They plonked her in a soft interview suite and bustled off to 'get the boss'. She wasn't in trouble then, Eden thought, as she glanced around the room. Armchairs, a shelf of toys for children to play with, a box of tissues on a low table. A soft carpet in pale apricot. It was the sort of room where bad news was imparted. Her stomach clenched. Surely they would have told her inside her flat if someone had died? Not bring her all the way over here?

After she'd fretted for a couple of minutes, the door swished open and two plain clothes officers came in. They introduced themselves as Inspector Ritter and Sergeant Ford. Ritter's jacket was rumpled and flecked with dandruff. By contrast,

Ford's pencil skirt was so sharp you could slice cheese on it. A female officer present: that always presaged bad news. Eden pulled her shoulders back and braced herself.

Ritter plonked himself in an armchair opposite Eden and foraged in his jacket for a pen. He clicked the end a few times before he said, "Thank you for coming in, Miss Grey. We appreciate your help."

She made a noncommittal noise. It wasn't bad news, then. From Ritter's tone it was more like 'helping the police with their enquiries', though from her experience, this was not necessarily as benign as it sounded.

"I'm sure you know why you're here," Ritter said. His skin was ashy and pouchy: a double-whammy of eczema and over-work.

"No," Eden said. "Two officers met me at my home and brought me here. They didn't say why."

Ritter and Ford exchanged a look. Someone was in for a bollocking later.

"You heard what happened in Cheltenham earlier today?"

Eden shook her head. "I've been working all day."

"You don't listen to Radio Gloucestershire?"

Not if she could help it. Wazzack FM wound her up. She shook her head again.

Ritter sighed. Another few clicks of his pen before he explained, "You know the bubble fish in the arcade in town? Well, today instead of blowing bubbles it blew tear gas."

"My God, that's horrible." She'd been tear gassed herself as part of her training. The point of the exercise was to learn to get your gas mask on as quickly as possible and check that the seal was snug, but in those few seconds of exposure the pain was intense. The only way to get rid of it was to wash it away, but water made it worse.

"A child died," Ford added. She twisted her fingers together, the knuckles calcified to marble. She has children herself, Eden thought.

"This is awful," Eden said, "but I don't see why you're telling me about it."

Ritter nodded at Ford, who produced a slim smart phone and placed it on the table. "Someone rang in to Radio Gloucestershire with this message."

Ford jabbed at the screen and a voice clip filled the room.

"Next time it will be cyanide. Bring me Eden Grey."

At the first syllables Eden stiffened. Hammond. She'd know that voice anywhere; it haunted her, poisoned her dreams and mocked her. And that message. How like Hammond: not giving a shit who knew it was him, thumbing his nose at the law and the prison authorities who were supposed to be keeping him on a short leash. So much for high security; he had as much control as he had when he was on the outside.

"We'd like to know who this is," Ritter said, when the recording ended, "and what he is to you."

"His name is John Hammond, and he's currently in prison serving a life sentence for various offences including gun running and attempted murder." Eden gave the abbreviated version: Hammond's charge sheet ran to several volumes. "I helped to put him there, and he's been after me ever since."

"You should have told us he's been threatening you," Ford said, drawing her lips into a thin line. "We could have done something."

"I'm on the witness protection programme," Eden said. "And he still found me, has been ringing me and threatening me and sending people to mince me to bits for the past three years!"

23

"We'll speak to the prison governor, get this character locked down," Ritter said.

Eden snorted. "That won't work. Every time he gets his wings clipped, he comes back fighting. Hasn't it occurred to you that he must have someone working for him in Cheltenham?"

Ritter and Ford glanced at each other. "Obviously," Ritter said, "someone planted the tear gas."

"That person will be primed to set off the cyanide gas if Hammond doesn't give him the signal," Eden said. "If you grab that person, there'll be a back-up plan."

There was always a back-up plan. That was how Hammond worked: layer after layer of plotting and back-ups so that whatever happened, he was always several steps ahead. Her ribs ached as it dawned on her that there was only one way to avoid catastrophe. "I'll go and see him. Find out what he wants."

Ritter clicked his pen. She fought the urge to wrench it from his fingers and snap it in two. "I don't think that's a good idea," he began. "Better if you let us work out who he's in contact with, and pick them up."

"No," Eden said. "He knows that's exactly what you'll do and he'll be prepared for that. Ring the prison and get me in there to see him. I'll go and speak to Hammond."

CHAPTER TWO

"Good of you to join us," Aidan called, as Andy sloped into the staff room and flomped into a chair.

Andy grunted. A stale odour wafted from him, a mix of alcohol, sweat and unwashed clothes. He'd been late to work for a week now; he should send him home, tell him to shower and change and then come back, but was that workplace bullying these days? Telling someone they stank? He wavered for a second, then clamped his mouth shut. He'd make sure he didn't work down-wind of Andy today, and have a word with him later about his time-keeping and generally shoddy appearance. Right now it was all hands on deck and an emergency excavation to complete.

"Morning, campers!" Lisa Greene floated into the Cultural Heritage Unit trailing clouds of Chanel. "God, what's that pong?"

And the only reason *she* was here was he was desperate.

"Right, now we're all here, finally," Aidan said, with pointed looks at Lisa and Andy, "let's get cracking. We've got what look like Iron Age burials up near the Devil's Chimney. We need to record and excavate them all, and we've got two days before the bulldozers come in. Any questions?"

The team — Trev, Mandy, Andy and Lisa — shook their heads.

"Then let's not waste any more time. Trev, Mandy, Andy, you take the van with all the equipment. Lisa, you come with me. Meet you up there."

The team trouped out of the office, Andy avoiding his eye. Lisa hung back while he switched off the lights, set the answerphone, and locked up.

"It's lovely to be working together again," she said, as they headed towards the car park. Aidan's car, an immaculate black Audi, was parked in the corner.

"Don't read anything into it, Lisa," he said, zapping the remote locking from a distance of ten yards. "Two days and you're back to Oxford."

He must be bloody mad. Firstly telling her about the Iron Age burials, and being persuaded to let her join the dig. Especially when she'd announced, "I'm owed a few days holiday and I promise I'll only charge you mates' rates."

He watched her folding her coat onto the back seat and easing herself into the passenger seat. Even though she was in her digging gear of scungy jeans and a sweater, Lisa still got into a car as if she was Princess Grace, lowering herself into the seat before swinging her legs in, knees clamped together.

He grunted and started the engine.

"Do you remember that dig we did in Italy?" she asked, smoothing her palms over her thighs.

The one where she flirted with everything in trousers and made his life a misery? Yes, he remembered it. His skin crawled with remembered jealousy. "Which dig?" he asked, turning out of the carpark and heading towards the ring road. The lights were in his favour, but a prat dawdled across the road at the corner opposite Boots and Primark. Aidan bipped the horn and earned himself a two-fingered salute.

"Chav," Lisa said, foraging in her trouser pocket and pulling out a packet of Silk Cut.

"You're not smoking in my car!" Aidan snapped.

"All right, Mr Touchy." She ostentatiously put the fag packet back in her pocket, making her movements slow and deliberate as though she'd been stopped by the US police and didn't want them to shoot her. "Tell me about these burials."

"The conservation people want to widen the path and put in an all-weather surface so it's easier for wheelchair users to get up there," Aidan said. "The rangers went in with a mini digger and scraped off about two tons of brambles and grass, and in doing so, scalped what look like Iron Age burials."

"Could be quite a mess, then? Everything scattered all over the place by the digger?"

"And by the brambles themselves. It's the erosion I'm worried about — it's pretty windy up there at the best of times."

"And we've got two days?"

"Yes, then the whole lot gets grubbed up."

The town centre was clogged with commuter traffic and the car inched along. A woman with a double buggy stepped out into the road and squeezed between his bumper and the back of the van in front. He held his breath, anxious in case she scraped his paintwork, only letting it go when she hefted the buggy onto the opposite pavement. If they'd left at seven, like he wanted, they would have missed the general public ambling and cursing their way to work. Aidan jabbed at the car's CD player, and the interior filled with the haunting cadences of the Sixteen singing Allegri's *Misere*.

Lisa was looking him over like a horseflesh trader at an auction. "Is that your digging outfit?"

He glanced down at his black moleskin jeans and dark grey shirt. "What's wrong with it?"

"Bit smart for grubbing in. You used to wear ripped jeans and a horrible t-shirt like a normal archaeologist." She prodded

27

him in the ribs with a sharp finger. "Being management has made you stuffy."

When he didn't reply, she said, with fake casualness, "I suppose whatshername likes you to look smart."

"Yes, she does, and as you well know, her name is Eden." At this rate, as soon as the Iron Age burials were excavated they'd be filled with a much fresher corpse: Lisa's.

"Still together, then?"

"Yes, thank you for asking."

"How long is it now?"

"Four years."

"Four years? That's jeweller's window territory." Still getting no response, she added, "Make or break, four years."

"If you say so."

Lisa folded her arms and glared at the traffic. "I haven't done Iron Age for centuries. All my stuff's much more recent."

Oh God, she was going to bang on about the war graves work she'd done. She'd already got that tell-tale look in her eye, the one that was half-proud, half-haunted. To deflect attention, he cut down a back street, accelerated over a run of sleeping policemen, and cut back into the traffic well ahead of the jam. "Not far now," he said, powering up Leckhampton Hill.

They toiled up the steep, narrow road and turned off at the top, the car bumping along a rough track that led along the side of a field. The Cultural Heritage Unit van was already there and Trev and Mandy were dragging out the gear. The grime coating the back of the van was inscribed with the message, 'Also available in white'. He'd have to speak to Trev about that. Aidan nosed his car into a space beside the van and made sure the hand brake was firmly engaged.

As he stepped from the car, the wind caught the door and snatched it out of his hands. This dig wasn't going to be fun.

Already Lisa was battling to get her arms into the sleeves of her anorak as it flapped around her. Mandy was unloading plastic finds trays from the vans: they'd need weighting down. He had a nightmarish vision of rare Iron Age artefacts being blown over the side of the hill.

"Where's Andy?" he asked Trev.

Trev — solid, in his forties, with a thatch of unruly grey hair — hitched his head towards a clump of beech trees. Andy was puking copiously, groaning after each spasm.

"What's wrong with him?"

Trev mimed bringing a pint to his lips, his face grim. "You're going to have to deal with him, Aidan."

Aidan sucked in a breath. "Let's go check out the site, OK?"

The walking path ran parallel to the field track, separated by a tumbled down dry stone wall. They clambered over and headed down the path. To one side was a waste of strewn nettles and brambles, to the other the edge of the escarpment. Cheltenham spread across the valley below, punctuated by glinting glass and church spires. GCHQ's green and silver doughnut squatted on the outskirts, an alien spaceship. Aidan's eye travelled beyond the town to the Malvern Alps bruising the horizon. Grey clouds tumbled the sky, a shaft of God-light beaming benediction in the distance.

They rounded the edge of the hill and were confronted by the umber stone spike of the Devil's Chimney.

"What the hell's that?" Lisa asked. A cigarette hung from her fingers and her breath fogged with smoke.

"Devil's Chimney," Trev said. "This area used to be a quarry, and for some reason they cut all the stone round it and left that pillar."

There was a viewing platform next to the Chimney. Lisa scampered down to it and peered over the edge. Aidan joined her more warily — he'd never liked heights and looking down made his head swim. After a moment gazing at the drop, he climbed back up to the path. "The graves are along this way."

He'd come to see the graves and make an initial assessment a week before. Five small, stone-lined shapes set into the ground. To the untrained eye, they were just random stones; luckily, the ranger who'd stripped the area of vegetation was a keen *Time Team* fan and thought there was a pattern to the stones, and called Aidan in. He'd poked around with a trowel with rising excitement. The area was rich in Iron Age history — barrows and forts all round the valley rim — and these looked like cist burials. He'd asked the ranger to cover them with the cut brambles to protect them from wind erosion and dogs, and now he gingerly removed the dead branches to reveal the cists.

"Lovely," Trev breathed, rubbing his hands together. "In the right place, too, just outside the hill fort."

"Let's not jump to conclusions," Aidan said, though he, too, was assessing how well the cists fitted the general pattern of occupation and known archaeology in the region. "Looks like five cists, that's one each. Let's get to work."

Hunkered down beside the cist, he forgot about the chill and the cramp in his legs, as he gently brushed at the earth covering the burial. Four of the graves were clustered together, one was further apart. He'd sent Andy to do that one, to keep the whiff as far away as possible.

The morning passed to the gentle percussion of trowel against stone and the swish of brushes. Mandy sat cross-legged with a sketchbook across her knees, measuring and recording. Trev toiled away, humming under his breath, then suddenly sent up a shout. "You beauty!"

Aidan raised his head. Trev was red-faced with excitement. "What you got, Trev?"

Lisa unfolded herself and went over to peer at the excavation. "Nice," she breathed. At the bottom, budged up against one of the stones lining the hole, was a bone. "Fragment of tibia," she said.

"Excellent," Aidan said. "Confirms that it is a cist burial."

"Amazing to find any bones at all," Lisa said. "Congrats, Trev."

Trev beamed like a new father, gently brushing the soil away from the bone until it could be levered free and placed in a finds box lined with bubble wrap.

"Drinks are on you, Trev," Mandy called.

"Happy with that," he grunted.

Aidan hid a smile, knowing that Trev's find had introduced an element of competition to the exercise. They'd all be praying to find something in their grave, now. And actually finding human remains might just buy them more time for the excavation. He cast a look towards Andy. The lad was green and sick looking, and had sneaked away to puke his guts up more than once that morning. He hadn't bothered to come and see what Trev had found, just toiled away in his own little world.

"All right, Andy?" he called.

Andy's head shot up. "What?"

"You doing OK over there? Found anything?"

Andy shrugged. "Dead un."

From the corners of his eyes he caught Lisa, Trev and Mandy snap to attention. They emerged from their trenches like zombies.

"You've found another bone?" Aidan said. They all arrived at Andy's trench at the same time, gazing into the hole in horror.

"Fucking hell." Lisa voiced what they were all thinking.

For a moment his mind was numb, then it went into overdrive. "Put the trowel down and get out now!" He turned to Lisa, glad she was there with the gravitas of her learning and reputation, to guide him. "Lisa, what do you think?"

Her face was white. In the trench was a partially excavated skeleton: the dome of the skull, scapula, and clavicle visible. The grave was lined with stone, the skeleton lying on its side with its hands tucked up beside its face, just like an Iron Age burial, but this was wrong, all wrong.

Lisa studied the skeleton without touching it for a long time. Then she eased into the trench and gently brushed soil from the skull, peering at the jaw. She hunkered back on her haunches, groaning, then climbed out. "Call the police," she said. "Have you got a groundsheet to cover this with until Forensics can get here?"

Aidan nodded at Mandy and Trev, and they ran back to the van. At least he could rely on them, he thought, wearily, as he turned to Andy.

"What the hell have you done?" he said.

"You said excavate the graves." Andy folded his arms tight over his chest.

"And I said they were thought to be Iron Age graves," Aidan said, his jaw tight. "What do you typically find in an Iron Age grave? Bugger all, that's what."

"Never mind that," Lisa exploded. "You should know that no one ever, ever, excavates a skeleton alone. That's the protocol, and it's to stop exactly this kind of almighty fuck-up. The moment you found bone you should have shouted."

"What's the problem?" Andy said. "A skeleton in a grave. Big deal. You said we had to get them out quick."

Lisa caught Aidan's eye. Her cheeks were blotched pink with fury. "The problem, you imbecile, is if that skeleton's Iron Age then I'm the Queen of Sheba. Look!" She pointed at the skull, where the jaw flapped open. "See anything odd there? That skeleton's got mercury fillings and braces."

Aidan pulled her aside, afraid she might lamp Andy, she was so angry. "What do you think?" he asked in a low voice.

She rounded on him. "I think it's recent, suspicious, and we'll be charged with tampering with a crime scene."

He feared that, too. As Trev and Mandy returned with a groundsheet and bricks to hold it in place, he went back to his car to ring the police and reflect on the end of his career. When he returned to the site, Lisa was standing guard over the trench.

"I'm protecting the integrity of the forensics," she announced, without being asked, shooting a venomous look at Andy, who hung his head, face flaming scarlet.

"The police say they'll be a while," Aidan said. "Something about a major incident in town. We'll have to cover this, then wait until they get here."

The groundsheet snapped and bucked as they stretched it over the trench and weighted it down with bricks. Even so, it tore free and Mandy scampered over to the collapsed wall to forage for more stones. Shrouded, the site was strangely spooky, and they all stared at it in silence, cocooned in their own thoughts.

"Andy and Trev, take a lunch break. We'll wait here for the police, then swap over," Aidan said. Normally he'd have sent Mandy to join the others, but he wanted her to play

33

gooseberry, a decision he thanked when he saw Lisa's eyes flash at him and her mouth open to protest.

It was two hours before a police car toiled up the track and two coppers clambered out.

"What you got?" one of them said.

"A fresh one, by the look of it," Lisa answered. She extended her hand. "Dr Lisa Greene, University of Oxford, forensic archaeologist. I've done war graves excavations before: I know the drill."

That put everyone else in their place, Aidan thought, grimly. A right bunch of amateurish prats, blithely digging over a crime scene that was so blatant it couldn't be more obvious if there was sign saying 'Crime Scene' pointing to it.

The policeman shook Lisa's hand and gave her a covert once-over. She was worth the look, Aidan conceded, with her petite frame, reddish pixie cut, and pert features. And she was deploying her devastating charm to full effect, touching the older policeman on the elbow while she talked earnestly up into his face.

"Let's have a look at it, then," said the other, and they peeled back the groundsheet. The police squatted to look at the skeleton. "Modern, is it?"

"Certainly post Second World War," Lisa said, "judging by the quality of that dental work. Could be very recent indeed."

The policeman straightened and whistled through his teeth. "Let me call it in."

He moved away to mutter into his radio, turning back to look again at the site and all of them standing around. What a bunch they must seem, Aidan thought, a grubby pack of archaeologists. Five go mad in a trench.

"Right," the police officer said. "The pathologist's on the way."

"Can we carry on with the other burials?" Aidan asked.

"No, they're part of the scene until Forensics clear them."

Great, they'd lose the whole day. The contractors were coming in to construct the walkway in two days' time, and by then, the graves could still be in exactly the same condition as they were now. Aidan went back to his car and rang the ranger who'd found the cist burials, updating him on what had happened, and begging for more time. "They could be significant," he pleaded. "I'd like to get them out if we can."

The ranger promised to see if he could put back the contractors, and Aidan rang off. He flopped his head against the headrest and let his mind go still, focussing on simply breathing in and out until the voice in his head was silenced. Just as he'd achieved calm, a troop of police vehicles parked behind him. They were followed shortly after by a Mercedes driven by a smart-looking woman with a severe haircut, who started barking orders before she'd even got out of the car. The pathologist, he surmised. She opened the boot of her car and climbed into a white plastic forensics suit, grabbed a hard silver case, and trudged up the path, still rattling instructions to the officers trailing behind her. In their white suits, they looked like survivors of a nuclear holocaust; the last people left on earth.

He was shaken from his reverie by Trev tapping on the window. He lowered it and Trev leaned in.

"Boss, we've given statements to the cops." Trev jerked his thumb at Andy and Mandy standing beside the van. "They won't let us near the site. Shall we go back to base?"

"Good idea, Trev. I'll stay here and keep an eye on things."

Trev cleared his throat. "You might want to keep an eye on Lisa, too. She's trying to help."

Bloody hell, that was guaranteed to get up the pathologist's nose. He groaned and climbed out of the car. "All right. I'll see if I can prevent further bloodshed." Trev grinned and waved as Aidan headed back to the site.

Lisa was indeed interfering. He pulled her aside, hissing, "You're not the only one who knows how to get a stiff out of the ground, Lisa."

She shrugged him off and lit a cigarette, blowing the smoke at him, and watched the movements at the grave with narrowed eyes. A tent was erected over the skeleton and shadowy shapes moved within, cameras flashing and capturing the tableau in a series of frozen glimpses. Hours later, the forensics team came out with a series of large cardboard boxes, and the pathologist emerged and tugged down her white hood. She spoke to the crime scene manager, who then came over to Aidan and Lisa.

"You think that grave is Iron Age?" he said.

"Looks identical to the other cist burials," Aidan said. When incomprehension muddied the officer's face, he explained, "Graves that are lined with stone."

"OK, this is the problem we've got," the officer said. "None of us knows about Iron Age whatsits. We've removed the skeleton and taken samples, but we don't know what we're looking at in that trench. You do. How do you feel about suiting up and digging up that grave, with one of my CSIs keeping an eye on you?"

Aidan shrugged. "No problem."

Lisa, of course, was gagging to be in on the action, and within minutes they were both peering into the hole where the skeleton had been. Aidan tapped the flat stones lining the grave with his trowel. "The placement looks Iron Age. Let's get them out and see."

"What are you doing?" the CSI asked.

"There's no way to date stone," he explained. "If we take out the stones we might find dating evidence underneath."

"Like what?"

"Pottery shards, metal traces." Aidan puffed out his cheeks. "Or there might be nothing at all."

"Brilliant."

They took opposite sides of the grave, but it was a squeeze with all of them in the tent, and Aidan studiously avoided touching Lisa. She'd got that look in her eye that presaged trouble. The smell of cigarette smoke clung to her, filling the tent unpleasantly, mingling with the fading traces of Chanel. They scraped and brushed at the stones, removing them one by one, photographing and recording as they worked. No artefacts emerged; no objects that could tell them when the stones were put in place.

Just as Lisa straightened and eased the kinks out of her spine, declaring, "Nothing," Aidan's trowel removed a lump of soil and revealed something red and ragged. Whatever it was, part of it was trapped underneath one of the stones.

"Got something here," he said, and the CSI sprang forward to see. Gently he levered out the stone and brushed away the soil until the object was fully exposed. He stared at it for a moment. "Definitely not an Iron Age burial," he said, as the camera flashed, recording the find.

It was a Mickey Mouse watch.

CHAPTER THREE

Eden stood on her balcony, a glass of gin and tonic in her hand, and gazed out over the rooftops to the Suffolks. The shops were closed and shuttered, but the bars sparkled with coloured lights, a year-round Christmas tree. The houses in the square were fading to grey rectangles in the gloom, their windows glowing with reflected TV light. Beyond it all, the ring of hills that gripped Cheltenham in its embrace loomed as a darker shade against the navy sky.

She sipped her drink and hugged her arms tighter around her. She didn't like this new case and her investigator's instinct prickled. A boy who killed himself thirty-five years ago should be well and truly forgotten apart from the occasional sigh in his mother's breast. So who was leaving floral offerings at his grave, and why did the cards attached say 'Sorry'? Sorry for what? And why the remorse now, all these years later?

Another sip, the ice-cubes bumping against her lips. The dead boy was tragedy enough, but that one of his close friends disappeared only days before, presumed murdered, raised a lot of questions. Questions she wasn't entirely sure she felt comfortable asking. Sometimes it was better to leave the past to its own devices.

Her mobile rang, number withheld. She answered it warily, her mind still reeling after her conversation with the police and afraid in case it was Hammond. "Hello?"

"It's me." Miranda. Her old boss from her undercover days. Eden could imagine her with the phone clamped under her chin, her hands free to riffle though files or light a cigarette, the giant tiger's eye ring on her middle finger flashing her domination over a largely masculine team. Miranda had bigger balls than all of them.

"What's up?" Eden said.

"I heard about the tear gas today," Miranda said. "And the kid in the shopping mall."

Eden sighed a sigh that came from the depths of her soul. "Poor kid. The mother must be distraught."

"I heard there was a message."

"Yep, naming me."

"Our old friend?" Miranda said.

"*Your* friend, you mean." Eden had neither forgotten nor forgiven Miranda for selling out.

"I'm trying to make amends."

"By ringing me and telling me what I already know?" Eden snapped.

"Look," Miranda said. "I've got some intel on this."

"Tell the police."

"The word I've got is he's planning something big."

"Bigger than releasing cyanide in a shopping mall?"

"A way to get you, once and for all."

"No change there, then." Suddenly Eden was dog tired. How many years now had she been on the run, afraid of Hammond catching up with her? Fear was exhausting.

"Look, Eden, don't get sucked into his game," Miranda said. "Keep a low profile."

"That would be easier if someone hadn't told him exactly where to find me," Eden said. "Bye, Miranda."

She hung up, scratching the side of her head where she'd pressed the phone. She had a tattoo there, on her scalp. A permanent souvenir of her time undercover, when she'd shaved one side of her head and let the hair hang loose on the other. The tattoo was to show she'd been in prison, a mark of hardness. Now it was hidden by her hair and she rarely thought of it, apart from times when it prickled and itched and she remembered it lurking there. Like the scars that marked her body — a parting gift from John Hammond — it was a reminder she couldn't escape her history.

The doorbell rang and jerked her out of the murky waters of the past.

"Started without me?" Aidan said, coming in with the scent of cold night air clinging to his clothes. He nodded at the gin and tonic. "Can I have one? It's been quite a day."

"Me, too," she said, pouring a large one for him and topping up her own glass. "You go first."

"It's been a total nightmare." Aidan flung himself onto the settee, long legs stretched out. "We were supposed to be excavating some Iron Age burials, and instead we got a crime scene."

"A body?"

"A skeleton. Not that old. The teeth had fillings and braces."

Eden folded herself onto the sofa beside him. "Do the police know who it is?"

"Not yet." He slugged back the gin and turned to her. "What about you? How's your day been?"

"New client, seemed at first to be a total waste of time, but now I think there might be something going on there that's worth investigating." She took a breath. "But when I got home the police were waiting for me."

His eyes met hers.

"Have you seen the news this evening?" When he shook his head, she continued, "Someone put tear gas in the bubble fish in the arcade. A child died."

"Bloody hell. What's that to do with you?"

"It was Hammond. And next time it will be cyanide if I don't go and see him."

Horror raced over his face. "That's evil," he managed, eventually.

"That's what he's like. I don't know what he wants, but I'll find out tomorrow."

It was a few seconds before he connected the dots. "You're not going to see him?"

"I have to! When he says next time it'll be cyanide, he means it. He's obviously got someone who can plant tear gas; he'll have someone who can plant cyanide, too."

"But, Eden, the man's a monster!"

"Exactly. And he'll kill people if I don't do what he says."

Aidan breathed in noisily, visibly trying to compose himself. "I don't want you to go."

"Neither do I, but I have no choice."

"Let the police deal with him. They must have enough to lock him up forever."

Eden banged down her glass. "I provided enough evidence to lock him away forever, and it made no difference. He's got people everywhere. People who look honest but are in his pocket." She swallowed a lump of anger and fear. "I have to find out what he wants."

"And if he attacks you?"

"Been there, done that." She was trying to lighten things, to persuade herself she wasn't terrified. Hammond launching himself at her across the prison interview room was exactly what she feared; Hammond killing her while screws on his payroll looked on blindly.

"I'm glad you're taking it so seriously." Aidan carried his glass into the kitchen and poured the remains down the sink.

"Let me know when you've come to your senses."

He picked up his coat and stalked to the door.

"Thanks for your support," she called, as it banged shut behind him.

CHAPTER FOUR

What do you wear to meet the man who tried to kill you?

Eden stood before her open wardrobe and shuffled her way through the clothes hanging there. There weren't many: a few pairs of dark trousers and a couple of skirts; four blouses; a leather jacket; a favourite pair of jeans that had been worn and washed into thin softness; a handful of brightly coloured tops.

She pulled out the jeans. They were comfortable and familiar, and if she wore them she wouldn't give Hammond the pleasure of thinking she'd gone to any effort. But then again, he might think that the way he'd hunted her over the past few years had ground out her self-esteem and she habitually slouched about in tracksuit bottoms and fag ash.

Long sleeves were essential: she had to cover the scars he'd left on her arms. Her mind shuddered at the memory of the knife in his hand, the way he swung it to and fro before her eyes, like a stage hypnotist with a fob watch, watching her watching the blade swing back and forth, before with a swift movement he sliced across both her arms, across her thighs, and then plunged the knife into her stomach. She couldn't sit across from him with her scars visible, knowing he'd stare at them until they itched, and when she scratched them, that smug smile would spread across his face.

Dressing too smart was out of the question. Couldn't let him think she'd taken any trouble over her appearance, that going to see him was a special occasion for her. Where was the balance between trying too hard and shattered self-esteem? After more dithering, she finally selected a pair of black trousers — not the newest pair — and a long-sleeved blue blouse with tiny yellow flowers.

She could barely eat breakfast, though she knew she ought to force down something. She chewed endlessly at a slice of toast, trying to distract herself with the early TV news, but the bolus of food went round and round her mouth, getting drier with every circuit, and each swallow stuck in her throat. Eventually she gave up, swilled back a now cold cup of coffee, grabbed her bag and went out to her car.

Inspector Ritter had offered to drive her to the prison and she'd declined. It was a long journey and she didn't want to be trapped in a car and forced to make conversation when the only thing they had in common was wanting to nail the vicious shit they were going to see. Her thoughts on the journey would be dark and forbidding enough, and she needed the distraction of driving to prevent her wallowing in the past.

Ritter was going to meet her there, but for now she tuned her car radio to a poppy channel churning out oldies but goodies, and yanked up the volume ready to sing along. The streets were just coming to life as she pulled out of Cheltenham and headed towards the M5, then turned the car north and sped towards the high security prison that had the pleasure of hosting John Hammond.

Three hours later she pulled into a motorway service station, drank a coffee and went to the loo. In her experience, prison governors were poor at remembering that official visitors had travelled a long way and might need to refresh themselves before interviewing a dangerous little scrote. The last thing she needed was to arrive bursting for the loo and being ushered in to a showdown with the man who wanted her dead.

The rest of the journey went too quickly. When speed restrictions appeared she prayed it meant a long hold up, an accident that would mean she had to turn back. But she remembered the message Hammond had left her and thought of the child he'd already killed, stretched her spine and tried to ignore the dread that was clotting in the pit of her stomach.

"All right?" Ritter was standing in the visitors' carpark beside his car, a Mondeo that was as dusty as his suit, sucking on a cigarette so hard his cheeks collapsed into hollows.

"Fine." She swung her handbag over her shoulder. "Good journey?"

Ritter screwed up his face. "Would rather be heading to Devon than coming up here into gobshite land," he said, chucking the fag onto the ground and squidging it with the toe of his boot. He squared his shoulders. "Come on, then, let's get this over with."

They walked to the visitors' entrance and gave their names, and were shown into a dingy waiting room whose walls were covered with posters warning about venereal disease, illustrated with high definition photos of manky genitalia.

"I prefer a Monet, myself," Ritter said, and despite herself, she laughed. "You ready for this?"

"The posters? I've seen worse."

"Hammond. God knows what he wants."

"He wants me." *Next time it will be cyanide. Bring me Eden Grey.* "The question is what he wants me to do before he has me killed."

"I could rip his throat out for what he did to that kid."

"Me, too. You have children?"

"Three boys. Drives the wife mad."

Eden smiled. "How old are they?"

"Thirteen, eleven and six." He made a rueful face. "Last one was a bit of a mistake. It's something we can hold over him when he becomes a stroppy teenager."

45

Eden smiled, appreciating that he was trying to ease the tension as they sat here waiting to speak to a man who had no qualms about killing.

"You got kids, Eden?"

"No." Her mind chased back to the baby who died; Molly, who never lived, and whose death set in train a series of disasters that led her here, to this dingy waiting room with its scabby dicks; to a new life that never shook itself free of the old.

"The governor would like a word." A prison officer led them up a flight of stairs and along a corridor that was hung with watercolours and was carpeted in a thick, deadening grey wool. The room they were shown into had a large, oval polished table and executive chairs. A tall, ascetic man occupied the chair at the head of the table, a thick cardboard folder open in front of him. He rose to shake hands with them, and gestured towards a coffee pot and tray of biscuits.

"Thank you for seeing us so quickly," Ritter said. "Obviously with a threat like this we want to nip it in the bud as soon as possible."

"I'll do everything I can," the governor said. "I take a very dim view of prisoners controlling illegal activity from within these walls."

"The mobile used to call the radio station was unregistered," Ritter said, "but we traced it to the cell tower closest to the prison."

"Smuggled mobiles are a problem we're trying to tackle," the governor said. "Not easy when some people fly them in with drones."

"Does Hammond know we're coming?" Ritter asked.

"No," the governor said. "I should tell you that he's been ill for some days."

"What's wrong with him?" Eden said.

"Stomach flu. He's been in the infirmary since the weekend."

Eden leaned forwards, her elbows on the desk. "But he rang the radio station yesterday."

The governor spread his hands. "As I said, we've got a problem with smuggled mobile phones."

"Is he well enough to be interviewed?" Ritter asked.

"Yes, he's being taken to the interview room now."

Unease crawled in Eden's stomach. Hammond was a devious little shit and this all felt too convenient: taken to the infirmary where prison life was much easier, the regime much slacker, just in time for him to drop his bombshell. "He has stomach flu?" she said.

The governor pressed the tips of his fingers together. "We're not unaware of his calculation. We treated his complaint with a healthy dose of scepticism, and made sure he was seen by a doctor."

Eden drained her coffee and put down her cup with a clatter. Her fingers trembled "Let's get this over with."

She rose to her feet. Ritter snaffled the last pink wafer biscuit and slotted it whole into his mouth, then stood and buttoned his jacket. As they reached the door, a prison officer hurtled inside.

"Governor, problem," he said.

The governor frowned. "What is it?"

"Hammond. Gone."

A cold finger ran down Eden's spine. "Gone?" As she spoke, a siren sounded. The prison was going into lockdown.

"What's going on?" the governor asked.

"The officer who was bringing Hammond from the infirmary was found tied up and gagged."

"His keys?" the governor asked.

"Missing."

Eden dropped her head into her hands. "The whole thing was a trick," she said, "and we fell for it."

The governor hurried away to help search the prison, and Eden and Ritter were ordered to stay put. Three hours later, after every prisoner was locked into his cell and accounted for, there was still no sign of Hammond. The governor returned with a prison officer three years off retirement. The man was juddering with fear.

"He said he'd cut my granddaughter's fingers off if I didn't help him to escape," he said. "I told him to fuck off, and a week later I got a package through the post. There was a finger in it. A little girl's, wearing a gold signet ring. He said if I told anyone, he'd cut off her ears as well."

"What did he want you to do?" Eden said.

"Go along with his story that he was sick, and get him into the infirmary," the officer said. "Then I had to let him beat me up, put my own cuffs on me and take my keys." His face twisted. "I'm sorry, governor, but I knew he meant it about my granddaughter."

Eden turned to Ritter and muttered, "That's Hammond's style, all right. He probably did the same to whoever put the tear gas in the bubble fish."

Eventually, they were allowed out of the prison. The air outside, clogged with diesel fumes and dust, had never smelled so sweet. As they crossed the car park, Ritter patted his pocket and extracted a vibrating mobile phone. "Ritter. Speak."

He twisted his lips together between finger and thumb while he listened. Eden looked away, trying not to eavesdrop, but her attention was called to a name he repeated. "Adam Jones? You're sure?"

When Ritter ended the call, she said, "Adam Jones? Didn't he disappear thirty-odd years ago?"

"He did, and he's been found."

"Where?"

"In an Iron Age grave up at the Devil's Chimney."

CHAPTER FIVE

Helping police with their enquiries. Aidan wondered if that was shorthand for 'soon to be cuffed and remanded in custody'. His stomach was churning as he drove up Leckhampton Hill towards the Devil's Chimney. Greg Taylor, in his green ranger uniform and a navy baseball cap, met him in the carpark and they walked together up to the site.

"Unbelievable," Greg said, repeatedly.

"It's a new one on me, certainly," Aidan said. "Don't think I'm ever going to live this one down."

The site was cordoned off with blue and white police tape proclaiming it a crime scene. The tent that had been erected over the grave was still in place, the plastic snapping in the wind, and a police officer stood guard over it, his hands tucked inside his utility vest. As they approached, he called into the tent, "They're here, ma'am."

A plain clothes officer emerged and eyed them up and down. She was in her early forties, slim built with dyed blonde hair in a crop. "Detective Inspector Stewart. Thanks for coming. Just want to go over the timeline."

Looking for errors and omissions, Aidan thought. Thinks we know something we're not admitting to.

"Mr Taylor, you called in the archaeology team. Why was that?"

"We knew we had Iron Age deposits in the area," Greg said. "When the brambles were stripped off, I thought it looked like Iron Age burials here."

"And you agreed?" A pair of sharp dark eyes turned on Aidan.

"Yes. I came up for an initial look, and they looked exactly like cist burials. And in fact, they were cist burials."

"But one was more modern than the others?" DI Stewart asked. "Has anyone taken any interest in what you were doing up here? Anyone asking questions, hanging around?"

"No," Aidan said. "There were a couple of dog walkers who went past when we were excavating, but they had a peer in the hole and went away. Gawpers are quite common on digs."

"Gawpers?"

He shifted uncomfortably. "People like to have a look." Hoping to see skeletons. If they'd come past later, they'd have been in luck.

She turned back to Greg. "What about you? Any colleagues who took an interest in what was up here?"

"We all take an interest in what's up here." Greg bristled. "It's our job. But no, there was no unusual curiosity."

"So this fake cist, how was it made?"

"My guess would be the dry stone wall," Aidan said. He led her to where the wall was eaten by ivy and lying tumbled in a heap. "This looks very similar to the stone that lined the fake cist."

"And it's convenient," she said. "We've been able to narrow down the timeline through the watch that was found. The manufacturer says they started production of that model in 1979, so we're looking at potential victims from that date to now."

"The watch?" Greg said.

Aidan answered first. "There was a Mickey Mouse watch found with the skeleton."

A spasm crossed Greg's face. "Really?"

"How often do you clear the area?" DI Stewart asked.

Greg shrugged. "It depends on funding, and how overgrown it's got. The last time would be about ten years ago."

"So our skeleton must have been planted between 1979 and 2006? Only a quarter of a century of missing persons to check," Stewart said glumly. "Who does the clearance?"

"Sometimes it's a team of rangers, sometimes we get volunteers from the public," Greg said. He gave a short laugh. "In fact, I used to help out up here when I was in the Scouts." He shoved his hands in his pockets. "We used to camp up here overnight, and hack back the brambles during the day. Never had so many scratches. My mum went through three bottles of iodine treating those scratches."

"How old were you?"

"The last time I must've been about seventeen, I guess."

Stewart raised an eyebrow. "You were seventeen and your mummy put iodine on your scratches?"

"Some of them were nasty, and they weren't easy to reach!" Greg said, hotly.

Stewart evidently bit back what she was about to say, and changed it to, "Do you have records of volunteers and rangers who have worked up here?"

"I suppose there must be some, somewhere."

"I'd be grateful if you could check and let me have anything you turn up." She turned to Aidan. "What about the archaeology? The person who did this, were they a professional?"

"Possibly, or an enthusiastic amateur," he said. "Anyone who's watched TV documentaries on Iron Age burials could probably make a good stab at it." He winced inwardly at 'stab'.

"OK, that gives me enough to start on," she said. "If you think of anything —" a stern look at them each in turn — "then contact me immediately. Thank you, gentlemen."

She stalked back to the crime scene and hoisted the blue and white tape. Aidan watched her go, professional indignation burning in his chest. Someone had made a fool out of him. Someone had constructed a fake Iron Age grave that was so convincing it had taken him in completely. He, with his PhD and years of experience in the field, had been duped by a fallen dry stone wall.

He looked again at Greg. "Which bit did you clear when you were here with the scouts, getting scratched?" he asked.

"The whole stretch of the path from the road past the Devil's Chimney," Greg said.

"So you hacked back the bit where the graves are?"

"I guess so."

"Do you remember seeing them?"

Greg stroked his chin, where he had a wispy beard on the very tip like a goblin. A horrible, hairy postage stamp. "Yes, I do remember, now you mention it."

"How many were there?"

Greg looked startled. "What?"

"How many graves were here then?"

"I don't know." Greg's face twitched. "Why? What's your point?"

"Just that if there were only four, we know that the fake grave was made between the time you were here with the scouts, and yesterday," Aidan said. "If there were five, it was put in earlier."

Greg walked away without answering.

First things first, issue a bollocking to Andy for making a total fuck-up of yesterday's dig.

"I think you know what I'm going to say," Aidan said, when Andy slouched into his office. He was young, only a few years out of university, and had a blonde quiff that folded back from his forehead. A ring glinted in his eyebrow.

"I took you on because you were a first rate archaeologist, and because you loved the subject," Aidan continued. "What's happened? The past week you've been coming in late, hungover, and your work's gone downhill."

Andy stared at his feet.

"Is it the work? Or the people?" Aidan asked, getting increasingly irritated. "I know Trev can be a bit much, what with the singing and being so bloody bucolic all the time, but he's not bad really. And if you tell him to shut it, he usually does. Eventually."

Andy swallowed.

"Is it me? Am I being a git to you? Because I know I'm not easy, Trev and Eden remind me often enough."

"It's not you," Andy said, his voice muffled. He wiped his hand across his nose. His shoulders jerked.

"Andy?" Christ, he was crying. "What is it?"

Andy mumbled something incoherent and broke down completely. Aidan took one look and knew the situation was beyond his capabilities. Striding to the door, he opened it and called for Mandy. When she came in, lurid plaits bouncing on her shoulders, he simply pointed.

Mandy crouched down beside Andy's chair. "What is it, Andy? Tell me what's going on."

The story came out in a series of jerky sobs and vocal explosions. "I've been seeing this girl, and she's got pregnant, and she says she's not going to keep it."

"You want her to have the baby?" Mandy asked.

Andy sniffed. "She wants an abortion."

Mandy's eyes met Aidan's; there were tears glinting on her lashes.

"All I can think about is being a dad, except she won't let me."

"Have you tried talking to her?"

"She won't listen. Hangs up the phone if I call her. Slams the door in my face any time I go round." He swiped his hand across his face. "She's made up her mind."

"Now listen to me," Mandy said. "I'm going to take you home, and you're going to have a long hot bath and I'll make you something to eat. You haven't been eating properly, have you? And then we're going to have a chat and see what can be done." Mandy mouthed instructions to Aidan over the top of Andy's head.

"Take a couple of days off," Aidan said, grateful for the prompt. "It won't come out of your holiday."

"Thanks, Aidan."

"It's OK if I go with Andy, isn't it, Aidan?" Mandy said. "I'll make the time up."

"Don't worry about it," he said. "Off you go."

The two of them left, pausing only for Mandy to pick up her furry teddy-bear backpack. A long-smothered sensation tugged at Aidan's chest. "I've got to pop out for a few minutes," he told Trev. "I won't be long."

Before Trev could comment, he scooped up his jacket and scarpered, across town and into a Catholic church. He'd been coming here, alone, for the past few months, since the embers of his latent faith had been whispered into flame by a case that pitted belief against science. It was his secret, this escape to the church, to kneel in incense-heavy air and mouth the words of prayers he thought he'd left behind years ago. Strange how the words remained, sliding unbidden yet not unwelcome into his mind. Hail Mary. Our Father. I believe.

This time his mission was clear and his footsteps quickened as if he were a parched man running towards water. Inside, his fingers in the holy water stoop, his heart loud, and the ache in his chest expanding and releasing, the relief drenching him as he let go and surrendered. To the statue in the corner, the Virgin with outspread hands, a bank of candles at her feet, some still lit, others burnt to stubs. He poked a coin into the slot and took a candle, lit it, and placed it in a holder, then stood back to speak into the statue's face.

"Help Andy and his girlfriend. Help them sort this mess out." The words came out in a stream, a one-way transmission and plea. After a few minutes, the words subsided, and peace enveloped him; the words were gone, dissolved into a single golden stream of emotion that flowed both in and out.

A last look at the statue, a dip of his fingers into the holy water, crossing himself, the drop of water beading on his forehead. Then out into the street and the traffic and the bus passing by. Out into the world again.

"You took your time," Trev greeted him, when he returned to the Cultural Heritage Unit.

"Sorry. Did I miss anything?"

"Only some detective ringing up. A woman."

"What did she want?"

"To arrest you."

"What!"

"Keep your hair on, only kidding. Just wanted to say she'll let us know when we can finish the dig."

"Oh, right."

"And Lisa's in your office."

Great. Some of the peace he'd found ebbed away. It ebbed further when he entered his office to find Lisa cheerfully going through the papers on his desk.

"What are you up to?" he said, slamming the door behind him.

"Snooping," she said, unabashed, knocking the papers back together into a pile.

"Snooping for what?"

"Your availability."

"Why?"

"I have a proposition to put to you."

Not the baby thing again. Lisa thought it would be a good idea if he fathered her child. They'd been over it before, several times, and he thought it had been put to bed. As the words 'put to bed' flashed through his mind, he flushed. They'd been good together, once. A long time ago.

"I've got a friend with a seaside cottage," Lisa said. "It's just outside Brixham. Lovely coastal walks, gorgeous country walks, excellent seafood."

"You sound like a tourist brochure."

"And I've arranged to stay in it next weekend," Lisa continued. "Would you like to come with me?"

It took a moment for it to register. "Who else is going?"

"Just me and you."

"In a seaside cottage. Together."

"There's a Napoleonic fort nearby," she said, with an enticing lilt that, despite himself, made him smile.

"The thing is, Lisa, you know quite well that I'm with Eden. And one of the rules of being in a relationship with someone is that you don't go swanning off on mucky weekends with other people."

"I didn't say anything about a mucky weekend," Lisa said, "though those forts do get rather muddy."

He eyeballed her until she was forced to glance away.

"OK, I admit it, I hope that it will turn into a mucky weekend. We've had them before and I know I like them. But all I'm asking is we go away and see how we get on." She leaned across the desk. "I miss you, you twit, and I think you miss me."

"I've got Eden!"

"When did you last go on holiday with her?"

He glared at her. Never. They'd never been on holiday together, not in all the time they'd been dating.

Lisa evidently read his mind. "I thought so. Four years and you've never even been away for the weekend," She picked up her bag and headed to the door. "Time to make up your mind where that relationship's going, Aidan."

CHAPTER SIX

Eden took her time on the journey home, stopping several times to check she wasn't being followed, making diversions along backroads to allow space for her thoughts to swell and burst. Eventually, though, she had to turn for home, experiencing curdled relief and fear as she parked in front of her block of flats. Lights shone from the windows, and from one of the balconies came the sound of pop music and laughter. People living normal lives, not skulking in the shadows, dreading the strike of the assassin's knife. She wondered what a normal life felt like. What was it like to answer your doorbell without first holding your breath and peeping through the spy hole to determine that the person with his finger on the buzzer wasn't bent on killing you?

Hammond was out there somewhere. Could be watching her now from behind the cedar tree. Could have attached a tracker to the underside of her car, which was even now beaconing her whereabouts to him or to one of his minions equally lacking in restraint, compassion or humanity. Was it safer to lurk in the car all night? Or to step out towards the laughter and the music? She dithered, frozen with indecision, until finally, screwing up her courage, she opened the car door. As she locked it, she widened her field of vision to check who was loitering on the pavement nearby, and went into the block and up to her flat.

As she approached her door, a tall, dark figure unpeeled himself from the wall. Her heart faltered for a second, until she realised it was Aidan lying in wait for her.

"How did you get in?" she greeted him, aware as the words escaped her lips how churlish they sounded.

"Someone was going out as I arrived, and they held the door for me," he said.

So much for security, if the other people in the flats let in strangers willy-nilly.

"I'm sorry about yesterday," he said. "How did it go today?"

"Not good," she said, letting them both in. Her flat was gloomy with evening light, and she scampered round switching on every light, feeling safer in the bright cocoon. She went into the kitchen and filled the kettle, more to avoid having to confess what had happened than through thirst. "We waited for a long time, and then we were informed that Hammond has escaped."

"Escaped? I thought he was in high security?"

"He was, but he threatened one of the warder's grandchildren and hatched a plan to escape. I was just the audience to witness how clever he is. He never had any intention of speaking to me."

"But the tear gas. What was that about?"

"A ruse to get my attention." She slumped on the settee, bone weary.

The muscles in his jaw worked. "What are you going to do?"

"Be extra careful, and start praying."

"Do you want to move away?"

"I just don't know." Her voice cracked with helplessness. There was nothing she could do, nowhere she could go, nowhere she was safe while Hammond was alive. She was weary of running for her life. Desperate to change the topic, she brightened her voice with an effort and said, "I know something you don't know."

"Go on."

"That skeleton you found. The police have identified it."

"They haven't told me." He looked put out.

"No reason they should. Anyway, I only know because someone rang Ritter with the ident while I was with him."

"And? Who is it?"

"A boy called Adam Jones. He went missing thirty-five years ago. The funny thing is, there's a connection with the new case I'm working. Adam Jones and my boy were friends."

"You think the two deaths are connected?"

"That's what I want to find out." She unpeeled herself from the settee and made a pot of tea, arranged shop-bought cakes on a plate, and tucked a tube of crisps under her arm. "Battenburg with a Pringles chaser," she said, as he eyed the feast. "Can't face proper food. Tell me what you know about Adam's burial. There might be a clue there to Philip's death."

Aidan helped himself to a slice of Battenburg and broke it into four squares, each adorned on two sides by a trimming of marzipan. "There was a cluster of Iron Age cist burials. They're small graves, lined with stone, with the body placed in the foetal position. There were five of them — all of them looked right, and there's lots of Iron Age sites round there, so it all fitted in. We got a couple of bones out of the graves, but there was a complete skeleton in one."

"How was it positioned?"

"On its side, hands folded together up by the face. Apart from the fact it was wearing braces, it all fitted perfectly. The grave was lined with stone, just like the others." He paused to eat a square of cake. "But there was a watch tucked under one of them."

"What sort of watch?"

"A kid's Disney watch with a red strap."

"Adam was twelve when he went missing. That sounds a bit young for him." She licked her finger to dab up the sugar on the plate.

"Whoever buried that kid did a good job. If we hadn't had to excavate because they're developing the path, it could have stayed there forever, no one any the wiser. Even when we excavated, it looked genuine. It was only the watch that gave it away."

"What do you mean?"

"The watch was underneath the stones lining the grave — so we know it wasn't a body put in an Iron Age grave. The whole thing was faked."

"It was a body put in it, not a skeleton? How do you know?"

"Soil samples from under the skeleton. Plus, it would be quite hard to position the skeleton the way it was found."

"Any clothing?" she asked.

"A few shreds, most of it had rotted away."

"Anything else strike you?"

"Whoever buried him knew not only that there were Iron Age graves in the area, but also knew exactly how they were constructed." He thought for a moment. "And something else — the body was placed carefully. It wasn't chucked in. Whoever buried that boy took their time and did it properly."

Something else struck her: not only did whoever it was know about Iron Age graves, they were a cool customer. Most murderers get found out because they panic and make a mistake. This person fabricated a grave that fooled a bunch of archaeologists, and remained undetected for over thirty years. Surely that narrowed the field of suspects?

PART TWO: 1981

CHAPTER SEVEN

"Wait for me!"

"Quick! Before he catches up!" Adam shoves Philip in the back to make him move faster. They speed past square front gardens and parked cars; young, free, bubbling with energy.

"Wait for me!" Gregory's voice is starting to crack, tears threatening.

Adam turns, still running, and shouts, "Go away! We don't want you!"

Gregory sticks his lip out and raises his shoulders for an all-out epic fit.

"Come on, Adam," Tommo says. "Last one to the end is a poof."

Behind him, Gregory inhales a huge breath. It sounds like someone blowing up balloons, but Adam knows when Gregory lets that breath go, he'll unleash hell. Waving to Tommo and Philip that he'll catch them up, he slows to a jog, then stops and waits for Gregory's pinched pink face to reach him.

"You didn't stop!" Gregory wails. His voice sets Adam's teeth on edge; whenever Gregory whines, he yearns to pinch the soft skin under his arms and twist it. Hard. "I called and called and you didn't stop!"

"I'm with my friends, Gregory. *My* friends. Not yours."

"I want to come, too."

"But they don't want you. I don't want you. So push off home and play with your dollies."

Gregory screws up his face, ready to launch an onslaught. "Mum said you had to be nice to me. Mum said you had to play with me."

Adam thrusts his face close to Gregory's and hisses, "She's *my* mum, not yours. Yours is dead and being eaten by worms."

Gregory tips back his head and howls, giving it everything he's got. It's impressive: loud enough to stop a dog-walker in his tracks and make the dog cock its head and whimper, and there's a world record amount of bubbling snot and real tears. Gregory doesn't do things by halves. He keeps it up for a long time while Adam watches him, arms folded.

"I'm going to tell Mum!" Gregory swivels on his heel and runs back down the street.

Adam doesn't wait to see if Gregory makes it home. He sprints away, joining Philip and Tommo at the corner of the road, and the three of them head for the park. Each step he takes, he wishes it's Gregory's head he's stamping on. His, and Dennis's and Mum's. He hates all of them. Hates that they're all Taylors because Mum took Dennis's surname when they married, and he, Adam, is a Jones. The only Jones surrounded by Taylors. The odd one out. He kicks at a stone and grins as it nicks the back of a dog's leg. The owner rounds on him, scowling.

"Sorry!" Adam calls. "Accident! It caught my shoe." And he and the others scarper.

"Is that Fat Simon?" Tommo asks, as they approach the ornamental lake. "Is that his grandma and grandpa? God, they're even fatter than he is."

They slink towards the lake, dodging behind bushes like spies to get a better look at Fat Simon. His grandma is saying, "I saw it and knew you'd like it, Simon," and she strokes his hair back from his greasy forehead. "My best boy."

Tommo smothers a snigger. "Fattest boy, she means."

Simon has in his hands a large model yacht, holding it so tenderly it's as if it has magical powers. A magical yacht, Adam thinks, his guts crunching. He's longed for one like it for ages, hoping his mum and Dennis will get the message, but they don't. They barely notice he's there these days, always cooing and gazing at each other. He might as well be invisible.

Simon's grandparents waddle off to a bench nearby, while Simon dithers by the lake. Adam emerges from his hiding place. "What you got there, Simon?"

Simon turns, wary, then smiles when he sees it's Adam. "Hello!" He holds up the yacht. "She's a beauty, isn't she?"

"A beauty, isn't she?" Tommo mimicks, scrubbling out from the undergrowth, Philip close behind. "Let's have a go, then."

Simon hesitates. Emotions chase across his face, and Adam knows he's battling with the desire to keep the pristine yacht to himself, and the possibility of buying Tommo's friendship by sharing it.

"Let him have first go," Adam says. "When did you get it?"

"Just now."

"Is it your birthday?"

"No. Just a present." Simon flushes; he knows the price of the yacht and that no one else could hope to receive such treasure without it being a mammoth special occasion.

"All right for some," Adam sniffs.

"Want to help me launch it?" Simon says.

"You need champagne," Philip chips in. "And to make a speech."

"I've got pop," Simon picks up a can of lemonade from the grass. "I'll do the champagne bit, you do the words Philip, and Tommo and Adam can launch it." He blinks round at them, begging for acceptance. Adam exchanges a look with Tommo and grins.

Simon brandishes the lemonade like a Satanist brandishing a dagger and dribbles a small amount onto the yacht's gleaming white paintwork. Philip puts on a posh, high-pitched voice meant to be the Queen, and intones, "And all who sail in her."

Adam and Tommo take one end of the yacht each and inch to the edge of the lake. They carefully set it down in the water, wait until it stabilises, then give it a mighty push, sending it spinning into the middle of the lake.

"My yacht!" Simon cries. His grandparents shoot up from the bench.

"Oh, Simon, what's the matter?" his grandma says.

"Oh, Simon, my best boy, what's the matter!" Tommo squeals, scampering round him. "What you going to do now, Fatso!"

"Leave him alone, Tommo!" Philip says.

A gust of wind catches the yacht and twirls it further into the centre of the lake.

"That was a mean thing to do, Adam," Philip says, staring Adam in the eye until he flinches. He understands the look: Philip expects meanness from Tommo but not from him. A hot wave of shame crashes over him, and he hates Philip for making him feel like a worm.

Tommo is doubled over at the misery on Simon's face. Adam thumps him on the shoulder. "Race you," he says, and the two of them flee, flying like the wind out of the park.

At the gate, Adam glances back. Philip is hopping on one foot, tugging at his shoes and socks, then he wades into the lake and rescues Simon's yacht. Simon and his grandma stand on the edge, crying.

"That was ace," Tommo says, when they stop to get their breath back. "Fat Simon! Grandma's best boy. What a joke!"

"Yeah," Adam says. His stomach squirms as he remembers the look Philip gave him. "And Philip's wet, too."

"Even wetter now he's gone to fetch that yacht."

And the two of them laugh like drains.

It's not so funny when he gets home. Simon's mother has phoned his mum and complained about the trick with the yacht, and Gregory has evidently worked himself up so much he's made himself sick, because he's installed in front of the TV with an old washing-up bowl beside him 'in case'. He turns a triumphant, tear-stained face on Adam when he slouches in.

"You're in trouble."

"Still don't want to be your friend."

"Mu-um!" Gregory starts, but his mum's already pounding down the hallway, so he buttons it, an avid expression on his face, anticipating the fun. Adam's hatred goes up a notch.

"Where have you been?" his mum demands.

"Out with my friends," he says, with an emphasis on 'my'.

"Couldn't you take your brother with you?"

"He's not my brother."

"He's your step-brother. Like it or not, we're all a family now." She plants her hand on her hips. "Can't you let him go with you sometimes?"

"But Mum, he's nine, and we're twelve, and..." He stops. Surely she can see the problem here? But no, she can't. Or won't.

"Let him join in, Adam," she says. "I won't tell you again."

"Fine." If that's what Gregory wants, that's what Gregory will get.

CHAPTER EIGHT

"I told Tommo and Philip I'd meet them later," Adam says, scraping up the last of his baked bean juice and licking his fork. He catches his mum's eye. "Can I?"

She nods at Gregory, his knife and fork held upright in tight fists, jabbing away at his pizza and beans. He's always the last to finish, toiling away at the table long after everyone else's plate is cleared away, washed up, dried and back in the cupboard. Adam stares at him, too, deliberately refusing to understand.

Adam's mum clears her throat. "You can see your friends if you take Gregory with you."

Great. Just what he wants — Gregory tagging along like a whiny ghost. Gregory's looking at him, chewing with his mouth partly open, revealing the concrete mixer of teeth, pizza and baked beans churning round and round.

"*Top of the Pops* is on," Adam says. Gregory loves *Top of the Pops*, thinks it makes him grown-up.

Gregory shrugs, but Adam can see the torment: hanging around with Adam and his friends versus watching his favourite show and pretending to be a teenager.

"Duran Duran might be on. Or Adam and the Ants." Gregory likes all those groups with their floppy hair, flouncy blouses and eye makeup like a bunch of girls.

"So."

"You'd have to wait till next week, and they might not be on then." His gaze bores into Gregory, willing him to stay behind with Mum and the TV. It doesn't work.

"I want to come with you," Gregory states flatly.

"Finish up your tea and wash your hands," his mum says, eyeballing Adam so he understands he'd better be nice to Gregory or he'll be for it.

Fifteen minutes later, Gregory has finally eaten his tea and the two of them are wheeling their bikes out of the shed. Adam's is bright blue, with racing handlebars — last Christmas's big present, a bribe to force him to be nice to Dennis; Gregory's is a squat yellow bike with thick tyres. A little kid's bike.

"You'd better not hold us back on your toy bike," Adam says, as they cycle over to Philip's house. Philip and Tommo are already waiting. Their faces drop when they see Gregory in tow, and push away from the wall and cycle off before Adam and Gregory reach them. Adam soon catches up but, as usual, Gregory trails behind, wailing.

"Let's play a trick on him," Adam whispers to Tommo. He doesn't want Philip to overhear: he still smarts at the memory of the disgusted look Philip shot him over Fat Simon's yacht. "You know how we go to the top of Leckhampton Hill and freewheel down?"

Tommo gets him straight away. "Nice one!"

They wait for Gregory to catch up. "We're going up the hill," Tommo says. "You want to come?"

Gregory nods, his eyes huge at being part of the group, and the four of them start the long toil up the hill. The first part isn't too bad, but when the houses peter out and the ground drops away to the side, they dismount and lean over their handlebars, puffing with every step. Steeper and steeper, they push on, lungs screaming, until eventually they come to the turn-off for the Devil's Chimney.

"Want to say hello to the Devil?" Tommo says, and strikes off up the track.

At the top of the ridge, they climb back on their bikes and jolt over the stony path. Adam glances back at Gregory. He's beetroot from the effort of the climb, his legs pumping up and down trying to keep up with them. He feels a reluctant surge of admiration. Not that it means he can come again. No one wants a child tagging along.

The path skirts the edge of the hill, the drop dizzying. Far below, Cheltenham sprawls across the plain. In the distance, clouds gather over the horizon, a beam of sunlight piercing through, like a spotlight. Godlight, his mum calls it. She has a lot of daft sayings like that.

Ahead, Tommo skids to a halt, spraying pebbles. Philip comes to a gentler halt behind him, Adam and Gregory bringing up the rear.

"You seen the Devil before, Gregory?" Adam says.

"The Devil?"

"Yeah. Old Nick. Satan. You know."

"No." Gregory's face pinches with suspicion. "And neither have you."

"Oh yes I have. Look!" Adam points to the Devil's Chimney, a stark orange finger of stone jutting up from the side of the hill. "Can't you see the Devil? Clinging to that rock?"

Gregory narrows his eyes and squints. Stupid kid's really trying to see the Devil. Adam pokes him. "Go on, get closer and you'll see him."

"I can see him," Tommo chips in. "Can't you, Philip?"

"Yes, I can see him."

Gregory drops his bike and inches towards the edge of the hill, his eyes fixed on the Devil's Chimney. Adam's heart thumps. They're really going to do it.

"Go on, Gregory!" he calls. "Go right up to the Devil!"

Gregory's sandals skid and he slips closer to the edge.

"Can you see him yet?" Tommo shouts.

"I think so." Gregory minces closer still.

"He's there, Gregory. Look at his eyes — burning — and looking right at you!" Adam bellows.

"Don't let him look you in the eye," Philip calls. "He'll turn you to stone!"

Gregory squeals and whisks round, just in time to see Adam, Tommo and Philip pick up their bikes and pedal away. A scream follows them down the track. Adam doesn't waver. The next bit's going to be good.

He waits where the track joins the road until a tear-stained Gregory with two scuffed knees appears. "You left me!" he howls. "And I got stung by nettles."

"You want to come out with us, this is what we do," Adam retorts. "If you don't like it, don't follow us."

Gregory juts his lip, tears sliming his face.

"You'll like the next bit," Adam says. "It's fun."

They mount their bikes at the top of the hill and wait until a van whooshes past, then at Tommo's signal, they set off, pedalling hard, then take their feet off the pedals, freewheeling down the hill. It's steep, very steep, and the breath is knocked out of him by the speed. He's as fast as a car, as fast as an aeroplane, as fast as a rocket. A car zooms down the hill beside him; he keeps pace with it for a long time before it accelerates past. His feet fumble for the pedals, holding them steady as he steers the bike round one corner, then another. He tries hard not to look at the drop beside him. One pebble in the road, one wobble and he'd plunge over the side. His heart is bursting through his chest. Faster, faster. The bottom of the hill looms ahead. Tommo's already there, whooping. Philip slides to a halt seconds later, and then Adam's at the bottom, gently tugging on his brakes and gliding to a standstill.

He jumps off his bike, panting with exhilaration, and turns to see where Gregory is. He's screaming as his little bike speeds down the hill, his thick legs jabbing up and down.

"Brake!" Adam yells.

Gregory brakes, the bike wobbles, his tyre hits the pavement, and he sails over the handlebars and lands in a heap in the road.

Time stands still, then goes very fast. Adam is running up the road to Gregory, Tommo and Philip at his shoulder. A car stops, brakes screeching, and a driver's getting out, waving his hands and shouting something. Gregory lies in the road, unmoving.

"Gregory!" Adam reaches him, doesn't dare to touch him. Is he dead? Has he killed him? He can barely breathe as the driver elbows him aside and checks Gregory over. Gregory groans and tries to move. Whimpers. Thank God he isn't dead.

"Where are you hurt, son?" the driver's asking. Gregory mumbles something. "You boys with him?"

Adam nods. "I'm his brother."

"You stay with him. I'm going to call an ambulance and I'll be right back."

"An ambulance? Is he … is he going to be all right?"

"Don't let him move. I'll be right back."

They stand in a circle round Gregory, staring at him.

"There's no blood," Philip whispers. "He can't die if there's no blood. Can he?"

The driver returns, and a short while later, an ambulance flashes a blue light up the road. Gregory's strapped to a board and loaded into the back of the ambulance.

"You go with him," Philip say. "I'll tell your mum what's happened."

Misery and fear engulf Adam and he can't speak. He climbs into the back of the ambulance after Gregory so terrified he thinks he might wet himself.

"You his brother?" the ambulance man asks. "Don't worry, he's in good hands."

They make him wait on a hard seat outside while the doctors work on Gregory. His mind conjures up horrible pictures of Gregory dying, or spending the rest of his life in a wheelchair, and Mum blaming him. His fault. He's planning his escape — he knows which day Mum gets her housekeeping money, he'll pinch it from her purse that day so he has enough to get to London, will pack his jeans and his anorak in case it's cold, sleeping in a park — when Mum and Dennis bustle in.

"Where is he?" Mum looks wild, her eyes scattering tears. Anyone would think Gregory was *her* child, not him. Beside her Dennis has his hands shoved in his jacket pockets, that awful grey blouson thing he wears all the time that stinks of dirt and cigarettes. The collar's stained dark with grease. He sniffs, his eyes darting around the hospital corridor.

"Where is he?" Mum's in charge. Despite his terror, Adam clocks that neither of them have asked how he is, if he's all right.

He jerks his head at the door. "In there. They wouldn't let me in."

Mum straightens and sets her mouth. "Stay here," she tells Dennis. "I'm going to find out what the doctors say." And she pushes her way through the doors.

Dennis takes the chair right next to Adam. Neither speaks. Neither looks at the other. Adam wonders if they were having it off while he and Gregory were out. He's heard them at night, when it's late and he's supposed to be asleep. The two of them

74

groaning and banging against the wall until he has to wrap his pillow around his head, wanting to scream it's so disgusting.

His mum materialises a few minutes later. "He's gone for x-rays and they say they'll keep him overnight. Concussion."

She suddenly deflates and starts to sob. Dennis wraps his arms round her, patting her shoulder uselessly. "He'll be OK."

"We don't know that!" she shrieks at him. "A head injury, that's what they said. That can be serious! And who knows what they'll find on the x-rays." And she breaks down completely, sagging at the knees and has to be steered towards the chairs.

"Go and get your mum a cup of tea," Dennis says.

Adam hesitates. He doesn't have any money and everyone knows you have to put coins in the machine.

"What you waiting for?" Dennis gives him a look that's full of loathing, a look that says clearly, *What have you done to my son, you little shit?*

"I haven't got any money."

Dennis pats his pocket and glances helplessly at Mum. She sighs and passes him her handbag. His fingers are in there like rats, hunting for her purse, unzipping the change pocket and slipping out some coins. He passes them to Adam. "Take your time."

So they can talk about him. Decide whether to send him to Borstal for letting Gregory get hurt. Well, he isn't going to Borstal, he'll run away and go to London and they'll never see him again and then they'll be sorry.

He loiters by the drinks machine, trying to decide which is more horrible, the chicken soup or the hot orangeade. After he's played this game for a while, he thumbs the coins into the slot and selects a tea with sugar. The machine discharges a beige plastic cup filled with hot beige liquid. It sloshes over the side as he carries it back to the waiting area, leaving a trail of spots on the lino.

By the time he gets back, Mum has calmed down and is sitting with Dennis's arm slung round her shoulder. Dennis's eyes are wet and he passes his hand over them and pinches his nose. The two of them crying together over Gregory. Mum takes the tea and gives him a weak smile. "He's got a broken arm," she says. A broken arm is all right. He had one a couple of years ago and it was great getting people to draw cartoons on the cast. "And a couple of broken ribs, but nothing more sinister."

"Will he be OK?"

"Yes!" she laughs, as if ten minutes ago she wasn't panicking that Gregory would die. "Of course he'll be OK. He's made of tough stuff, your brother."

Dennis smiles at her. "The whole family's made of tough stuff," he says. "You, me, Gregory."

He won't run away just yet, Adam decides, but he'll still pinch ten pounds from the housekeeping money. Serve them right.

PART THREE: 2016

CHAPTER NINE

"You should try to eat something."

"I'm not hungry," Kate said. She pulled her blue fluffy bathrobe around her and tightened the cord at the waist.

"You need to keep your strength up. The next few days and weeks could be difficult." Patty, the police family liaison officer planted a hand on her shoulder. She was always touching her, Kate thought, as if she was reassuring herself Kate was still there, not been vaporised in the five minutes since she last asked if she wanted a cup of tea.

"She's right, Kate," her mum said. "I know you don't feel like eating, but you should have something in your stomach." Her mother turned away and wiped at her cheeks with her fingers. Tears leached from her eyes constantly. Why's she crying, Kate thought, it's my daughter who's dead.

Gareth seemed to have no problem filling his stomach. He sat across the table from her, stuffing his face with scrambled eggs on toast. Patty couldn't tell them who had killed Jessica or why, but it seemed she was a dab hand at scrambled eggs. Gareth scraped his plate clean and slid his knife and fork into parallel lines.

"That better?" Kate asked, hating him. How could he eat when Jessica was dead?

"Come on, now, Kate, it's a tough day ahead," her mum said. She was always sticking up for Gareth.

Patty scribbled in her notebook.

"And what are you writing down now? 'Suspect's husband ate scrambled eggs on toast'?"

"You're not a suspect. I just have to keep a log of all my visits."

"Your visits! You're here because you think I've got something to do with Jessica's…" She couldn't say the word. "You think I did it, don't you?"

"Not at all, I'm here to support you and answer any questions you may have."

"Then answer me this. When can I have my daughter back?"

Patty folded her face into a sympathetic mask. "I know it's difficult, but there has to be a post-mortem. I understand that will be carried out today. After that, we'll have to wait for the coroner to release Jessica's body for burial."

"And how long will that take?"

"They'll be as quick as they can. Everyone understands how painful this is for you."

"Understand! You understand nothing! You sit here, in my house, hour after hour, doing nothing except writing in your little book," Kate screeched, grief giving way to pure, white hot cleansing anger. "Get out of my house! I don't want you here, spying on me."

"I'm not spying…"

"Kate!"

"All of you! Get out!"

"Come on, now, Kate," her mum said.

"I want to sleep. I can't sleep with all of you fussing round. I want you all out. Gone."

"Go where?" Gareth said.

"I don't care! Just go!" Kate hurtled out of the room and upstairs, where she flung herself on the bed. A few minutes later, there came a gentle knock on the door, as she knew there would. "Go away!"

The door pushed open a fraction. "Kate, it's me, Mum. Gareth and Patty are going out. There's just me."

Her mum glided up to the bed. Kate kept her face turned to the wall, her heart breaking as her mum's hand patted her shoulder. Distantly she heard Gareth putting on his coat and the front door slamming. A few moments later a car drove away.

"They've gone," Mum said. Her hand rested on Kate's forehead, smoothing back her sticky hair just as she had when Kate was tiny and running a fever. For a long time she lay there with her mother's hand on her head, wishing and wishing she was eight again, and tucked up in bed with her mother spooning tomato soup into her and stroking her back to wellness.

"I'll just be downstairs," Mum said.

Kate turned over and saw her mother's face, grey and haggard with grief. "No, Mum, you go home. I'll be fine. I just need to sleep, that's all."

"I don't want to leave you."

"I promise I'll be all right."

Her mother hesitated. "I'll be back in two hours." She bent and kissed the top of Kate's head. "Get some rest, you'll feel better. Call me any time, I'll be right back."

She left as quietly as she'd entered, and soon Kate heard the front door open and close, and her mother's shoes clicking down the path. Kate flopped back on the pillows, hunting for a cool spot. The house settled around her, relapsing into silence. As silent as the grave, Kate thought, the words sliding into her mind like insidious worms. She tried hard not to think about Jessica's body, her tiny, waxy body locked in a fridge at the mortuary; the little body that might already have a stitched ridge heaving up through her torso. The little body she wasn't allowed to see yet.

Kate picked up Gareth's pillow and pressed it over her face to smother the howl that erupted from her. The doctor had given her some pills to calm her down. It was still hours before she could take the next ones and already the misery was sweeping back in a gigantic wave that smashed down on top of her; grief scouring her hollow. Why had they all listened when she told them to go away? The house was too quiet; creeping her out.

She stumbled from the bed and into the bathroom, where she was sick into the hand basin. Beige blobs and a lot of hot beige liquid. She daren't look in the mirror, afraid to see Jessica lurking behind her, her eyes accusing. How could you let this happen to me, Mummy? She sleep-walked back to the bed and switched on the TV, letting it chunter on in the background. She couldn't make out a word of it, but it held the silence at bay. Then the doorbell went.

It might be flowers for Jessica. There had been lots of flowers, and friends calling round, and total strangers with tear-splotched faces and sympathy cards and teddies. Even that would be better than this suffocating silence. She padded downstairs to see: this one was a stranger, but he brandished neither teddy nor card, and his face wasn't tear-stained with second-hand grief. It was quite a nice face: good looking, clean shaven, blue eyes. He was tall and fair haired, in a smart dark suit and navy shirt without a tie. Respectful yet not maudlin, not like Patty in her black skirt and grey jumper, pretending she was part of the family.

"Kate Smithson?"

"Yes."

"I'm sorry to disturb you at this time, but I wondered if I could have a word? It is important, I'm afraid." A sympathetic smile and no tears: maybe he was here for her and not himself.

"I'm not dressed." She waved a hand at her dressing gown.

"I can wait if you want to get dressed," he said, and half-turned away, as if giving her privacy there and then.

"I'll just be a couple of minutes."

"Take as long as you need." That gentle, understanding smile again, and he was still smiling when she reappeared in leggings and a green top.

"What was it you wanted?" she asked.

He fixed her with a look. "Call me presumptuous if you like, but can I make you a cup of tea? You look as if you could do with it."

"Tea?" Suddenly tea was the one thing she wanted. Her mouth was acrid from vomiting and her stomach clenched like a fist. Tea, a good strong cup of tea would sort her out. "Yes, tea." She stood aside and let him in, ushering him into the sitting room.

He plumped up the cushions. "You sit here, Mrs Smithson, and I'll be right back with some tea. No, I can find my way round a kitchen."

"It's Kate," she called after him. "Everyone just calls me Kate."

He came back with a tray, teapot, cups and saucers, all arranged neatly. She and Gareth always used mugs, some of them chipped.

"Are you from the police?"

"Not exactly," he said. "I'm here about what happened to your daughter. It upset me very much when I heard about it. I can't imagine how desperately sad you feel right now."

Kate foraged in her pocket for a tissue. The stranger handed her a crisp white cotton handkerchief that smelled pleasantly of aftershave. "I understand about grief, Kate."

"Are you a counsellor?"

"No, but I've experienced a lot of death." He held her gaze. "And the thing is, grief can take us by surprise."

"How do you mean?" The tea was hot and strong, washing away the foulness in her mouth.

"Everyone thinks it's all about sadness. About crying and loss, but it isn't always like that." He paused as if waiting for her to comment. She nodded, wanting him to go on. "Sometimes grief can make us hollow. Or we can feel as though nothing's real and we're in a dream. Sometimes you can feel panicky. Or guilty."

She certainly felt that. Guilty. Tears stung her eyes as she thought of that morning. Kicking the pushchair. Shouting at Jessica. "I was horrible to her," she said, in a small, devastated voice. "I didn't know she was going to…"

"Of course you didn't. How could you? But she knew you loved her."

He waited until the tears subsided, a gentle presence beside her. "Guilt is normal when you lose someone," he said. "Guilt, and anger."

Kate leaned forwards. "I know exactly what you mean. I feel sad and horrible and scared and really, really angry, all at the same time. I could murder the person who did it. And I'm not a violent person, Mr … what did you say your name was?"

"Just call me John," he said, topping up her cup. "The anger can be quite shocking, can't it, Kate? I don't know if you're religious at all?"

"Are you a vicar?"

"No, just someone who's hoping to help you get through this." He studied her for a moment. "If you want me to help, that is."

A bubble exploded in Kate's chest and the tears flowed down her cheeks. She scrubbed them away with the handkerchief, but more fell, until the hanky was sodden. "Gareth, he's my husband, he doesn't understand. He's just sad about Jessica, but he wasn't there. He didn't see her struggling to breathe. He didn't watch her die. He can't see why I'm so angry."

"It's not his fault. This anger is yours, and it's your friend, Kate. You just need to express it in the right way."

A sob built in her throat.

"The anger is because you know that all of this need never have happened. I'm sure you've thought that," John said.

She glanced up at him, frowning. "How do you mean?"

"Let's look at it this way. There you were, having a perfectly pleasant morning with your lovely daughter, and you get caught up in something that is nothing to do with you. So who is to blame?"

"The person who put the gas in the fish!"

"A truly wicked thing to do. And why would someone do that. Who made him do that?"

Kate shook her head. "I don't understand."

"The woman in the message."

"Eden Grey," Kate said, slowly.

"That's right. Eden Grey. Have the police told you anything about her?"

"No, nothing."

"Ah. I suspected as much."

"Do you know her?"

"I know of her, Kate, and I know what she's capable of."

"Is she a terrorist?" Her voice came out as a whisper.

"I'm not allowed to speak about it." He made a zippering motion across his lips and mouthed, "Official secrets."

"Are you a spy?"

"I can't tell you that, either, I'm afraid, Kate." He adjusted his cuffs. "Just believe me when I tell you you have no idea what some people are capable of." He rose and walked over to the fireplace, where a family photograph hung: Kate, Gareth, and Jessica. "What a beautiful child." He turned to face her, his eyes blazing. "I can see why you're angry, to lose someone so precious."

"I won't ever get through this, will I?"

He returned to his seat next to her on the settee and her gaze fixed on the crisp creases in his immaculate suit. He smelt of classy aftershave and reassurance. "You will," he said. "Trust me, I know what to do."

CHAPTER TEN

Armed with her private investigator's I.D and a contract of engagement signed by Susan Wakefield, Eden presented herself at the coroner's office. Situated on the edge of Gloucester, it was a modern, light building with pale woodwork; sterile and impersonal. She was shown into a side office housing just a desk and chair, and waited while the clerk fetched the file she'd requested. When it came, her heart sank.

"That's it?" she said.

The clerk shrugged. "We don't keep the whole file, just the essentials."

'The essentials' turned out to consist of three sheets of paper: a proforma recording the name of the coroner, the witnesses and the verdict; a police statement; and a pathologist's report. Eden flipped to a clean page in her notebook, and read the documents through.

Philip Wakefield died on the 25th August, 1981. The middle of the summer holidays, Eden reflected, remembering her own schooldays and the wish that the holidays would last just another week, and another. He was found hanging in woods outside Cheltenham; the coroner's verdict was that his death was suicide.

The police statement offered sketchy details. Susan Wakefield had contacted the police on the evening of 25th August, concerned that Philip had not come home. He'd announced he was going out but hadn't told his mother where. The next day, when Philip had still not returned home, police questioning his friends came up with the detail that the boys often went to a camp in the woods. Upon visiting the camp, the police found his body. Philip was lying prone on the ground, a noose around his neck. Scuffs on the branches of a nearby tree suggested the rope had come loose some time after he'd died.

The pathologist's statement was equally thin. It stated that Philip was a well-nourished, average-sized twelve year old. Examination showed several old bruises and contusions on his body, and there were fresh cuts on his left arm. The pathologist surmised that these were attempts to slit his wrists. There were also scratches and bruises around his throat, probably caused by his clawing at the noose. His eyes were peppered with petechiae — small burst blood vessels — not uncommon in hanging. There was bruising around Philip's mouth, the colour of it suggesting it was several days old, and also fading bruises around his wrists and ankles. These were considered irrelevant to the current enquiry.

Eden jotted some notes and circled the questions that the reports raised. Why did he kill himself? Anxiety about his friend's disappearance? And what about the bruising round his mouth? Had he been in a fight a few days before he died? And if so, did it have any bearing on his suicide? And what about the bruising on his wrists and ankles? Why did no one offer an explanation of the old bruises?

She slotted the papers back in the folder and returned it the clerk, then drove into Gloucester city centre and parked at the records office. Calling up the rolls for the 1981 Gloucester and Cheltenham newspapers, she settled herself at a microfiche machine and braced herself for eyestrain.

It was worth it, though. The papers had much more detail than the stark coroner's records, and sprinkled their accounts with photos of the scene and major protagonists. A journalist had attended the inquest and provided a much more fulsome account of the witnesses.

Starting with 26th August, when the newspapers first reported Philip's disappearance, Eden traced the story from its beginnings. The newspaper reports talked of a quiet but well-liked boy, and reprinted his school photo: Philip in a V-necked school jumper, pimples just starting to mar his skin. The reports said he was always home by six o'clock, as that was when he had his dinner, and when he wasn't back by seven, Susan Wakefield rang round his friends. None of them had seen him. She called the police who put out an all units description for him.

The next edition covered the discovery of his body in the woods and reran the story of Adam Jones' disappearance. That the two boys had been friends since primary school piqued the journalists' interest, some of them speculating that Philip killed himself because he was so distraught that Adam was missing.

She followed Philip's story through the newspaper reports: the identification of his body and later, the funeral. There was a massive turn-out, the church crowded with people, many of them, she suspected, muscling in on the grief of two lost boys and unable to express the horror and disorientation they felt in any other way. Safety in numbers.

There were several pictures of Philip's friends and classmates at the funeral, a gaggle of boys unable to hug each other in their grief; wide-eyed that it had all happened so quickly. She zoomed in on the microfiche. That was odd. She blew the picture up as high as possible and studied them. Two of the boys had dark shadows around their mouths, and one's eyes looked unnaturally dark. Bloodshot from crying? Or was it a black eye from a fight? She zoomed back out and studied then again. Not unusual for boys to scuffle about, even if they were mates, but strange that they had identical injuries. The same injuries Philip had when he died.

The inquest was a couple of months later. Susan Wakefield testified that Philip had been upset in the days before he died, withdrawn and uncommunicative. Teenage hormones and natural moodiness? Or something worrying him? There was a picture of her leaving the court with her husband, a short man with a round, kindly face; both of them had their hands up to shield themselves from the press.

Eden skipped through the newspapers for another few weeks, noticing that Adam Jones' disappearance moved further and further back in the pages until he was mentioned no more. A missing boy with a dead friend: old news.

Eden made her way back to Cheltenham, parked in the Bath Road shoppers' carpark with its recycling skips and clothing banks, and headed along the street. She loved the bustle of the Bath Road with its independent shops, cafes and wholefood stores. She paused and gazed in the window of the second hand charity bookshop, thinking of the times she'd popped in just to browse, only to come away with a carrier bag full of treasure. Interesting books, in good condition, sold cheaply. Her idea of heaven. Aidan's, too. He was always rummaging around in the Classics section at the back, emerging triumphantly with an obscure book of Latin poetry and looking as though he'd won the lottery.

She kept her field of vision wide, noting who was where and whether they noticed her. Counter-surveillance. She ducked into a second hand furniture shop at the top of the street and made straight to the back. Reflections in shop windows had shown her a man in a black hoodie behind her. She watched him pass the shop and waited in case he doubled back, relieved when he joined the queue at the bus stop and got on with the other passengers. She killed another few minutes pretending to look at the ugliest wardrobe she'd ever seen, just to check black hoodie wasn't in a tag team, then left the shop and went down a side street. Ahead was a large Art Deco church with a peaceful garden. The daffodils were blooming blousily, a great sward of them that would have pleased Wordsworth, and she sat for a moment in silent reflection before making her way to Susan's house.

Susan was in black leggings and a grey thigh length tunic with patch pockets. She didn't seem surprised to see Eden, just opened the door wider to let her in, and showed her into the sitting room. Pot plants drooped over shelves and mantelpiece, and a giant fig dominated one corner of the room. A jug of milky water and a cloth were next to a rubber plant: evidently it was having its leaves polished.

The chair in the window was covered with a blue fleecy blanket, and in the middle, curled up asleep, was a large tabby cat.

"You're not allergic, are you?" asked Susan.

"No, I love cats. We had them when I was growing up." Eden bit the inside of her cheek. Were the cats still alive? How absolute it was to disappear from your old life. Her family and friends were told she was dead, and had no idea what she was up to now; equally she had no idea what was happening to them, even whether they were still alive. It hit her that one day her mum and dad would die, and she would never know, would spend the rest of her life ignorant of whether they were well, or suffering, or lonely. Grief kicked her in the guts, and she bent to stroke the cat to give her time to recover herself.

By the time Susan returned with two china beakers of the palest tea Eden had ever seen, the cat had taken up residence on Eden's lap.

Eden chose her words carefully. "Susan, I've been reviewing Philip's case at the coroner's court, and there are a few things that I think need explaining."

Susan tucked herself into the chair opposite. "Go ahead."

"There were a number of old bruises on his body," Eden said. "Around his mouth and on his wrists. Do you know how he got those?"

"He said he was in a fight."

"Who with?"

Susan licked her lips. "Adam Jones."

"When was this?"

"A few days before Adam disappeared. He said Adam hit him."

"Had they fought before?"

"Philip wasn't a scrapping sort of boy. He'd never even had a torn sweater."

"What was the fight about?"

"Philip wouldn't tell me," Susan said. "But he was very upset, didn't want me to put ice on the bruise. In fact, he tried covering it up with toothpaste so I wouldn't see. Adam hit him in the eye, too, because his eyes were all bloodshot."

"And the bruises on his wrists and ankles?" Eden asked.

"I didn't see the ones on his ankles," Susan said. "He told me the others were from this fight with Adam."

"Did you tell the police about the fight?"

Susan studied her hands, twisting her fingers together in a Gordian knot. The joints were swollen with arthritis. "No," she said, eventually.

"Why not?" Eden waited for the answer, her nerves taut with the tension in the room as the silence bloomed. A tear dropped onto Susan's hands. "Susan?"

"He was very upset after that fight with Adam," Susan said at last. "I was worried about him. He wouldn't talk to me, wouldn't tell me what was wrong. A couple of days later, he still hadn't talked to me, so I went up to his room after he'd gone to bed, to see if I could get anything out of him." Her eyes met Eden's. "He wasn't there. He'd gone."

"Gone where?"

"I don't know. Roger, Philip's dad, got in the car and drove round the streets, seeing if he could find him. I rang Adam's mother, and she said that they'd just discovered Adam was missing, too, but they thought they knew where he'd gone and his dad had gone to fetch him home. She rang me back a while later to say the boys were refusing to come home, but they were OK. Eventually, Philip sneaked back into the house. I heard him come up the stairs and go into his room."

"What did he say?"

"He denied it. Said he hadn't left the house all evening, that I was imagining things." Susan wriggled a tissue out of her pocket and scrubbed her nose. "The next day we heard that Adam was missing. Philip was even more upset than before, but wouldn't talk. The day after that, he killed himself."

"Why do you think he did it?"

Susan's voice was muffled by the tissue. "I told people it was because he was worried about Adam, but that's not true. They'd hardly seen each other over the summer." Her voice trembled as she said, "God help me, I thought it was guilt, that Philip knew what had happened to Adam because he'd … hurt him."

"You thought Philip killed Adam?"

"He lied about sneaking out of the house, they'd had a fight a few days before, and Philip was very, very upset. I thought … I thought maybe they'd had another fight, and it'd got really out of hand, and you know sometimes terrible accidents happen … and Philip just panicked."

"And you never said any of this to the police?"

"Of course not! I'm his mother!" She fought to bring herself under control. "Do you know, we got burgled the day of his funeral? We came back home and found the place turned over. Every room ransacked. They took my pearl necklace I got for my twenty-first birthday."

"Was anyone caught?"

"Eventually. He was only about sixteen, the lad who did it. He confessed and returned my necklace. Brian Armitage, that was his name. Not the full shilling, by all accounts. I hated him for what he did to us, when we were going through all that."

"It sounds terrible," Eden said. What a shock, to come home from burying your son, only to find your home ripped open. She knew that thieves scoured the notices in newspapers for details of funerals as they indicated when a house was likely to be empty for a few hours, but this half-witted lad didn't seem a likely candidate for that sort of targeted burglary. Unless he was working for someone else. She made a note to find out more: it was probably nothing, but the more she learned about this case, the more perplexing it was.

"I kept my suspicions about Philip to myself," Susan said. "Didn't even say anything to Roger. I didn't want to make things worse for him. He adored Philip. We'd tried for a baby for years, and had started to think it wouldn't happen for us, when Philip came along. Roger was delighted, couldn't have been a better father. I wasn't going to crush that by suggesting his son was a killer."

"It must've been hard."

"I loved Philip, and I loved Roger. I was just protecting them," Susan said. "But then a few years after Philip died, the police arrested someone for Adam Jones' murder."

"Who did they arrest?"

"A man called Ray Thompson. He was the uncle of one of Philip's friends, Dave Thompson. I didn't like Dave much."

"Why not?"

"I always felt he was laughing at me for being older than the other mothers, and because I was strict about good manners."

"What happened to Ray Thompson?" Eden asked.

"He was put on trial and acquitted. No body, you see. Hard to prove it's murder when there's no body." Susan's shoulders trembled as she continued, "I started to worry that I'd made a terrible mistake. If Adam was killed that night, and Philip was with him, was Philip killed, too, to keep him quiet?"

"And who else knows this, and is that why they're leaving the flowers on Philip's grave?" Eden finished, as Susan slowly nodded.

CHAPTER ELEVEN

Susan Wakefield had shown Eden a photo of Philip with his friends: Adam Jones, Dave Thompson and Lance Cotter. Only two of them left: surely they had opinions on why one of their friends died and another went missing? Lance Cotter wasn't hard to track down. A few minutes on Facebook and Eden knew that he'd spent his whole life in Cheltenham, lived in Charlton Kings, and was the manager of a homewares store on the Tewkesbury Road.

She rang the store and arranged to meet him, arriving a few minutes early and browsing around the pots of paint, rugs, and oven gloves until Lance came over. He was several inches shorter than her, and his gingerish hair was starting to recede. He approached with an air of flustered overwork and sweat patches circling his underarms. For a moment she felt a pang of regret: what she was here to ask him wouldn't help his stress levels.

"Thanks for seeing me, Mr Cotter," she said, shaking hands. His palm was wet and she surreptitiously smudged her hand down her trousers. "Is there somewhere we can speak privately?"

He took her into a dingy staff room furnished with chairs and tables from the shop's stock. Coffee rings adorned the table top, and someone had scattered sugar over the floor in a crunchy coating. A post-it note threatening to kill the wanker who was stealing yoghurts was stuck in the middle of the fridge door.

Eden took a seat opposite Lance and handed over her card. "I'm investigating the death of Philip Wakefield," she said. "You two were friends?"

"Sort of," Lance said. "We hung out together for a while."

"Who was he friendly with?"

"There was a group of us," Lance said. "Me and Philip, and Adam and Dave, called Tommo. Philip, Adam and Dave had been friends since primary school. I moved into the area during first year at secondary."

"Did he have any other friends?"

"There was a lad called Simon." He gave a short laugh. "We didn't like him, but Philip, he was soft hearted. Kinder than us. Little sods we were sometimes."

"Philip was friends with Simon?"

Lance's face creased. "It's a long time ago, and I haven't thought about those days much since." He seemed to snap to attention. "Philip killed himself. What are you investigating?"

"Some things have come to light that suggest it's not as straightforward as it first seemed," she said.

"Like what?"

"I can't say," she said. "You were friends with Philip, and Adam and Dave?"

"I hung around with them for a while when moved here," Lance said, "but I stopped being friends with Tommo and Adam."

"Why was that?"

He rubbed his sweaty hands down his trousers. "Tommo, he wasn't a nice lad. Could be mean, to that Simon, for one, and Adam, he joined in. Philip didn't like it, and I didn't, either. Some of it wasn't just teasing, it was nasty. And then Tommo got into stuff that I didn't want part of."

"What stuff?" Eden asked.

"You know what lads are like."

"Tell me."

Lance cleared his throat. "It was just rumours, but I already didn't like him by then, so I stopped hanging round with him." Eden held his gaze and waited. Eventually Lance said, "People said Tommo was into something dodgy."

"What kind of thing?"

"That he took drugs and stole stuff, and you know, hung around with dodgy people."

"Did Philip hang around with them, too?"

"I don't know," Lance said. "But he always liked Adam, so if Adam was into it, maybe he was, too."

"And was Adam into it?"

Lance licked a bead of sweat off his upper lip. "I don't know," he said. "I was only friends with them for a bit, then Adam got very thick with Tommo." He shot her a fierce look. "That's all I remember."

Liar.

Dave Thompson was harder to find and Eden had to resort to trawling the electoral register to track him down. She was surprised the family had stayed in the area: with his uncle charged with Adam Jones' murder, she would have expected them to flee, but it seemed they didn't drift far. Convinced of his uncle's innocence and determined to brazen it out? Or confident that whatever happened it would be a nine day wonder and life would return to normal? For herself, she would have gone much further than the handful of miles to Gloucester, but then, she knew too much about running away and starting a new life.

Dave now lived in Abbeymead, on the outskirts of Gloucester, with his wife and three children. The house was a yellow-brick semi with a triangle of close-cropped grass outside and space to park three cars. One of them was obviously Dave's: a neat little plum-coloured hatchback, it was painted with an advertisement for his cleaning company, Dave's Clean 'N' Shine. Dave himself resembled a whippet, with a thin face and wiry, taut body. His eyes were small chestnuts, darting to her face then scanning the road behind her.

Eden stuck out her hand. "Mr Thompson? I wonder if I could ask you a few questions, please?"

"I'm UKIP and proud of it, and nothing you say will change my mind." He pointed to the large St George's flag that hung at an upstairs window. "England for the English."

"I'm not here about politics," she said. "It's about Philip Wakefield."

"Never heard of him."

"You were friends at school."

A car went past and he waved to the driver. In the interval it appeared he'd suddenly remembered Philip. "Wakey-Wakey? Yeah, I remember him."

"Could I ask you a few questions about him?"

Dave glanced over his shoulder into the hallway. "We've got a bit of family trouble."

"It'll only take a minute."

He looked her up and down and she fought the urge to step back a pace. "You can't come in."

"That's fine."

"So what's this about Wakey-Wakey? He died yonks ago. Killed himself, stupid bastard."

"I'm investigating it." Eden handed him her business card. "There are questions that should have been asked at the time." She let this sink in for a moment, then asked, "What do you remember about Philip?"

Dave scratched his left armpit. "He was a bit of a pansy. I remember that."

"He was gay?"

"No, not gay. Just a pansy. A wimp. Hung around with the nerds."

"Who were they?"

"Some fat lad … what was his name." Dave repeated the scratching operation on the other side. "Philip was a bit of a wet blanket." His gaze fixed on the middle distance. "He came to the woods with us a few of times. Didn't like skinning a rabbit."

"The woods?"

"Me and Adam and my uncle Ray used to go. He taught us camping and survival stuff. How to tie knots and build shelters and light fires with sticks. Philip was shite at all of that. Maybe that's why he didn't come out with us much."

"Do you remember what Philip was like in the weeks before he died?"

Dave slowly and deliberately shook his head. "I can't remember him much at all."

God, he was an annoying sod. Time to jolt him. "Why did he fall out with Adam Jones?"

Dave went very still. "Adam Jones?"

"Yes, someone told me Adam and Philip were friends, but they fell out," Eden said. "I wondered if you knew what it was about."

"I think I've answered enough questions," Dave said, and shut the door in her face.

CHAPTER TWELVE

Back in her car, Eden engaged central locking. Ridiculous. If Hammond wanted to abduct her, he would, even if he had to get one of his goons to jemmy her out of the vehicle. Where was he now? What was he plotting? The one thing she knew about Hammond was that there was always a plot, and that he possessed the patience to wait for years until he brought it to fruition. Years where he bullied and bribed and pressed the weak points until he was fortified by a network of people who were beholden to him, too terrified of his revenge to deny him anything, even at the cost of their souls.

What was it Miranda, her old boss from her undercover days, had told her, months ago? *Be careful, Hammond's plotting something big.* Was the tear gas in the bubble fish the 'something big', or was there worse to come? Was Hammond waiting for his moment to exact revenge on her, or was he now far away, drinking cocktails in some old lags' paradise without an extradition treaty? She prayed it was the latter.

Time for some relief from churning this over and over. Eden started the engine and headed back towards Cheltenham, turning off the main road and heading towards the railway station, then negotiating her way up a narrow street of terraced Victorian houses. The street was lined nose to tail with parked cars, and she had to drive the length of the road before she found a space to park.

Her friend Judy's house was a haven of chaos, echoing with the shouts of her three boys as they all competed to tell her first about what they'd done that day. Judy herself was in the kitchen, presiding over the washing up and smacking the knuckles of the youngest boy as he scavenged the leftovers from the dinner plates.

"Those child experts who tell you to communicate with your offspring and encourage them to express themselves have a lot to answer for," Judy said. She was a tall, statuesque woman, in green linen trousers and an embroidered top. Her hair — dyed almost black with red tips — was cut short and lay in feathered wings over her cheeks. "Have you eaten, Eden? I could do you some toast."

"Have you got Marmite?"

"We have everything. Jam, marmalade, peanut butter, chocolate spread, nutty chocolate spread, Marmite."

"Marmite's horrible," declared Judy's youngest son, scrunching up his face in disgust.

"No it's not, heathen," Eden said, squeezing herself up to the kitchen counter between the boys, who were sloshing milk in and around a row of coloured plastic cups. She pinched a tangerine from Judy's fruit bowl.

"Off with the lot of you. That pet programme is on," Judy said, shooing the boys out. A moment later the TV blared with a kids' jingle. "It's an educational programme," Judy explained. She caught two slices of toast as they pinged out of the toaster. "So don't dob me in to the paramilitary wing of Mumsnet for letting my kids watch crap on telly."

"Your secret's safe with me," Eden commented, drily.

Judy plonked two mugs of coffee and a plate of toast on the kitchen table. "What have you been up to lately? Have they banged up that nutter yet?"

Judy had rung her the moment she heard about the bubble fish and the sinister message on local radio, offering Eden shelter and protection at her house. "No one in their right mind would come and stay here," she'd said. "They'll never find you." The comment had brought tears to Eden's eyes, and she knew she would never, never forget Judy's kindness.

"There have been further developments on that one," Eden said. Unwilling to elaborate and worry Judy further, she said, "I've got an interesting case."

"WI cake fraud?"

"Not quite, though it seemed like it at first."

"Tell all."

"Mother in a tizz because someone's been putting flowers on her dead son's grave."

"Ri-ight," Judy said, slurping her coffee. "Is she…?" She twizzled her finger next to her ear.

"I thought so at first, but the plot thickens. The boy died thirty-five years ago, and the flowers have only just started turning up, left anonymously, with tags that just say, 'Sorry'."

"Creepy." Judy shuddered.

"The boy died only days after one of his friends went missing, and now the missing friend has just turned up."

"Dead?"

"Very."

"And you think there's a connection between the boys and the flowers suddenly appearing?"

Eden shrugged. "That's what I'm being paid to investigate."

Judy tapped her lips thoughtfully. "Thirty-five years ago. 1981. I was eight." She snatched up a slice of toast and spread it thickly with marmalade. "For the benefit of my diet we'll call this pudding," she said. "A policeman came to our school to talk to us about a missing boy. What was really odd was there were no teachers present, just us kids and the policeman, and he said that whatever we told him, we wouldn't be in trouble." She pondered for a moment. "Very strange." She turned to Eden. "Who's the missing boy in your case?"

"A boy called Adam Jones."

Judy snapped her fingers. "That's right! Adam Jones."

"Did you know him?"

"No, but he went to the same school as my sister. She was actually in his class. I think she must've fancied him a bit, because she was upset for ages when he disappeared."

"Your sister?" Eden said. "I don't suppose I could speak to her, could I?"

"Sure. She lives in Bristol — you happy to meet her there?" Judy caught Eden's eye. "You want me to ring her right now, don't you?"

"Yes, please."

PART FOUR: 1981

CHAPTER THIRTEEN

"This is the life, isn't it, lads?" Tommo's uncle Ray links his fingers behind his head and leans back against a mossy tree stump. Dense woods encircle them, ripening the air with the scent of vegetation, the ground a blanket of leaf mould and bluebell leaves. The camp fire spits and hisses, a blackened jerry can wedged in the heart of the flames. "No women bothering us, telling us what to do."

He winks at Adam and Tommo and starts whistling the Laurel and Hardy theme tune. Tommo grins back, flashing his rotten tooth. The tooth in the middle of his smile has got a cavity right in the middle of it, but Tommo won't see the dentist to get it pulled out and a new one put in. "I'm not wearing dentures like a little old lady," he announces, whenever someone asks, but the sight of it turns Adam's stomach.

He runs his tongue experimentally over his own teeth, wishing he's allowed not to go to the dentist, like Tommo. Earlier in the week he'd shuddered in the dentist's chair while his braces were fitted: a tangle of wire and rubber bands on a thick orange plate that fills up his mouth and thickens his speech. He's allowed to put them in their nasty plastic box if he's eating something really sticky, but otherwise they have to stay put. Even at weekends, even when he's seeing his friends. At least Mum had agreed that they could be fitted after his birthday, so he wasn't digging cake out of the wires in front of everyone. Now, when he pokes his tongue against far edge of the plate, he can taste the soft squishiness of chewed toast caught there, a reminder of breakfast.

"All right, Adam?" Ray asks.

"I hate my braces."

Ray claps him on the shoulder. "Never mind, mate. Be worth it in the end when you're in Hollywood."

"Hollywood?"

"My missus reckons you're going to grow up with film star looks. Make the most of them, I say." Ray props himself up on one elbow. "But don't let a woman get you under her thumb."

"How do they do that?" Adam asks. The only woman he knows is his mum. Course she's bossy, but isn't that what all mums are like?

"They have their ways, believe me," Ray says. He turns to Tommo. "Like your auntie May, always on at me to change nappies and mash up baby food. All day long it's, 'Katy needs her nap, stop playing your music so loud' and 'Keep an eye on Katy while I pop to the shop'." He sighs and rolls his eyes. "Women!"

"Women!" Tommo copies the eye rolling. "My mam's like that, too, isn't she, uncle Ray?"

Ray groans. "Your mam's a law to herself." He puts on a squeaky, female voice, "'Ray, the cupboard door's fallen off, come and fix it', 'Ray, I don't have enough to last the week, can you lend me a fiver?'"

Tommo shifts and prods at the fire. "You don't mind helping us out, do you, uncle Ray?"

"'Course I don't! We're family."

Ray ferrets in his jacket pocket and draws out a packet of cigarettes, taps one out and lights it, blowing a plume of smoke with a satisfied huff. Adam watches him, committing it all to memory so he can practise in his bedroom later. Strange to think that Ray is Tommo's uncle: he's much younger than Tommo's mam, and doesn't tell them off for swearing and burping like other grown-ups do.

"Want one, Adam?" Ray says, offering the packet.

Adam shakes his head, his eyes fixed on the tan tips poking out of the pack.

"Go on! I won't tell." He turns to Tommo. "I know you'll have one."

Tommo grabs a cigarette, lights it, and sucks hard, then breathes out long and deep with the same satisfied puff Ray did. "Try it, Adam," Tommo says. "You'll like it." He sniggers. "Only don't get it caught on your braces."

That does it. Adam snatches a cigarette and puts it between his lips. It feels weird: softer than he thought it would; he was expecting it to be hard like a plastic joke cigarette filled with talcum powder.

Ray leans in with his lighter, instructing him to breathe in through the cigarette, and eventually the end glows orange. The smoke catches at the back of his throat and his eyes water with the effort of not coughing. Ray plants his hand on his shoulder. "Just breathe in nice and slow, Adam. You'll get used to it."

And after a few puffs, he does. He holds the cigarette between his thumb and first finger, and sucks in and puffs out, and it's brilliant.

"This is the life, eh, lads?" Ray says again, and belches a smoky belch. "Better out than in."

They sit around the camp fire, smoking and not talking, and a deep peace settles over Adam. Out of Gregory's reach for once, with his mates, being treated like a grown-up. No Gregory whining and threatening to tell. Gregory's broken arm is set in a cast and that means no cycling for him and six weeks of freedom for Adam.

"Thirsty?" Ray hooks his hand into the inside pocket of his jacket and pulls out a flat bottle full of colourless liquid.

"Is that water?" Adam asks in dismay, hoping for cola.

Ray and Tommo laugh. "'Course not! What do you think I am, a poof?"

The blood rushes to the tips of his ears. "'Course you're not a ... poof. What is it, then?"

Tommo punches his arm, hard. "Vodka, you twat."

Ray cracks open the bottle and hands it to Tommo, who takes two long swigs and swallows them with a shake of his head, like a dog coming out of the sea. He rubs his palm over the top of the bottle and passes it to Adam.

"I dunno," he begins.

"Go on, do you good," Ray says. When Adam still hesitates, he adds, "Vodka doesn't smell. Your mum won't know a thing."

Adam tips the bottle to his lips. The vodka slips down cool and oily, hitting his stomach in a ball of flames, making him gasp. Another gulp and after a few minutes his head's lighter and the sunbeams bouncing off the trees are brighter.

"You know we were talking about Hollywood earlier?" Ray says, flopping back against a trunk with his arms crossed behind his head. "About you being a film star and that?"

Adam can't remember, but he nods and says, "Uh-huh," in a grown-up way.

"Wondered if you'd like to help me with something."

"Help with what?"

"A sort-of film I'm doing. Need some actors."

Tommo smirks and the black tooth makes a reappearance. Adam swallows down a wave of nausea.

"What sort of film?"

"Well ... you like horror films, don't you? Dracula and mummies from the tomb?"

Ray has a video recorder, an amazing machine that he lets Adam and Tommo and their friends watch, and he goes to the video shop and rents all sorts of movies for them to see: *The Omen* and *The Texas Chainsaw Massacre* and *The Exorcist*. Films that have frightened the life out of him and make him check under his bed every night in case something evil's lurking there waiting to get him. And Ray has also sourced other films for them to enjoy, x-rated with sex in where you saw *everything*.

"Yeah, I like films," Adam says.

"Like to be in one?"

"Yeah."

"I've been in one of uncle Ray's films," Tommo chips in. "It was great."

"You'll get paid," Ray says. "Only fair."

"What part would I have to play?" He was in a play at primary school, the Christmas concert for mums and dads; the little kids in tinsel and angel wings; the bigger kids doing plays, and he was a squirrel in a hot furry costume with a big red tail and everyone laughed at him. He's not doing it if it's in a stupid costume, even if he does get paid.

"Nothing too hard," Ray says, airily. "Just have to be yourself."

"I'm not sure."

"No problem." Ray smokes his cigarette in silence for a few moments. "How long have we been coming here, eh, lads? You Adam, you Dave, Philip, Lance. All your friends."

No one answers him.

"Me bringing you up here in my car, teaching you lads how to tie knots and make fires and build camps and trap rabbits." Another hard suck on the cigarette. "Must be six years. Seven, maybe."

Again no answer.

"You with no dad at all —" a nod to Tommo — "and you with no dad to speak of —" he stares at Adam — "just me showing you all the things that dads should show you."

"Thank you, Ray," Adam says.

"You know, this film, I do need someone to help," Ray says. He flicks away the cigarette end. "You don't have to remember lines or stuff, and it'll be fun. Won't it, Dave?"

"I liked it."

"And there'll be more of this." Ray taps the vodka bottle. "Plus the wages."

And so Adam agreed.

"Just one thing," Ray adds. "Don't tell anyone. It'll be our secret, eh?"

That's fine with him. If his mum doesn't know she can't tell him to take Gregory along. "Course," he says. "I can keep a secret."

CHAPTER FOURTEEN

Adam glances across at Gregory. He's lying on his back, his thick hair in a mop over the pillow, his mouth open and his lips puffing on every out breath. In the room next door, his mum and Dennis are groaning and squealing, the wall shuddering as the bed bangs against it.

He slips out of bed and shucks off his pyjamas. Underneath he's fully dressed. He opens the bedroom door a crack, listening to check Mum and Dennis are too busy to hear him creeping about, and tiptoes downstairs, his shoes in his hands. A stolen copy of the back door key is in his pocket. He lets himself out, wincing at the door's creak, locks the door behind him, tugs on his shoes, then sprints down the yard and out.

A car's waiting for him at the end of the road. Tommo's uncle Ray and Tommo himself in the passenger seat.

"Anyone notice you've gone?" Ray asks.

"Nah," Adam says casually, though his heart's still banging with the thrill of creeping out. He clambers into the back of the car and Ray sets off, through the quiet, dim streets, up Leckhampton Hill and out along the road to the Devil's Chimney. They pass the turn off to the car park and head right to the top then trundle down an old farm track next to a tumble down stone wall. When the engine stops, the air is thick with silence. Lighting their way with a torch, Ray leads them to a clump of trees. The torchlight casts the branches into eerie shadows and transforms his face into a goblin. Beyond the trees is a small circular clearing.

"Here's your costumes." Ray hands each of them a carrier bag. Adam draws out a long, white garment, like a superhero cape. He drapes it round his shoulders

"No, you spaz," Tommo says. "Take your things off first."

Tommo's already stripped off his jeans and sweater and t-shirt, and is standing in just his pants and socks, as though he's about to have a school medical. Slowly Adam peels off his jeans and top, looking away when Tommo pulls off his pants and socks.

"Do we have to take it all off?" he says, trying hard not to look at Tommo's pale naked body.

"You'll have the cloak on," Tommo says, wrapping his around him and tying it under his chin.

If he can hide in the cloak it won't be too bad, he reasons, taking a deep breath and stepping out of his pants. The night air's cold, and he hurriedly drapes the cloak round him, glad it drapes down to his wrists and grazes his ankles.

"Now what?"

"Just wait, uncle Ray will come and get us," Tommo says.

They huddle in their cloaks like two abandoned ghosts, the trunks of the trees sheltering them from the wind. Clouds scud across a tiny paring of moon, like a curl of soap under a fingernail. Just when Adam thinks he's going to freeze to death, Ray approaches, wearing a long black robe, and dangling a mask from one hand.

"You're on, kiddo," he says to Tommo. Tommo sticks back his shoulders like a soldier and heads towards the clearing. A few minutes later a low chanting floats on the wind.

"You cold?" Ray asks. "Try this."

He passes a bottle to Adam. He unscrews the top and takes a small sip, gasping as the liquid sears his stomach.

"Have a bit more, it'll keep you warm," Ray says, tipping the bottle as Adam puts it to his lips so it sloshes into his mouth. Adam swallows, his eyes watering, as the whiskey burns down his throat.

"Don't choke on that," Ray warns. "That's the good stuff." After a while, he asks, "Feeling a bit warmer now?"

"Yeah." Warmer and less nervous. It's all a bit of a lark, not scary at all.

"You like a bit of this?" Ray takes a fat joint from a tin. He drags deeply, then hands it to Adam. He puffs and breathes out the smoke in a long gust. "Not like that," Ray says. "You've got to hold the smoke in your lungs. Like this."

He demonstrates and passes the spliff back to Adam. This time he captures the smoke in his lungs, trapping it for as long as he can, and when he finally exhales, his limbs are floppy and a deep sense of well-being sinks over him.

"Have another. Nearly your time to shine."

Adam puffs again, relishing the warmth and ease that are melting his body. When Ray holds his hand, he doesn't shake him off, just lets him lead him to the clearing. To one side is a large camera on a tripod, a box on the ground beside it.

"What's that?"

"Camera and recorder. Don't think about being filmed," Ray whispers.

A group of robed figures huddle around a table set in the centre of the clearing. They're all wearing long black robes and masks: wolves and crows and hyenas. Lanterns hang from the tree branches. It's creepy and hokey at the same time.

"Up you get," Ray says, helping Adam onto the table. There's a black velvet cloth on it, very soft. He lies down and adjusts his cloak around him, fighting the urge to giggle. This is silly, but he's getting ten pounds for this and he doesn't want to annoy Ray. Briefly, he wonders where Tommo went, and how anyone is going to see anything in the dark. The scratch of rope round his wrists and ankles startles him and he tries to sit up. Ray presses him down again.

"It's just for the film. To make it look authentic. I won't fasten them tight." When he's trussed up, Ray hisses in his ear, "Whatever happens just lie still and don't say a word. Got that? Think of the money."

The men form a circle round the table and suddenly they're all bathed in bright light. Adam glances over his shoulder and makes out car headlights. The lights glint on the masks, showing the eye holes as bottomless black pits. One of the men raises his arms, and they all start chanting. Adam can't follow what they're saying. Something about the Devil, being his servants, being infused with power. He doesn't understand it. It doesn't matter — all he has to do is lie still; he doesn't need to know anyone else's lines.

The chanting grows louder, and from out of nowhere comes a tall figure in black. It moves to the top of the table, near his head, and he makes out a red devil's mask, terrifying and grotesque. Suddenly he hears what they're chanting: *sacrifice him, sacrifice him* and before he knows what's happening, the Devil has torn open his cloak and his naked body is exposed to the cold night air. He twists and tries to flip onto his stomach, to cover himself up. The ropes hold him in place, helpless. Before he can cry out an objection, a plastic bag's over his head and twisted tight at his throat. Adam struggles, his heart banging in his chest. Each breath sucks the bag tighter onto his face, moulding itself to his nose, his lips, his eyeballs. The ropes scour his wrists and ankles.

A hand on his mouth. He bucks and squirms, desperate. The air in the plastic bag is gone. He's blacking out, and the hand keeps pressing down on his mouth, stopping his breath. He twists and kicks, then everything goes black.

When he opens his eyes, the masked man is looming over him, and he screams.

"You're fine," a muffled voice tells him. The Devil is loosening the ropes, freeing him.

He squirms into a sitting position, rubbing his wrists and sucking in great lungfuls of the chill night air, coughing and spitting blood. A jolt like electricity surges through him, firing his veins and exploding in his head. When he stands, he's embarrassed by the hardest and most painful boner of his life, and he rearranges the cloak to cover it up. Ray pops up with the whiskey bottle. Adam grabs it, his throat raw, and knocks back a slug, then another, his heart hammering and his breath ragged.

"What happened?" he croaks.

"You did brilliantly," Ray helps him back to the shelter of the trees. "You all right?"

Adam tests himself: he's in one piece, but his mouth hurts, and he fingers his lips and runs his tongue around his teeth. His braces have dug into his lips and made them bleed. He dabs at them with the cloak. "I'm fine."

He retrieves his clothes and climbs back into them. Tommo is back, dressed, and smoking a joint. He offers it to Adam. Its cool smoke calms him. He's fine, he's all right, it's all a bit of a game, that's all.

"Here you go, Adam," Ray says, thumbing a note from a wodge he extracts from his back pocket. "Ten pounds. And a bonus if you'll come back and help us make another film." His thumb hovers over another tenner nestling in the pack. Adam stares at it. Twenty pounds for sneaking out of the house, drinking whiskey and smoking a joint. And his lips will heal in a couple of days.

"Yeah, I'll do it."

"One thing, Adam," Ray says. "Don't tell anyone about this, eh? They wouldn't understand and they might make you give the money back."

"I won't tell." Telling was Gregory's speciality, not his.

"Just you'd get in trouble cause of the whiskey and the weed, that's all."

"Yeah, sure," Adam says. "When's the next time?"

"I'll let you know."

He drops Adam at the end of his street. Adam lets himself in through the back door, and stands on the threshold for a moment, listening. Sleeping breaths, everyone totally unaware he's been gone. He closes the door with a smile and creeps to bed.

CHAPTER FIFTEEN

"If it happens again I shall go round and speak to Dave's mother," Adam's mum says, speaking through her teeth so every word hits his cheek like pebbledash. "It's not on. Smashing your braces like that."

"It wasn't Tommo's fault," Adam mumbles. "It was an accident."

"Last time was an accident. There's no excuse for this."

They're in the dentist's waiting room, again, the broken bits of wire from Adam's braces wrapped in a tissue in his mum's hand. The second time in a fortnight, no wonder she's mad. The first time, the wires had simply bent out of shape and the dentist tweaked them with pliers. This time, they'd sheared off altogether in his mouth, and he'd come round at the Devil's Chimney with his mouth cut and bleeding. Lucky he didn't swallow the wires. It could have been tricky to explain: going to bed with the braces intact; next morning braces all mangled. Fortunately she barely looks at him these days — each evening she and Dennis gaze at each other and watch the clock until it's time for him to go to bed, then he hears them pounce on each other.

The lie came easily: Dave. Rough and tumble. Boys' play. And then being afraid to tell her when the braces got broken a second time because he knew she'd react like this. She'd gone ballistic, as predicted, but at least she doesn't suspect. None of them suspect anything. Especially not Gregory, and that's the sweetest part of going up to the Devil's Chimney with Tommo and Ray: Gregory doesn't know a thing about it: doesn't know that Adam sneaks out in the middle of the night, and especially doesn't know that Adam has a roll of cash hidden in an old shoe at the back of the cupboard.

The dentist examines the braces. "Hm. You've been fighting," he says, mildly. "Bruised the inside of your lip and cheek."

"That was the braces," Adam says.

"Hm." The dentist looks at him for a moment and Adam makes a flicking movement with his eyes towards his Mum. The dentist understands, and winks. "Yes, I see. Never mind, I can fix this up."

Twenty minutes later, the wires are replaced and Adam's climbing down from the chair. "I'll see you again in six months," the dentist says, pointedly. Adam nods. He'll be more careful. Next time he goes to the Devil's Chimney, he'll remove the braces altogether, leave them behind in their nasty plastic case.

PART FIVE: 2016

CHAPTER SIXTEEN

The body was too tiny. A little puppet, wrapped in white cotton and lying on a bed. It, too, was draped in white, like a tableau in a department store window. Presenting the body of her daughter. Jessica's lips were pursed slightly, as if she were puckering up for a kiss, or blowing a bubble. Kate bent her head and kissed the rosebud lips, shuddering at the cold and hating herself for it.

"What's wrong?" Gareth asked. His shoulders were hunched up around his ears, his hands rammed into the pockets of his jeans. How many times had she told him to put on something decent for visiting their daughter, and how many times had he just turned away, brushing his palms across his eyes and shrugging?

Kate was in her green skirt and pale blue blouse. The two didn't match, but they were Jessica's favourites. Whenever Kate put on this blouse or this skirt, Jessica's eyes were sure to light up, and she could never tame her hands from pawing at the fabric. It was bloody annoying at times, Kate conceded, wishing with a pang that rent her soul for the smear of jam and banana that adorned every outfit. What she'd give now for Jessica to wake up and say, "I like your top, Mummy. I like that green, Mummy, it reminds me of seaweed."

Seaweed was another of Jessica's favourite things, along with snails, doing a poo, and licking the embossed wallpaper in the dining room because it felt funny on her tongue. How many times had Kate shouted at her to stop licking, it was disgusting and dirty and what was wrong with her anyway? For all the good it did. Jessica would cry, hold her breath until she was purple in the face and then throw a tantrum, and once the tears were mopped and she'd been bribed into quietness with a piece of chocolate, the licking would start again. Chocolatey streaks down the wallpaper and endless wiping with antibacterial spray.

Kate wished she could have brought a snail or a piece of seaweed to offer Jessica, to keep her entertained while she waited to sail through eternity. Eternity was too long; Kate had reckoned her own life at eighty years, and was counting down the years and months and hours until she, too, would be drifting through eternity and could be with Jessica again. Sometimes, the thought of the wait winded her, and she had to halt and clutch whatever was nearby to steady herself, desperately wondering how the hell she would ever make it through.

So no snail, but a posy of flowers. Little ones, blue and yellow, tied with a white ribbon. She slotted them into Jessica's folded hands and patted them down. She half expected Jessica to open her eyes and ask, "What are you doing, Mummy?" and Kate gazed at her, not daring to breathe in case she broke the spell, waiting for her sleeping princess to wake.

"Ready?" Gareth said, beside her.

"No, I'll never be ready."

"We've got to," he said, not daring to meet her eyes.

"Just another minute."

"You said that twenty minutes ago."

"You want to go, then go!" she cried. "I just want a minute with my daughter."

Gareth unpicked her fingers from Jessica's. "We've got to go," he said. "It's time." He dipped his head and kissed Jessica's cheek, then looked expectantly at Kate.

"Night night, sweetheart," she whispered, kissing Jessica and standing back, trembling, as the mortuary assistant drew the sheet back over her daughter's face. She knew he'd remove the flowers she'd brought before he slotted Jessica back in the fridge on her shelf, another body waiting for permission to be buried. As they walked away, Kate was convinced she heard Jessica cry out, and it was only Gareth's arms about her that prevented her running back. At the door, she turned to look again at the lonely body and the two candles burning either side of it.

They didn't speak on the journey, each stared straight ahead through the windscreen at the dull grey road and the medley of roundabouts. As they turned into Abbeymead and made their way through a jumble of curving streets to her parents' house, Kate said, "Will we ever survive this?"

Gareth didn't answer, but slid his hand across the seat and gripped hers.

Her mother was waiting when they pulled in, standing at the window holding the net curtain aside, her face pinched and old. Beside her stood her dad, his shoulders hunched.

"How did it go?" her mother asked.

Kate shrugged. Impossible to describe what it felt like to watch the sheet being drawn over your three year old daughter's dead face.

"You all right, kid?" her dad asked.

"Not really, Dad."

"Dave's come over to see if we need anything."

Her cousin Dave ambled in from the back garden, a whiff of cigarette smoke clinging to his clothes. "How you doing?" he asked.

She nodded, unable to speak. "Still on the fags, Dave?"

"Yeah." He gave a shamefaced grin out of one side of his mouth. "Why, want one?"

"Actually, I do."

"Come on, then."

She ignored Gareth and her mother protesting and followed Dave into the garden.

"How was it?" he asked in a low voice.

"Horrendous." She shuddered. "Hurry up with that cigarette, Dave."

His hand went to his pocket, pulling out a packet of cigarettes and a pile of fluff and depositing them on the windowsill. "I've got a lighter in here somewhere."

"What's that?" Kate said, pouncing on a business card with a boiled sweet stuck to it.

"Oh, some woman came round earlier in the week."

"What did she want?" They'd had a lot of journalists asking questions and pretending to be part of the police investigation. Sharks, the lot of them.

Dave shrugged. "Asking questions about years ago." There was a pause and they caught each other's eyes.

"Asking about what?"

He flicked the lighter and cupped his palm round the flame to light her cigarette. "About your Dad."

"What about Dad?"

"About years ago and Adam Jones."

"Not again! I thought that was all finished long ago." Her vision blackened round the edges and she clutched at the doorframe.

"I told her I couldn't help her."

Kate looked again at the card and felt the blood rush to her face and then drain back out again. "Dave, have you looked at this card? Seen who it is?"

It was the woman. The woman whose fault it all was. Kate's pulse quickened. It was a sign. A divine inspiration telling her to take revenge. The universe had delivered her up. The woman who had taken Jessica and was now after her dad. She glanced again at the name on the card, the same name that had haunted her since Jessica's death: Eden Grey.

CHAPTER SEVENTEEN

Judy's sister Alison agreed to meet Eden at the Watershed Café in Bristol. Those having breakfast meetings were just departing, and the morning lunch rush hadn't yet got underway, so they were able to find a quiet table overlooking the river, out of earshot of the counter.

Alison was tall and statuesque, like Judy, but her hair hung in waving golden locks to her shoulders. She wore navy linen trousers and red pumps, and her arms jangled with bracelets.

"Thanks for coming to meet me," Eden said.

"Happy to help, if I can," Alison said. "Plus, I've never been questioned by a PI, so I have to admit I'm a bit intrigued."

Eden laughed. "I'll try not to make it too inquisitorial," she said. "Judy told me that you were at school with a boy called Adam Jones?"

"Adam? Gosh, yes, that's a blast from the past." Alison dropped two nuggets of brown sugar into her cup. "We were in the same class. Mrs Temple's. She wore perfume so thick it made your head swimmy."

"Adam Jones's body has been found." The police confirmation of the identity of the skeleton found up at the Devil's Chimney had been announced on the local news, behind late bin collections, a teenager with anorexia, and a stabbing in Stoke on Trent.

"Really? After all this time?" Alison spooned up the froth from her coffee. "Was it foul play?"

"Looks like it. The body was in a fake Iron Age grave."

Alison's spoon stopped. "How bloody weird is that?" she cried, sounding so like Judy it made Eden smile.

Eden unwrapped the cinnamon biscuit that accompanied her coffee. "What do you remember about Adam?"

"He was good-looking," Alison said. "One of those boys that all the girls fancy. Probably would have turned into a right porky slap head now, but back then he was dishy. I doodled his name in my maths book. Got detention for it." She made a sheepish face. "Don't tell Judy, I'll never hear the last of it."

"Did you go out with him?"

"No!" Alison choked on the laugh. "He wasn't interested in girls."

"He was gay?"

"Looking back on it, he wasn't anything, neither straight nor gay, just a twelve year old boy. You know how some of them stay at the trainset stage for a long time? He was still at the trainset stage. Hung around with his mates, scuffling in the corridor, that kind of thing."

"But that's not what you thought at the time?"

Alison stared out at the river below them, marshalling her thoughts. A yellow tourist boat glided past. "I haven't thought about this since, and back then things ... attitudes ... were very different."

"Different, how?"

"How we think about right and wrong. Who the victim might be."

Eden stayed very still, unwilling to break the flow.

Alison continued, "There were rumours about Adam, that he was into something rude. That was how it was put. He was doing something rude. I'd never heard the term 'rent boy' before. I thought it meant someone who lived in a rented house." Alison blushed at her young naivety. "I asked my dad what it meant, and let's just say he went ballistic. Didn't explain it of course, I had to ask someone at school, and they told me it meant boys having sex with men and being paid for it." Her eyes were pained when she looked at Eden. "Back then, we didn't think that this was abuse, that those boys were victims, we thought they were dirty. Greedy. In the wrong. God, it makes me shudder to think of it now."

Eden gave her a moment to collect herself. "Which boys? You said 'those boys were victims'."

Alison spread her hands. "It was all just rumours. You know what it's like at school. One teacher says good morning to another in the corridor and before you know it there's an affair and a secret love child. It was the same with Adam."

"There were rumours he was a rent boy?"

"Him and a few other boys."

"Which others?"

Alison thought for a while. "Some people said Dave Thompson."

"What, exactly, did the rumours say was going on?"

"They said that Adam and some other boys went up to the Devil's Chimney and did rude things with men for money." She groaned. "Those poor children."

"Judy says that a police officer came to her school to ask about Adam."

"The police came to our school, too. I don't know whether anyone told them anything. Wouldn't surprise me if everyone was too embarrassed to repeat it."

"What about Philip Wakefield? Do you remember him?"

"Vaguely. Quiet, a bit swotty but not particularly clever."

"Were there rumours about him?"

"Not that I can remember," Alison said. Her bracelets clattered against the table top and she pushed them further up her arm.

"Do you remember Philip's death?"

"I remember crying about Adam going missing, worried about how the hell I was going to become Alison Jones if he never turned up again. Everyone thought he'd run away, gone to London maybe." Alison made a face: the hopes and naivety of the young. "I remember feeling really shocked when I heard Philip had killed himself. Imagine feeling so terrible you did that."

"Anything else that might be relevant? About either Philip or Adam?"

Alison rubbed at the lipstick smudge she'd left on her cup. "This is probably nothing, but one day I decided to follow Adam home from school. I wanted to see where he lived so I could hang about on the pavement and accidentally bump into him."

Eden smiled, remembering the love tactics of a smitten schoolgirl.

"Anyway, I kept well back — I didn't want him seeing what I was up to — and I saw a car was following him, too. It kept pace with him along the street, then stopped just ahead of him, and a man got out and started shouting at him." Alison rearranged the salt and pepper shakers on the table to demonstrate where all the players were in the drama. "He was yelling at Adam to get in the car, and Adam was shaking his head and shouting no, he wouldn't. The man grabbed his arm and tried to hustle him in, but Adam wriggled free and ran away, up one of the alleys behind the houses. The man shouted after him and then got in the car and drove off."

"Who was the man?"

"I don't know, but years later when they accused someone of murdering Adam, I just assumed it was him."

"Could you describe the man?"

"No idea." She clicked her fingers as a thought sprang to mind. "Tell you one thing, though. He was driving one of those old cars made of wood."

Alison left to go to work, and Eden went to the counter to order Portobello mushrooms on toast and to ask for the café's Wi-Fi code. The mushrooms came on a pristine white plate with a packet of fruity piquant brown sauce made by an independent food manufacturer. Smearing a dollop on a forkful of mushrooms, she wondered if the days of her addiction to HP sauce were numbered.

Her lunch plate to her right hand, her tablet to the left, she ran a quick internet search on Mrs Temple — Adam, Philip and Alison's form teacher. There were a couple of archived items from the *Gloucestershire Echo* of Mrs Temple retiring from the school, and a later article where she appeared as secretary of a local literary society. It appeared she'd stayed in the area, at least.

Eden then searched for the school, Tennyson Comprehensive, reasoning there was likely to be an old pupils' association of some description. There wasn't, but there was a Facebook group that received several posts a day, so she typed a question, asking if anyone could put her in contact with Mrs Temple, who taught there until 2005. By the time she'd finished her mushrooms and another nuclear-strength flat white, she had a response.

"I'm Mrs Temple. How may I be of assistance?"

Eden typed her response via direct message. She didn't want the whole world to see what she was up to, and be besieged by nutters wanting in on an investigation, when they had nothing of interest to contribute. The herd mentality, the need to feel one was joining in, however dubiously, reminded her of a local radio phone-in she'd once heard, about a dead whale that had washed up on a beach. The creature had been taken by lorry to a specialised site dealing with biological waste, a journey of many miles, the whale trailing a pong of decay every inch of the way. The phone-in asked people who'd been affected by the smell of the whale to call in with their experiences. For the next two hours, the radio waves hummed with callers who prefaced their story with, "I didn't actually smell the whale or see the whale, but I do know that road it went down." Announce on Facebook that you're reopening a case into a dead boy, and 'I didn't smell the whale' curio hunters would be out in droves.

"I'm investigating the death of Philip Wakefield," Eden wrote. "I understand you were his form teacher, and it would be extremely helpful to hear your opinion and memories of him. If you're willing to meet me, please feel free to state a time and place most convenient for you."

Quarter of an hour later she received a reply. "2pm at the Coffee Dispensary in Cheltenham. I'll be the only one who isn't staring at a screen."

She wasn't the only one not staring at a screen. The Coffee Dispensary — a small, hip café, which softened its wooden seats with furry cushions — was occupied by a troupe of arty types engaging in an expansive conversation. A harried freelancer, evidently desperate to complete a project, looked up frequently from his laptop to cast them agonised glances. In the far corner, commanding a view of the room, sat a nimble, alert woman in her late seventies, wearing a navy pleated skirt and a cream blouse with a pearl brooch. She rose when Eden entered.

"Miss Grey? I'm Clarissa Temple." A cut-glass accent and an air of absolute authority that Eden could imagine being mocked mercilessly by those pupils who were most terrified and cowed by it.

"Thank you for meeting me, Mrs Temple."

"I don't mind if you want to call me Clarissa, if you can bear it." Mrs Temple twitched an ironic eyebrow. "My father was too fond of Richardson, something I couldn't ever quite forgive him for."

"Especially when he could have chosen Pamela," Eden said.

"Precisely."

Eden took a seat opposite Clarissa and showed her private investigator's identification. "Philip Wakefield's mother has engaged me to investigate his death," she said. "I'm intrigued by the fact his friend Adam Jones disappeared around the same time."

"An unhappy coincidence," Clarissa said, "and one, I suspect, you don't trust any more than I."

"Philip's mother suspects that someone knows something about his death. Someone's been leaving her messages suggesting as much," Eden said. "That only makes sense if someone knows, or thinks they know, that Philip's death wasn't suicide."

"Quite, and I for one, do not believe it was suicide."

"Why is that?"

"I'd taught Philip for a whole year. He was a careful boy, a sensitive boy. He was not a rough and tumble sort of child. And that sort of child doesn't take himself up to the woods to hang himself when he decides to shuffle off." She pronounced it 'orf'. "He takes to his bed and throws the covers over his head after swallowing a bottle of aspirin."

"People can act out of character in extremis," Eden said.

"That's what the police told me when I raised the question with them." Clarissa poured her tea. It was Darjeeling, light and aromatic. "I also told them that Philip was cack-handed and it made him less than dextrous. Couldn't even do up his shoelaces properly. That sort of boy doesn't hang himself."

"What did the police say?"

"They told me, very politely, to mind my own business, and that I didn't know what I was talking about."

"You think Philip's death was suspicious?"

Intelligent blue eyes sparked. "I think there are questions to be asked, that have not so far been asked."

"The coroner was happy to bring in a verdict of suicide," Eden said.

"Because he was told all about two boys who were friends, and one of them went missing and the other was devastated, and about a woodland camp where they used to play, and where it seemed the boy left behind couldn't bear life without his friend."

"You were at the coroner's inquest?"

"I was."

"I've been told that Philip and Adam were friends but they fell out some time before Adam disappeared. Do you know why?"

Clarissa laughed. "They were growing up! Philip was slower to grow up than Adam, and I suspect he found him rather tedious and childish. Adam was rather a sporty boy. He was in the school teams for football and cricket. Philip just wasn't interested."

"What was Adam like?"

"I think at heart he was probably a nice boy, but his mother remarried and he hated his step-father, and then he fell in with a boy who had trouble written all over him."

"Dave Thompson?"

"Quite. He was already known for shop lifting and graffiti, and I suspect that Adam joined in, too. He could have done with a couple of weeks of Philip Wakefield's mother, that boy."

"How do you mean?"

"He started to look a bit, not neglected, but not quite up to snuff. Big dark circles round his eyes, he fell asleep in class, and on more than one occasion he smelt of smoke and drink."

"What did you think had happened when he disappeared?"

Clarissa studied her hands. Her nails were short and neat with pale pink varnish, and she wore a large old-cut diamond ring on the little finger of her right hand. "It was during the holidays, so I wasn't in the thick of it as I would have been if it had happened during term time. I thought he'd run away, possibly just to teach his mother a lesson. It's quite usual for children to feel they've been rejected when a parent remarries."

"And later?"

"Later a lot of very unpleasant rumours went round about Adam." She caught Eden's eye. "All gossip of course, and ultimately, of course, someone was charged with his murder."

"Dave Thompson's uncle," Eden said, and Clarissa nodded. "Did that shock you? Were you surprised?"

"No," Clarissa said. "I'd had the misfortune to teach Ray Thompson myself, and nothing he did would surprise me. That boy gave me the shudders."

CHAPTER EIGHTEEN

"Trev, do we keep records of everyone who's worked on digs in the past?" Aidan stood at the door to his office and called across the corridor.

Trev materialised, a banana in his paw. "Some of them. If they got paid there should be records," he said. As he spoke, he slowly unpeeled the banana fully and poked it into his mouth. Aidan watched, appalled, wondering if Trev would wash off the soggy bits of banana that clung to his fingers, or if he'd simply wipe them down his jeans, as he'd been witnessed doing on previous occasions.

Trev chewed and talked simultaneously, the masticated banana making a wet, sloppy sound. "'Course if they were just volunteers, we'd have a record for health and safety."

"And where are the records kept?" He dug his fingernails into his palm. The sound of that banana was revolting.

Trev nodded towards the stairs to the basement. "Down there, somewhere. Unless they got sent to County Office." The last bit of banana was posted into Trev's mouth, and he rubbed his hands down his jeans. "What?"

"Nothing," Aidan said. "Just doing some detective work."

He went down the metal staircase and flicked on the strip lighting. It threw the corners into spooky shadows and over-illuminated the rows and rows of boxed skeletons and artefacts filed on metal shelving. He moved along the lines of shelves, casting an eye over each box, searching for anything that could be records. He had to hand it to the team: they labelled everything assiduously. There were no boxes marked 'Stuff, misc'; it was all sorted and filed and the boxes tagged. Working up and down the rows, he found a set of brown archive boxes, and inside were folders of accounts, grant applications, receipts, and staff records. Opening the top folder, he was amused to find his own application to work at the Cultural Heritage Unit: an earnest covering letter and an overlong CV. Presumably Trev and Mandy had also read it; no one had any secrets round here.

Working through the boxes was very like conducting a dig: the newest material was towards the top, then as he dug deeper, he turned up the ancient records, including an antiquated accident book, last inscribed three years previously, when Trev reported a papercut sustained from looking through the accident book. The entry previous to that was October 1998.

A clatter on the stairs behind him made him turn, and Lisa trotted towards him, her heels clacking.

"Here you are!" she said. "Coming for lunch?"

"I'm busy right now."

She hunkered down beside him. "What are you up to?"

"Trying to get together a list of people who might have known about those Iron Age graves."

"Why?"

"The police asked me."

Lisa studied him for a while, her head cocked on one side like a bird in front of a mirror. "Your pride's hurt," she said.

Aidan snapped the current folder shut. "True." He threw it onto the pile of folders he'd already examined. "Someone not only knew what an Iron Age grave looked like, but also that there were cist burials up at the Devil's Chimney."

"And they made one good enough to foil the finest brains in the Cultural Heritage Unit," Lisa added, drily.

"And one of the world's top war graves investigators," Aidan added.

"Fifteen all," Lisa said. "Now you put it like that, I'd like to get my hands on the little bastard who fooled us. Don't forget I took this week off as part of my annual leave, just to help you."

"Grab a box then, and dig in."

Aidan lifted a box down from the shelves and plonked it in front of Lisa. Side by side, they pored over the contents of the boxes, until Lisa let out a cry. "Here's something!"

"What?"

"A grant application made in 2001."

"It's too late," Aidan said. "The grave was dug by then."

"But it references a previous dig on the site, and there are photos," Lisa said, shoving the folder into his hands.

He flipped through the pages. It was a grant application to conduct a dig up at the Devil's Chimney, specifically to excavate a set of Iron Age graves that had been discovered several years before, in 1978. Accompanying the grant application was a set of photographs of the area, and details of the previous dig. Aidan spread the pages over the floor, and they crouched over them, shoulder to shoulder.

"The original dig was done by the University of Bristol, led by one of their professors," Lisa said, scanning the pages. "They excavated further along, and found the Iron Age graves on the last day."

"Isn't that always the way?" So many digs ended that way, turning up little until the last moment, almost as if the artefacts weren't ready to be discovered yet, and wanted to be left in peace just a little longer.

"It seems they covered them up with brushwood to protect them, and applied for funding to come back the next year."

"And the funding never came through?"

"No, and the professor in charge got a post in America, so it all got forgotten about."

Aidan sifted through the photos. "This is interesting. There are photos from the original dig, showing the graves." He waved the photo at her. "Notice anything?"

"There are only four of them."

"Which means the fifth grave was put in later," Lisa said.

"We knew that," Aidan said, "but here's where it gets really interesting. Look at this." He laid down a photograph. "This was part of the grant application in 2001. How many graves?"

"Five." Lisa glanced up at him, her face flushed with excitement. "So we can prove the fake grave was put there between 1978 and 2001."

"Exactly."

"It says here that the conservation department was told about the graves, and the local office asked to keep an eye on them," Lisa said.

Aidan sat back on his heels. "That complicates things. Not for us, for the police."

"How so?"

"It widens the field of people who knew the graves were there: everyone who worked on that dig, plus anyone who worked at the conservation offices." He pulled another box down from the shelf. "Let's find out how many other people knew about those graves."

CHAPTER NINETEEN

Bernard Mulligan had helped on a previous case and Eden liked his bluff, no nonsense approach. When she rang him, he readily agreed to see her, and within the hour she was heading up the M5 to Birmingham, turning into the Jewellery Quarter, with its smells of bacon rolls and hot metal, and making her way to Bernard's office.

"Hello, stranger," he greeted her, in his pleasant Geordie burr. In his late fifties, he was wearing trousers, a shirt, tie, and V-necked sweater, all in Air Force blue. "Been keeping out of trouble?"

"Of course," she said, wondering if the blood would ever flow back into her hand after Bernard's meaty grip. She wouldn't fancy anyone's chances against him in an arm wrestling competition.

"A likely story. Tea?"

She'd prefer coffee, but knew that Bernard's background of signals and police force meant that tea was the only hot drink he could make, so she nodded and said, "Strong, splash of milk, no sugar, please."

"NATO standard minus two coming up."

She eased her arms out of her electric blue leather jacket and propped it over the back of a comfortable chair. Bernard had his desk, filing cabinet and a single client's chair set up at one end of the room; at the other were an easy chair and two-seater sofa in oatmeal, which matched the overall oatmeal, beige and taupe colour scheme of his office. An anodyne print in muddy colours of cattle at the edge of a river adorned the wall behind her.

Bernard set down two mugs of builder's tea and propped a notebook on his lap. "What you up to this time?"

"Strange case. Two boys, friends, one goes missing and is never found, the other hangs himself a couple of days later."

"And you don't think it's a common or garden tragedy?"

"There are things that don't add up. There are questions that should have been asked at the inquest that weren't — such as explaining old injuries on the boy's wrists and ankles. Plus there's the fact he couldn't tie his shoelaces, so how did he manage a noose?"

"People can be resourceful when they're desperate."

"I'm surprised that the suicide wasn't investigated more thoroughly, at least to see whether the boy killed himself because he knew what happened to his friend." Bernard fixed her with an astute stare. "His mother fears he was involved somehow. And now there's a possibility that someone else knows what really happened."

"What else?" Bernard asked.

"There were rumours that the missing boy was a rent boy. That's 1981 speak. He was only twelve."

Bernard winced. "Nasty. And you're thinking that plod weren't as enlightened back then as they are now, and that they shovelled it under the carpet."

"Exactly." She flicked back through her notes. "Oh, and there's another funny aspect to this case. It might be nothing more than a little scrote seeing a chance, but the parents of the boy who killed himself were burgled while they were at the funeral."

Bernard groaned. "Some people are scum, they really are. Right, let's have the details."

Eden gave him the names, dates and details of the two cases, and Bernard transcribed them into his notebook in a laborious script. "What do you need me to do?" he asked.

"You were a copper, you know people," Eden said. "Can you ask around a bit, find out what was going on back then?"

Bernard tapped his lips with a thick forefinger while he thought. "I've got a mate, retired now, is a bit of a busybody. Knows everyone, or knows a bloke who knows. I'll see what he can dig up. But you know what these old coppers are like, Eden, they close ranks."

"Even if it was years ago and it stinks?"

"Especially then," he said. He studied her for a moment, then asked, "I heard you were in a spot of bother. Tear gas in your honour, wasn't it?"

"An old nemesis," Eden said. She felt Bernard's gaze on her face and was overwhelmed by the urge to unburden herself. "I've got an unconventional past, as you know."

"Takes a spook to know a spook," he said. "What's the story?"

"I got him put away for a long time, only he's a devious bastard with lots of favours to call in, and getting me killed is not going to be difficult. He's already tried a couple of times." She looked at the picture of bucolic tranquillity and thought how strange it was that she'd got used to talking about her own death. Her shoulders slumped. "You know, I can't feel afraid any more. I've been in fear for my life, literally, for so long and now it's come to crunch time I just don't feel anything. Does that make any sense?"

"Fear fatigue," Bernard said. "I've seen it on operations before. Just watch it, though, Eden. It can make you careless."

CHAPTER TWENTY

Bernard Mulligan didn't hang around. He called Eden on her mobile and she was still scrabbling for a pen when he was part way through his report.

"Hang on, Bernard, I can't keep up!" she grumbled. "Start again."

"I've got the low down on how those two cases were handled — the boy who disappeared and his friend who committed suicide," he said. His voice was breathier than usual and her pulse quickened: if it excited Bernard then he'd dug up some meaty stuff. "Turns out they *were* investigated together, under the eye of a copper called Inspector Godwinson, and pretty soon he decided there wasn't a link between the two cases. Once the suicide case went to the coroner, it was shelved, job done. Suicide, no further action."

"But the Adam Jones case?"

"Went cold-ish. Apparently some people mentioned Ray Thompson as a dodgy character and the boys in blue did some digging. The original investigation didn't find enough evidence to go to trial. Bloodstained clothing in the back of his car, blood type the same as Adam Jones, but also the same blood type as Ray and a million other people."

"So they ditched it?"

"No body, no evidence of a crime. Seemed to be a missing child case. End of." Bernard paused for dramatic effect. "Anyway a few years later, a bright young lad, graduate fast tracker or some-such, came in and was given the cold cases to keep him out of the way. So he starts poking into the Adam

Jones case, and asking questions about why it wasn't investigated alongside the Philip Wakefield case."

"It was because of the coroner's verdict."

"Exactly, but the coroner can only find on the basis of the evidence put before him, and our coroner retired a year after the Philip Wakefield inquest with dementia."

"So maybe he wasn't entirely on the ball when Philip's case came up?"

"Seems likely. Apparently there were a few dodgy decisions that later got reopened and the verdicts changed."

"Which leads to the question of who wanted a verdict of suicide, and why?"

"Coming to that," Bernard said. "This Inspector Godwinson tried to interfere with the new investigation. The young chap didn't like it, and there was an altercation."

"They sacked the new chap?"

"That's the interesting thing," Bernard said. "They kept him on, and put Inspector Godwinson on gardening leave. He retired on the grounds of ill health a little while later, said it was stress. But here's the thing." She heard him unwrapping a sweet: keeping her on tenterhooks. "Inspector Godwinson's name has since come up in historic child sex abuse allegations."

"*What?*"

"Not to put too fine a point on it, the copper investigating a rumoured twelve year old rent boy was a kiddie fiddler."

"Jesus," Eden breathed. "Someone needs to interview him about what he knew about the Adam Jones case."

"Need a ouija board," Bernard commented, drily. "He died a couple of years ago." She heard the sweetie clacking against his teeth. "Cirrhosis of the liver."

"What about the case files?"

"Third party, the lot of them."

"Sorry?"

"Fire and flood. It seems there was a burst water main near the room where old case records were held and they lost the lot, including the files for the original investigation into Adam Jones's disappearance and Philip Wakefield's suicide."

"What about the case files for the case against Ray Thompson?"

"Sealed, and kept by the CPS. I asked about having a gander at them, but now this skeleton's turned up the files are needed by the new investigation. It's no can do, and that's final. I do have something else to report, about that burglary during Philip Wakefield's funeral," Bernard added. "Brian Armitage, a small time young thief, been done a few times. He confessed to the crime, returned the necklace he stole, and asked for a number of other offences to be taken into consideration. Quite a clear-up rate." Eden warmed to the dry sarcasm of his tone. "And as a bonus for his good behaviour, none other than Inspector Godwinson spoke up for him when he was sentenced."

Eden chewed the side of her thumb, her mind whirring. Godwinson had decided not to investigate Adam Jones' disappearance and Philip's apparent suicide together; Godwinson had persuaded the coroner to bring in a verdict of suicide; and Godwinson argued leniency for the burglar who turned over the Wakefields' home. It was all stinking like haddock. "And the fast-track copper, the one who had a bust up with Godwinson?"

"Cooper's his name. An excellent bloke, by all accounts. Straight as they come. Bright spark decided to try out that new-fangled DNA testing, and low and behold, the blood stained clothing in Ray Thompson's car was covered with Adam's blood."

"But it wasn't enough for a conviction."

"No," Bernard said, "not without a body. Problem is, you can't prove he's dead, and that's enough for a reasonable doubt. Kid could've simply run off to London. I hear the streets are paved with gold down there."

"And where's Cooper now?"

"Retired recently. He runs a livery stables, apparently."

"Whereabouts?"

"Up the road from you."

"Do you think he'll see us?"

"He'll see you," Bernard said. "Pop over this evening and give him a hand with the mucking out."

"Thanks. I'll pack my wellies."

Bernard chuckled. "I warned him you were a queer customer and not to ask questions. He's a good lad, he'll see you right."

CHAPTER TWENTY-ONE

Eden was expecting heaps of dung and straw everywhere, and was pleasantly surprised to pull up in a neatly tarmacked carpark with a view over white painted fences. Across the evening air came the harrumph of horses cropping grass in the fields. Next to the carpark was a smart green trailer with a sign stating it was the office. Beyond was the yard, lit by a line of ornamental lamp posts, horses lolling their heads over the half-doors and hopeful for an apple. All of them were sleek with patrician noses. No riding school hacks here; these horses belonged to the upper crust and cost a mint.

A light shone in the office window. She tapped at the door and a voice called to her to come in. Ian Cooper sat at a desk, a large diary and a spike of invoices in front of him. In his mid-fifties, he was tall and sandy haired with high cheekbones. He wore cream riding breeches, a checked shirt, and tweed jacket.

"Eden Grey? Bang on time." His accent held a Scottish lilt. He closed the diary and slotted it into the desk drawer.

"Thanks for seeing me."

"Not at all. You're just in time for mucking out." His eyes held hers for a second, then he burst out laughing. "Mulligan told me to say that. You two are working together?"

"He's been helping me with a case I'm doing." She hitched her head towards the stables. "I'm happy to help out while we talk."

"You any good with a curry comb?"

"I was when I was a teenager. I'm sure I'll remember."

"Come on then, meet Stan."

She assumed that Stan was a groom, but Ian led her to a loose box which housed a large black stallion.

"Beauty, isn't he? Can clear six feet with his legs hanging down." Ian let them into the loose box and slapped Stan's side. "Got big hopes for you, old boy, haven't we?"

Eden stroked the horse's neck. "He's gorgeous. Show jumper?"

"Eventer," Ian said. "Totally fearless, this one." He handed Eden a rubber curry comb. "You take that side, I'll do this. What can I help you with?"

Eden filled him in on her investigation into Philip Wakefield's suicide. "I know you led the second investigation into Adam Jones's disappearance. Did you ever think that the two cases were linked?"

"Of course I did!" Ian said. "My problem was that we couldn't say definitely what happened to Adam, and that coroner's verdict didn't help."

"You couldn't reopen Philip's case without a new inquest?"

"None of my bosses were keen to go down that route. The suicide verdict was plausible, but my guts were telling me there was more than met the eye."

"But you reopened the investigation into Adam Jones?"

Ian stopped brushing for a moment and leaned his forearms on the horse's back. "By the time I started looking into it, nine years had gone by, and I had to try and track people down. Some of the people who were interviewed originally had moved away. Some of Adam's classmates had gone to college, and when I spoke to them, they were hesitant to commit themselves. Said it was a long time ago and they weren't sure; didn't want to make statements."

"But some did?"

"Yes, some did. Repeated what we'd been told before: that there were rumours about Adam Jones, that he was into dodgy sex games with dodgy men."

"Did you believe it?"

"Yes, but I couldn't prove it."

"I've spoken to some of Adam's friends, and they told me the same rumours," Eden said, knocking the dust out of the curry comb. "And they all mentioned Ray Thompson."

"He had a record. Not for sex crimes, but a couple for handling stolen goods, a couple of cannabis possessions. Always small amounts. He seemed pretty small fry, that's what I thought." He paused.

"Until?"

"Until it became clear that people didn't want me poking my nose into this case."

"Who? Inspector Godwinson?"

"Yes, and if he wasn't around, he sent one of his minions. I'm not sure they knew what he was covering up, they just did it because he was the boss and that's what it was like back then. No questions, absolute loyalty to the Guv. And I was a jumped-up, overeducated, promoted-too-soon Jock, so everyone was keen to trip me up."

"How?"

"I got a call from someone who said they had information. Said they'd tried to come forward in the original investigation but had been told what they had to say wasn't much use. Hadn't even given a statement. I arranged to meet them at a café in town, thought it might be a bit less intimidating that coming into the station. I went there and waited. No show." He swiped a brush over the horse's flank. It gleamed like polished ebony. "When I got back to the station, I found out someone had rung this informant and told him to come in.

147

He'd gone there and seen Inspector Godwinson, who told me the information was dud. Didn't even write it down."

"Who was the informant?"

"One of Adam's friends. A fat lad with glasses, according to Inspector Godwinson."

"What did you make of it?"

"I think Godwinson knew his evidence was good and squashed it."

Eden nodded, feeling depressed. Cover ups always made her want to scream. "You managed to get a case to trial, though?"

"It was mostly DNA. There was a cloak of some sort in the back of Ray Thompson's car. It had blood on it: DNA showed it was Adam Jones." Ian patted the horse's back and gathered up the brushes and combs. He led Eden out of the loose box and fastened the door. "The rest was circumstantial and rumour. Not enough to convict." He sighed. "I wish I hadn't tried."

"You gave it your best shot."

"It made me an outlaw in the station. Godwinson was shuffled out, and no one liked that. It was different later, when they found out he was a nonce, but until then I was the smart arse who thought he knew better and who bungled the case."

"Are you still convinced that Ray Thompson murdered Adam Jones?"

Ian fixed her with a steady look. "Yes. He did it all right. I just couldn't prove it."

CHAPTER TWENTY-TWO

Barbara Taylor's house was underheated and over-knick-knacked. Shelves set into the alcoves either side of the cold fireplace were crowded with china dolls in ballooning Victorian skirts, wooden dolls in national costume, and all the Olympic mascots back to the Moscow bear in 1980. A wall of eyes, blank and staring, enough to give you the willies. Eden took a seat with her back to the alcove and tried not to think about Orwell's Big Brother.

"Thanks for seeing me, Mrs Taylor," she said. "I can't imagine how difficult this week has been for you."

Barbara was thin and stringy, as if she'd been squeezed through a garlic press. Her hair hung in long strands on her shoulders, her narrow face accentuated by a centre parting. Deep grooves scored the sides of her mouth, like a ventriloquist's puppet. A small table near the window was covered with a cream linen cloth and held an array of photo frames: Barbara in a pink dress next to a man in a grey suit outside the Register office; a boy in a striped jumper blowing out birthday candles; a man with a postage stamp beard grinning at the camera. A large one, that surely normally lurked at the back, now took centre stage. It was of a boy in grey V-necked sweater, half turned towards the camera; the classic school photo shot, except that the boy's mouth was bruised and his eyes bloodshot. Barbara went to it and lifted it to her eyes, almost as if she was reminding herself what Adam looked like.

"I only had him twelve years, been without him thirty-five," she said. "Sometimes I think I dreamed him."

"I can't imagine what it was like, not knowing what had happened to him," Eden said.

"I knew all right, they just couldn't prove it." Barbara replaced the photo and took a seat at the end of the settee. A knitting needle poked out from behind the cushion and she prodded it back into hiding again. "Ray Thompson. He killed Adam. There's just no evidence."

Eden smoothed down the nap of her skirt. "I'm investigating Philip Wakefield's death. There might be a link with Adam's." No point telling her Philip's mother was terrified Philip killed Adam; she wasn't here to add to the woman's agony. "Do you remember Philip? He and Adam were friends."

Barbara scrunched up her forehead. "A bit shy. Used to go out on their bikes after school. Came home all scratched and bruised, said they'd been up the hill."

"The hill?"

"They'd go up the Devil's Chimney, and ride their bikes down as fast as they could." Barbara sighed, memories of the old days paining her. "Boys." She rose and went to a drawer in the sideboard and pulled out a photo album. She turned to the page she wanted and sat next to Eden. "Here they are. Adam and his gang."

A line of boys on bikes. Eden recognised Philip Wakefield, Lance Cotter and Dave Thompson, but there was also a small boy, younger than the others, his bike a child's beside the racers. "Who's that?"

"That's Gregory, Adam's step-brother."

On the opposite page was a photo of Barbara, a very young Adam, and a man. They were all leaning against the side of a Morris Minor Traveller: a crate on wheels. Adam was holding hands with the two adults, strung between them like a pearl. "Who's this?"

150

"That's me and Dean, Adam's dad. Not long before we split up." Barbara turned the page. "The old story. I got pregnant so we got married. Dean couldn't go to university like he'd hoped, so he joined the fire service. Doing all right till he had an accident and the only job he could get was in a metal works. Hated it. Got him thinking that if it hadn't been for me and Adam, well. So we split up and he went to university, just like he'd always wanted."

An everyday tragedy that kept on giving for this sad woman and her spooky ornaments. "Did he see Adam after the divorce?"

"Not really. He never paid any maintenance." In Barbara's eyes the two were connected. She continued, "Bit later he got a job in Birmingham, closer to Adam, see him a bit more. Adam didn't want to." She tugged at her cuffs: they were fraying and her thumb went through the seam. "Dean was here the night Adam went missing."

"How come?"

"Just turned up, demanded to see him. Went upstairs, woke up Gregory, and there's Adam's bed not slept in. Dean went to look for him, but Adam wouldn't come home." She closed the photo album. "Not surprising: Adam hated his dad by then."

"What was Adam like before he disappeared?"

Barbara shrugged. "Tired. I had to prise him out of bed in the morning, but that's boys, isn't it?"

"You mentioned Adam's step-brother. How would I get hold of him?"

"He lives local with his partner." Barbara blushed as she said this, and waited a moment as if expecting a follow-on question that needed a defence. Eden merely nodded. "He's a ranger up at Leckhampton."

Eden's scalp started to prickle.

"He was there when they discovered Adam's ... well, you know."

"Adam's step-brother was there when they found his skeleton?"

Another tug on the cuffs. "Strange, isn't it."

In the middle of a line of snooty Georgian buildings squatted a grey 1960s monstrosity: a duckling that had infiltrated the swans. It housed the offices of the conservation team that protected Leckhampton Hill. Eden went to the front counter and asked if Gregory was available to speak to her.

"Gregory?" the woman echoed. "Oh, you mean Greg."

Eden took a seat on the most uncomfortable plastic bucket chair she'd ever known and studied the posters on the walls: bats, dogs, ticks, lungworm, leeches. God, the countryside was dangerous. All those creepy crawlies waiting to suck your flesh and inject you with deadly poison. Just as her skin was crawling and she was having to fight the urge to scratch, a man came out and called her name. He was in his early forties, with a thatch of thick light brown hair, and was wearing a ranger's uniform of canvas pants and moss-coloured stocking stitch woollen sweater.

"You wanted to see me?"

"Is there somewhere private we can speak?" Eden asked. "I want to ask about your brother, Adam."

Greg's shoulders sagged a little. "Of course," he said, his voice low and sad. He punched in the combination on the security door and led her along a corridor and into a small meeting room that smelled strongly of tuna fish sandwiches. "I know it happened a long time ago, but I still miss Adam every day."

"You were close?"

Greg yanked out two chairs for them. "Not in the way you mean. I idolised him. I always wanted a big brother. Used to hassle my mum, God rest her, about it when I was tiny, and could never understand why she said it could never happen. A big brother was always on my letter to Father Christmas. It's what I told people I wanted for my birthday." He bent one leg over the other and gripped his ankle. "Then Mum died and the world ended for a while. I was only seven. But then Dad met Barbara and they got married, and low and behold I suddenly had an older brother." He chuckled to himself. "For a long time I thought I'd magicked him up."

"He was a wish come true," Eden added.

"For me, yes. Not that Adam saw it that way."

"He didn't like having a little brother?"

"Not one bit. I'm sure I was a pest, wanting to hang round with him and his friends all the time. Wanted to be part of the gang. They were way too cool for a brat like me, but Mum told him he had to be nice to me, and so he took me along sometimes. Not often. He had a big bike and lots of friends and they went off on their bikes and did stuff without adults being around."

"What sort of stuff?"

"Just boy stuff, going off exploring, that sort of thing. But I was pretty sure Adam was drinking and smoking, too. Sometimes I thought I could smell it on him."

"What about drugs?"

Greg fingered the square of stubble on his chin. "I didn't know it was drugs at the time, but Adam often had a sweetish smell about him. It was only when I was at uni I realised what it must have been."

"Didn't anyone else notice? Your parents, or his teachers?"

"I don't think Mum and Dad would have ever imagined that Adam would take drugs. I mean, we weren't that sort of people."

She'd heard that before when teenagers were caught with drugs. *We're not that sort of people.* It was easy to miss if you never thought it could come into your orbit. How many parents attributed mood swings and erratic behaviour to hormones, and were horrified to find later it was cannabis.

"Do you remember the night he went missing?" Eden asked.

"I was in bed, and suddenly the light went on, Adam's dad burst in, and they found Adam's bed was empty. A huge row erupted, and I told them he'd probably gone up to the Devil's Chimney. Adam's dad stormed out, shouting he was going to find him and bring him back."

"How did you know that's where Adam was?"

"He went up there a lot, sneaking out at night and coming back in the early hours, often a bit drunk and his mouth bleeding." Greg cast her a sideways look. "And he suddenly had a lot of money. A thick roll of it he hid in the cupboard."

"Where did he get it?"

Greg spread his hands. "I wasn't supposed to know about it."

"Did you tell the police about it when he disappeared?"

A crimson tide rose from Greg's collar and engulfed his face. "No."

Eden let the word hang between them, debating whether to ask the next question. From the anguish on Greg's face, he'd castigated himself enough over the past few years. Picking over the greedy actions of a nine year old boy wouldn't help her investigation. Instead she asked, "How did Adam get on with his dad?"

"Not at all," Greg said, crossing his legs the other way and looking relieved that the conversation had turned. "He didn't see much of him, and when he did, there was an argument. His dad turned up on his birthday once and gave him a present." He shook his head to himself. "It was exactly what I wanted at the time, but of course it was too young for Adam. It was one of those watches with Mickey Mouse on the dial, and his arms are the hands. One of my friends had one and I really, really wanted one, too. And Adam gets one and doesn't want it."

"Did he give it to you?"

Greg laughed. "No chance! He threw it back and his dad stormed off."

Eden paused before she asked the next question. "How did you know where Adam was buried?"

Greg started and flushed again. "I didn't … what makes you think…?"

"Your mum says you were there when Adam's remains were found. Rather a coincidence, don't you think?"

"Not really. This organisation protects lots of places around Cheltenham. Woodland, forest, wildflower meadows, wetlands. He could have been buried in any of them."

"But he wasn't buried anywhere, he was on your patch," Eden said.

Greg had no answer to that.

CHAPTER TWENTY-THREE

Eden didn't like coincidences, and the adoring step-brother of a murder victim accidentally discovering his brother's remains was too much for her. She needed to check out Greg's story, so first stop, the Cultural Heritage Unit. Mandy let her in and ushered her into Aidan's office. He was scowling at his computer screen. When she entered, he dragged his spectacles off his nose and folded them underneath a sheet of paper.

"The ranger who found the skeleton at the Devil's Chimney," she began, without preamble. "He's the boy's step-brother."

Aidan's mouth opened and closed several times but no words came out.

"I want to know how he knew."

Aidan yanked open the drawer of a metal cabinet and pulled out a file. "I found this a couple of days ago. The police asked me who might have known about the Iron Age graves so I did some digging. No pun intended."

"Let's see." Eden slid the file across the desk and flicked through the papers. "So there was a dig there in the seventies, and they recorded the existence of the graves."

"And reported them to the conservation office to protect them."

"Who let brambles grow over them."

"Undergrowth can protect sites better than signs saying 'keep out'," Aidan remarked. "But the really interesting thing is that a few years ago there was a grant application to excavate the graves, and someone went up there and took a look. Except now there were five graves."

"They didn't think that was odd?"

"The earlier dig only noted the graves they'd found. I wouldn't have been surprised if we'd found more graves once we started excavating. Once you start clearing and measuring, other sites often emerge."

"But the fifth grave turned out to contain Adam Jones?"

"Exactly."

Eden drummed her fingers on the file. "Who could have known about the graves?"

"Anyone who worked for the Cultural Heritage Unit, for a start," Aidan said. "And copies were sent to the conservation office, so anyone working there, too."

"I wonder how long Greg has worked there?"

"Only about six years," Aidan said. "We got chatting when we first went to look at the graves. But he would have had access to the records."

"He told me he didn't know Adam was buried up there."

"Maybe he didn't. Maybe it was just a hunch." Aidan bounced his fingertips against his lips while he thought. "But he couldn't have known that the new path would be put in right through the graves. That, surely, is coincidence?"

"Is it? Who decided to put in the path?"

"The conservation people."

"And who said it had to be there?" Eden asked. "Could it have been put somewhere else?"

Aidan rummaged in a drawer and brought out a large scale map and unfolded it on the table. Just as the map occupied the whole of his desk, Trev barged in clutching two mugs of coffee, and plonked them down on top of it. "Room service," he declared.

"Trev! Map!" Aidan lifted his mug and wiped his finger over the map, smearing away a drop of coffee. Eden removed her own coffee and cradled it in her palms.

"What you looking at?" Trev said, looming over the desk.

"The site of the new path at the Devil's Chimney."

Trev traced the route with a thick forefinger. "It uses this old farm track further up the hill, and loops back towards the existing track along the ridge. Bonkers, if you ask me."

"Why?" Eden said.

"Because there's another track round the other way, with much better access. Not so steep." Trev pointed out the other track. It approached the Devil's Chimney from the opposite direction, and avoided the Iron Age graves altogether.

"Who put in the planning application?" Eden asked.

Trev and Aidan looked at each other and shrugged.

"Let's go and find out," Aidan said. He picked up his cup of coffee and handed it to Trev. "Thanks, Trev."

Eden copied him. "Thanks, Trev. See you later."

As they bundled out of Aidan's office, Lisa came up from the basement. "Nothing more on that 1978 excavation," she said. Her eyes narrowed when she caught sight of Eden. "Oh, it's you."

"Indeed it is," Eden said.

"Show me when I get back," Aidan said. "We're following a lead."

"Heavens, you're even starting to sound like each other," Lisa said. "Be careful, it's only a step away from matching sweaters." As they reached the door, she called out, "Let me know about the cottage, won't you, Aidan?"

He wrenched open the door and they went out.

"What cottage?" Eden said. "You taking me on a mini break?"

"No," Aidan said. "Lisa wants me to go away with her for the weekend."

"Oh." Eden fell silent. Lisa was always scheming to get Aidan back. Not so long ago she'd announced she wanted to have Aidan's baby. Seemed she was trying a new tack. "So are you going to go?"

Aidan stared at her, emotions chasing across his face, and she could have kicked herself. Let sleeping dogs lie. "Do you think I should?" he said, at last.

"No," Eden said. "I think you should do what makes you happy."

She plunged her fists into her pockets and they walked in silence to the Council offices and up the stairs to the Planning Department. A trim young woman with a blonde ponytail fetched the folders they requested, and showed them a table in the corner where they could read them.

"Here's the planning application for the new path," Aidan said, fanning out the papers. Eden leaned close to him to read it, too. His jacket prickled against her wrist and she could smell the bergamot notes of his aftershave. A bubble of sadness swelled in her chest. For a long time she'd dared to think their relationship had a future, that they could be a normal couple, eventually. But her past wouldn't allow that, not with Hammond on the loose and any future at all looking increasingly unlikely. She ought to let Aidan go, let him find happiness and normality with someone else, someone who wasn't constantly looking over her shoulder for assassins.

"There's a question about archaeological importance," Aidan said. She dragged her attention back to the application. "That's interesting. Whoever filled in the form stated there's no known archaeology along the route of the path, nothing that would prevent the path being put in."

"Maybe whoever filled in the form didn't know about the archaeology."

Aidan shook his head. "They'd have to. The first thing you do is search the records. We know that the conservation office was told about the site so it could be protected. This —" he jabbed the paper — "is a lie."

"Who did the form? Is there a signature?"

Eden riffled through the pages. At the end of the application was an electronic signature: Greg Taylor. She sat back in her chair and chewed the side of her thumb. "Greg had access to the archaeological records that said there were graves there, and he decided to route the path through them rather than choosing the alternative."

"And he was the one who cleared the ground and uncovered the graves," Aidan said. "Told me he recognised them from watching TV."

"And one of the graves held the skeleton of his step-brother."

"Do you think he was the killer?" Aidan said.

"No, he was too young, and he was in bed when Adam disappeared." She thought for a moment, replaying her conversation with Greg. "Anyway, if he did it, he wouldn't want it being uncovered. He'd do everything he could to keep people away from those graves."

"So why has he gone to all this trouble?" Aidan said.

She remembered the light in his eyes when he talked about Adam. Thirty-five years was a long time to hold his memory so dear. She understood why he'd lied on the form, and why he'd insisted on being the one to strim the graves himself. Maybe he hadn't known for certain that Adam was buried there, but he had his suspicions. How many other avenues had he pursued over the years, in his search for the truth?

"Eden?" Aidan was staring at her. "We need to report this. He lied on the forms."

"If he hadn't," she said, "Adam's body would never have been discovered. Imagine living your whole life wondering what happened to someone you loved."

His expression made her shiver. "I can imagine that all too well," he said, a quiet sad tone colouring his voice. "Every time you go out after homicidal lunatics I wonder if I'll ever see you again."

"I know how to take care of myself, Aidan."

He snorted. "Right."

CHAPTER TWENTY-FOUR

Easy for Eden to say. Knows how to look after herself, Aidan seethed as he went back to his office. He'd seen the scars on her body, scars she got from that maniac Hammond. Scars that tell their own story of a woman who was trying to obliterate herself. His guts wrenched every time he thought of her attacked and left to die, saved just in the nick of time. Any normal person would have settled down to a safe, normal life after that; kept their head down and stayed out of trouble, but not Eden. Since he'd known her he'd saved her from being strangled by a thug; seen her plunge into danger to rescue a kidnapped girl; and charge off to confront a murderer. All in a day's work for her, but for him? His nerves were shredded. And if Hammond could get someone to put tear gas in a shopping arcade to get to Eden, what else was he capable of?

He churned all the way back to his office, despairing at his own impotence to either protect Eden or persuade her to keep a low profile. When he entered the building, a welcome sense of tranquillity settled over him. The offices were in an elegant Georgian building, and the high ceilings, symmetry and delicate plaster mouldings soothed him. There was a gentle hum of conversation. Discussion of excavations and preservation of artefacts. Normal conversation, not a psychopath in sight. He wandered into Trev and Mandy's office to join in.

"Hi, Aidan," Mandy said. "Any news on when we can get back up to the Devil's Chimney and finish off those Iron Age graves?"

"If they are Iron Age," Trev added. "Gave me the heebie-jeebies, that skeleton turning up like that."

"Usually you can't get enough of skeletons," Aidan pointed out.

"Only if they're a few centuries old."

"And don't wear braces," Mandy added.

Aidan perched on the corner of the desk. "The police haven't okayed it yet. I'll call them and see when we can get back up there."

"Good."

They all smiled, and he experienced a moment of calm and security. Here, there was order and control. Here, he knew the rules, he was appreciated and respected for his learning and opinion.

"You putting the kettle on then, Aidan?" Trev asked.

"No. I'll do better. Want a posh coffee?"

"Are you paying?"

"Yes."

"In that case I'll have a grande hazelnut latte."

"A cappuccino, please," Mandy said. "Lots of chocolate sprinkles on the top."

"And I'll come with you." Lisa materialised in the doorway. "You'll need a hand to carry that lot. And I want a double espresso."

He didn't argue. For once he felt genuinely pleased to see Lisa. She understood him, and he understood her. There was no worrying about whether she was running into danger and putting her life on the line.

"You all right, Aidan?" she asked, as they headed down the road. The café was on the corner, in a converted industrial unit. It had metal pendant lights and a funky feel to it, with squashy red booths like a diner, and ultra-cool tattooed staff.

The counter was spread with tray bakes and muffins. A cluster of yummy mummies occupied the lower level, four-wheel-drive prams blocking the way. Lisa's eye travelled to them and lingered, then she snapped her attention back to him. "You seem a bit discombobulated."

"I am, a bit."

"Want to tell me about it? We can have our coffee here and then get some for Twinky and Winky."

"Mandy and Trev."

"Whatever." The barista asked for their order. "Two double espressos, please."

"How do you know that's what I want?"

"It's what you always had."

He went to pay for the coffee but she waved him away, and took their drinks to a couple of soft arm chairs on the upper level of the café.

"Tell Aunty Lisa," she said.

"It's Eden. She's in danger," he said, and poured it all out, his worries for her safety and his inability to protect her.

"Does she want protecting?" Lisa asked, when he finally stuttered to a halt. "Because she seems to me like a very self-contained woman. Has she ever asked you to change a washer or look at her car?"

"No, but she's looked at mine a couple of times."

"And has she ever clutched at your arm at a horror movie?"

"Why's that relevant?"

Lisa fixed him with a look that clearly said 'you're a dolt'. "Because women who want protecting let you know they want protecting. Do you get rid of spiders, shin up ladders, carry heavy parcels?"

"No."

Lisa leaned forwards and spoke in a low voice so he had to bend to hear her. "She doesn't need or want your protection. She can take care of herself."

"But she can't! That's the point! There's this complete madman out to get her and —"

"And what can you do to make her safer that she isn't already doing?"

That stumped him. "She could hide in my flat until the police lock him up again."

"But from what you've told me, this Hammond won't stop even when he's back in prison. He's got people he can manipulate to do what he wants. He's bribed and coerced the prison officers. He's always in charge, and the only way that'll change is when he dies." She sucked in a breath. "I know it's terrifying, but Eden can't escape him. She could hide in your flat all day, but frankly, that wouldn't stop this Hammond. The question is, how do *you* come to terms with it?"

"She said she's sick of being afraid, and that's making her reckless."

"And what about you? Are you sick of being afraid for her?"

He met her shrewd green eyes. "I just want things to be normal," he said. How pathetic did he sound? Like a small boy who wished he hadn't been told about Father Christmas.

"Of course you do, but that isn't going to happen. If you wanted a normal life you shouldn't have chosen a woman like Eden. But now you have, the question is how do you live with it?"

He pressed his palms together. Suddenly they were clammy and trembling. "How do other people live with it? People whose partners are in the Forces? They must spend all day waiting for bad news."

"They accept the risk and carry on regardless. The relationship is worth the worry," Lisa said. She left the unspoken question hanging between them.

Aidan drained his cup and stood. "Come on, let's get those coffees for Mandy and Trev."

"You have to decide, Aidan."

"I can't leave her when she's in such danger," he said. "What would that make me?"

"When is she going to be out of danger?" Lisa asked. When he didn't reply, she said, "Exactly."

"Did you grow those coffee beans yourself?" Trev greeted them when they returned.

"Sorry," Aidan said. "We got talking."

"We brought cake to make up for it." Lisa offered her sweetest smile, and Trev beamed at her. Aidan had to hand it to her: she knew how to snap on the charm all right. When it suited her.

"You two busy at the moment?" Aidan asked.

Mandy snaffled a Bakewell slice before Trev's paws could get in the cake box. "What do you need?"

"It's pissing me off about those Iron Age graves," Aidan said. "Someone knew what they were doing, and that an Iron Age grave wouldn't look out of place. I want to know who."

"I've had a look through our records, but I thought perhaps we —" he indicated the four of them — "could dig a bit more. The police think the boy was killed and put in the grave in 1981. So we need to know who researched that area before 1981 and could know about the graves."

"That'll take weeks," Trev groaned.

"Maybe, but I already have a lead." He went into the meeting room and spread his papers over the table. "There's a grant application to excavate up there. It references an earlier dig which noted there were graves up there. Trev, you can help me with that."

"What about us?" Lisa said. Side by side with Mandy they looked an unlikely pairing: Lisa with her slender, petite frame, red-gold pixie and navy sheath dress; Mandy with her luridly dyed plaits making her look much older than forty, in ripped jeans and a candy striped sweater.

"Can you go through the published research and see what's recorded?"

"A literature survey?"

"Exactly. You remember how to do that?"

"I've not done one since my PhD," Lisa said.

"That's all right, Lisa," Mandy said, "I'll show you. I'm a whizz with Boolean."

Aidan smothered a smile at the indignation on Lisa's face. He'd put money on her ladyship reclaiming the high ground by wittering about her war graves cases the whole time they searched the databases.

Aidan clapped his hands together. "Let's get on with it, shall we?"

Mandy dragged a spare chair up to her desk. "Right, Lisa, I'll log into the system if you start sketching out some search terms."

Aidan and Trev exchanged a look, then headed down into the basement and the glory of the archives. Trev stood with his hands on his hips and gazed at the shelves of boxes with dismay. "There's yards of material down here," he said. "And none of it goes back as far as the 1980s. You remember the eighties, Aidan?"

"No, I'd only just been born."

"It was great. I was a New Romantic for a while. Eyeliner and a big shirt. Happy days." Trev rubbed his paunch, a misty look in his eye, and Aidan prayed that his New Romantic days were well and truly buried in the past.

"You start that end and I'll start this."

"I thought you said you had a lead."

"I have. Let's check what else there is down here."

They each hefted down a box, took a gurney each, and started to search.

After two hours, Trev rose and stretched, his vertebrae snapping. "This might be something." He held up a blue hard backed book. "It's the accident book from decades ago."

"I saw that the other day. And?"

"Someone put a spade through their foot at a dig on Leckhampton Hill."

Aidan scooted over. "Let's see."

The book was divided into columns: date, person injured, place injured, details of injury, name of person recording the entry. The cover was coming away and had been repaired with masking tape, and inside the pages were soft but decipherable. Trev's thick forefinger pointed to an entry made in 1977.

It recorded that on April 1977, Stan Pullman put a spade through his foot, on a dig up at Leckhampton Hill. Whoever filled in the report was anxious to get it right, because they also recorded that Stan was a student at the University of Bristol and was volunteering on the dig, led by Professor James Hawkins. The person recording the accident was D. Jones.

"It's the year before they recorded the graves," Aidan said. "I wonder if they did a survey?"

"Bristol might still have the records of what they found and who was digging." Trev paused. "I could pop over there and see what they've got. Bristol's my old uni."

"Check the records for 1977 and 1978," Aidan said. "And see what you can find out about Professor Hawkins, Stan Pullman and D. Jones."

"D. Jones?"

Aidan pointed to the accident book. "He or she recorded the accident. That means they were there."

CHAPTER TWENTY-FIVE

This equipment went out with the Ark, Eden thought, as she wrestled again to load the cassette into the microfiche machine. Her fingers were dotted with small cuts and bruises where she'd got her fingers trapped or the spool had spun round and thwacked her. Surely this stuff was all digitised now? Not when it came to the Gloucester archives and back copies of the local papers, it transpired. All still on microfiche, and that meant an afternoon hunched in an uncomfortable chair and wrecking her eyesight as she peered at the screen.

She moved the microfiche on a couple of pages, checking her notebook for the dates Ian Cooper, the retired police officer who had charged Ray Thompson with murder, had supplied. From the tone of his voice it seemed as though they were seared into him.

"I don't think there's anything to find there," he said. "But go ahead if you want."

"I won't rest unless I go through it all," she'd said. "You know what that's like."

There was a hollow chuckle. "I could probably recite the evidence to you verbatim. When that case was on, I was in court all day and dreaming about it all night."

The case files were sealed — the CPS was reviewing them in light of Adam Jones's body being found — and Eden couldn't get access to them, so she had to rely on the reports of Ray's trial in the local papers.

The trial started in April 1990 at Gloucester Crown Court. Ray was charged with the murder of Adam Jones on or around the 23rd August, 1981. He pleaded not guilty and it went before a jury. Eden followed the trial day by day, scrutinising the photographs of witnesses and friends arriving and leaving the court: Adam's parents, his step-brother Gregory, Simon Bird, Lance Cotter, Dave Thompson, Adam's form teacher Mrs Temple. They all helped to establish the time line she'd already constructed, and told of a boy who left his home at night and disappeared up to the Devil's Chimney with Ray Thompson. Rumours of what they were doing up there were presented in court and dismissed as hearsay. Nine years later, it was easy to demolish the evidence. How could witnesses remember what they were doing, on which day, after so much time had passed, and when they were so young when the events happened?

Next came the expert witnesses. When Ray was arrested, there was blood on his clothing, and mud all over his car. Inside the spare wheel was a crumpled white cloak stained with blood. Ray had scratches up his arms and on his hands, which he claimed were from pruning roses in the garden. Experts set to work testing the mud, the cloak, and the blood. The original investigation, in 1981, showed the blood on the cloak was the same blood type as Adam, but it was a common blood group, shared by the majority of the population, and proved nothing. DNA testing carried out years later refined the results: the blood was Adam's. Ray swore he had no idea how it got there. Further, the DNA expert couldn't say how the blood came to be there: it could have been a nose bleed.

When it came to the blood on Ray's clothing when he was arrested though, that was more of a mystery. DNA showed it belonged to neither Adam nor Ray himself.

Experts also tested Ray's car. There was mud caught in the wheel arches and trapped underneath, still wet at the time of his arrest. They compared it with soil from the Devil's

Chimney, and it didn't match. That demolished the prosecution's argument that Ray killed Adam, put him in his car and drove him to a spot on the Devil's Chimney to bury him.

The crux of the case, though, was the fact that Adam's body had never been found. The defence brought in an expert on teenage runaways, who testified to the number of young boys who run away from home each year. Some are never found; some are found but refuse to return home; and some come home after a few days, weeks or months. A runaway coming home after several years of limbo was not unusual, he said. The defence pounced. So was it possible that Adam could be waiting at home right now? Could he turn up tomorrow, or the day after, alive and unharmed? Yes, it was possible. Without a body, no one could say for certain that he was dead.

The jury retired for less than an hour before coming to a decision. Not guilty. Ray was released from custody, beaming and punching the air in victory.

Eden flicked back through her notes, chewing over what she'd uncovered. There was evidence here, but it was all unexplained. How did Adam's blood get onto the cloak found in Ray's car? Why was it hidden inside the spare wheel? Did Ray get those scratches from pruning roses, or were they defensive injuries inflicted when he killed Adam? And if he didn't kill Adam, who did?

She printed off copies of the more detailed accounts of the case and stowed them in a folder to study later. The archives were closing for the day and a harassed-looking archivist was sending her pleading looks begging her to finish up and go away, she was ready for the weekend. Eden rewound the microfiche cassettes and returned them to the desk with thanks, she had plenty to think about.

Eden's mobile rang as she was unlocking her car. The voice on the end of the line spun her back through the years, to when she was working undercover, and more than a little intimidated by her ebullient boss, Miranda Tyson.

"Eden? Miranda. You need to sit tight."

"I've been sitting tight for years now. Any tighter and I'll disappear up my own backside."

A throaty laugh and the click of a cigarette lighter the other end. A deep inhale and a cough. Miranda's forty a day habit was evidently catching up with her. "How are you?"

"I've been better. No doubt you're calling about Hammond."

"He rang me to gloat."

"Of course, you two are bosom buddies." Eden couldn't keep the vitriol out of her voice. If it weren't for Miranda, she wouldn't be in danger right now.

"I said I'm sorry."

"Well that makes it all OK. Thanks for calling." Eden went to hang up, but a squawk down the line stayed her hand. "What?"

"He's up to something."

"He's always up to something."

"He was boasting that he'd got a new tame monkey."

"What's that supposed to mean?"

"I think he means he's using someone to get to you," Miranda said. "Someone who can get close to you."

"Let me guess: he didn't tell you who?" Eden's kept her voice sarcastic but a chill ran through her. She knew Hammond, knew he could pile on the charm and manipulate people into doing what he wanted. What if he was cosying up to the people closest to her? Mandy or Trev, Judy, Aidan?

None of them would realise who he really was and how dangerous he could be.

"Just be careful, that's all." She heard the hopelessness in Miranda's voice.

"Too late. I'm sick of running scared."

"You're not going after him?" Miranda sounded horrified.

"No, but I've got years of tradecraft behind me. I'm not going to sit at home feeling afraid and sorry for myself. If it's time to die, it's time. But I'm living up to the end. Bye."

Eden ended the call, her hands trembling as she realised she meant it. She would live until the end. Until Hammond caught up with her.

CHAPTER TWENTY-SIX

No one would call him Fat Simon now. He was lean and muscular, with very erect posture and a long-legged, striding gait. His dark suit was well cut and showed off a trim torso. Gone were the thick black specs and nerdy boy haircut: Eden suspected his bathroom held an array of male grooming products, and that he didn't get much change from a hundred quid for his haircut. Quite the transformation.

Clarissa Temple had come good again, not only recalling Simon's full name, but supplying the additional detail that he was an estate agent. "Properties quite out of my price bracket," she'd added, in her cut-glass accent. "Nothing less than two million, I hear."

"Based in Cheltenham?"

"On the Promenade," Clarissa said. "Naturally."

A quick look at the company's website gave Eden all the information she needed — not only what her target looked like these days, but when he was likely to leave the office. She'd stationed herself on a bench opposite and pretended to read the paper while she kept the offices under surveillance. Simon had strode in about ten minutes ago. Seeing him striding back out again, she folded the paper and set off in pursuit.

He turned the corner at the end of the Promenade, and headed up the street parallel to it. As he approached a florist's, Eden hung back to watch. A woman in a long black apron with a daisy on the front came out of the shop and hefted up a galvanised silver bucket of gerberas. Simon ran the last few yards and came to a halt beside her. The woman lifted her hand to her head and pushed back her hair, her face tired.

175

Simon spread his arms, pleading. The woman smiled and twitched her head towards the shop, and he followed her inside.

He was a persuasive sod, Eden thought. Mind you, as an estate agent it pretty much came with the territory. That, and the ability to describe a grotty cupboard as a bijou studio ripe for development. She gave him a moment, then scuttled over to the shop and went in. A bell sounded above her head as she tugged the door open, and a voice from the back called, "We're just closing. Sorry."

"That's OK," Eden said, "I'm looking for this gentleman."

Simon swivelled round in surprise, slotting a credit card back in his wallet. He picked up a large bouquet of cream roses and pink lilies from the counter. They were wrapped in pale pink tissue paper and secured with raffia string. "Me?" he said.

Eden nodded at the flowers. "Philip would be pleased," she said.

Shock and misunderstanding chased across Simon's face. "I don't know what you're talking about," he said, eventually.

"Yes, you do," Eden said. She flashed her private investigator's identity card at him. "It's a nice thing you've been doing, remembering your friend. I just want to know why now?"

Simon's shoulders sagged. "How did you find out?"

"Your name came up from everyone I spoke to about Philip. And then a copper told me you'd tried to tell him you knew something about Adam Jones's death." Eden shrugged. "You want to take the flowers up to the cemetery now, or can I buy you a drink?"

"I can't be long," Simon said. "I have to get home." He hesitated. "But I'd like to talk about Philip."

There was a wine bar on the corner. It was too early for the beautiful people who were its usual clientele, and they easily found seats in a private corner where they wouldn't be overheard.

"Who hired you?" Simon asked. His drink was a lemon and lime with a dash of angostura bitters. Eden nursed a coke. It was made from syrup and had too much ice in it.

"Philip's mother. She found your flowers and the notes saying 'sorry' and was worried," Eden said. "The more I asked around about Philip and Adam Jones' disappearance, the more questions I had."

"Philip was my friend," Simon said. "I've never forgotten him." He opened his wallet. In the transparent slot for a driving licence was a photo booth snap of Simon with his arms round a man wearing a green sweatshirt. He poked the picture out of sight and fiddled around in the back of the wallet, drawing out a small rectangular photo: him with Philip Wakefield, the two of them holding a large toy yacht.

"This was taken not long before he died," Simon said.

"How long have you been leaving the flowers?"

"About six months."

"Why?"

Simon sipped his drink, his little finger curled as though he was drinking a cup of china tea. "I started thinking about Philip a lot, and felt guilty that I hadn't been able to help him."

"You went to the police."

He let out a humourless bark. "Didn't do any good. When Philip died, I told them what I knew. No one took it seriously, they treated me like a hysterical schoolkid."

"But you went back when the investigation was reopened," Eden persisted.

"I was at university and heard they'd reopened the case into Adam's disappearance," Simon said. "I rang the police and went to meet them, but again, they weren't interested. It was the same police officer I'd seen before, the one who told me I was making up fairy tales." His eyes burned with hurt and injustice.

"What was it you wanted to tell the police?"

Simon didn't answer immediately, and when he did, his voice shook with emotion. "Philip confided in me that Adam had persuaded him to go up to the Devil's Chimney and take part in a horror film. He was in a terrible state, crying and hysterical about what had happened. I didn't believe him at first, then when he kept on repeating it over and over, I said we should go and see for ourselves. I thought if there were two of us telling the same story, people would have to believe us."

"What did you do?"

"We went up there and hid. It was just as Philip had told me, men in masks and some sort of grotesque ritual going on. Now I'm older I know what it was, but then —" he shuddered — "I just knew it frightened the life out of me." He gulped at his drink. "We were crouched down, watching, and suddenly we heard Adam screaming and running past. Running blindly, like he was terrified. All the men scattered. I don't know if they thought it was a police raid or what, but they vanished, leaving the camera and the recorder. I lunged at it and took the film, then me and Philip ran, too."

"Adam was there?"

"It was the night he disappeared. We were terrified that if we told the police we were there, they'd think we'd hurt him, so we kept quiet." Simon swallowed. "And then Philip killed himself."

"Have you still got the film?" she asked.

Simon traced a design in the condensation from his glass. "I wish I had, it would prove what was going on up there, but Philip was terrified he was on the film, so I gave it to him."

"What did he do with it?"

"No idea."

"And you and Philip were together the whole night?"

"Until we went home, yes."

"And Adam was alive?"

"He went running past us."

"Do you remember what time that was?"

"Close to eleven, I think."

Eden's mobile rang and she made an apologetic face at Simon as she answered. She was dragging her jacket from the back of her chair as she ended the call. "I'm sorry," she said. "I've got to go. My client's been burgled."

CHAPTER TWENTY-SEVEN

Trev was beaming when he returned from Bristol.

"They were really nice," he said. "Gave me a desk, made me a coffee. I never got that when I was a student."

"You surprise me," Aidan said, drily.

"So what did you find out?" Mandy said. A day searching databases with Lisa had made her scratchy; Aidan could tell she was itching to get home and do whatever Mandy did to relax. Re-dye her hair a new shade of purple, presumably.

"Well, my lover, Bristol has got great records of that Professor Hawkins dig, and they let me photocopy them, on their machine, and they didn't ask me to pay for it."

Alarming how easy it was to make Trev happy, Aidan thought. A coffee and a free go on a photocopier and he was in a good temper.

"So what did you turn up?"

Trev plonked a cardboard folder down on the meeting room table and they all clustered round it.

"Here's the map of the dig site," Trev said. "As you can see, it covers the Iron Age settlement, the Devil's Chimney, and the Iron Age graves we were excavating. They did the dig in two stages: in April 1977 and September 1978. I've got a copy of the day book for the dig." Another lump of paper hit the table. "They were focussing on the settlement, but on the last day of the 1978 dig, someone noticed the tips of one of the cist burials. I suspect it was one of the students sneaking off to have a wazz and tripped over it. Anyway, they took a trowel to the area and saw there were potentially four cist burials."

"So they recorded them?" Aidan said. "We already know this, Trev. They found those graves and let the conservation team know. What we need to know is who knew about them?"

Trev gave him a hurt look. "Just being thorough," he said, in a wounded tone. "Here's the list of people who were on that 1978 dig." A sheet of paper with a list of names, Professor Hawkins at the top, followed by two experts in Iron Age pottery, then a list of students in alphabetical order. Towards the middle was the name 'Dean Jones'.

"And there's a team photo." A colour photo of a motley crew in seventies flared jeans and tank tops. "And some of them working individually." A fan of photos of people hunkered down, scraping away at the soil.

"Who's this?" Aidan picked up one of the pictures.

"The chap you were interested in. Dean Jones. The one who filled in the accident book."

"I've seen him before."

"Maybe you were at university with him," Mandy said, trying to be helpful.

Aidan shot her a freezing look. "I'm not that old, thank you." He frowned at the picture. Where had he seen that face before? He knew it from somewhere. "Why do I know the name Dean Jones?"

The others shrugged and blank-faced him. He looked again at the photograph. A tall, strong looking man with a narrow face and high cheekbones. He'd seen that face recently. Where? He sifted through his memory, flinging up images of people he'd seen in queues and offices, the police officers he'd spoken to, when suddenly it clunked into place. He had spoken to a man hanging around at the dig the other evening. When Aidan had asked the man what he was doing there, the man had replied, "Just come to see where they found that boy."

"You knew him?" Aidan had asked.

"Not really," the man had said. "You with the police?"

Aidan had told him that he was an archaeologist and had asked if he could help with anything.

"No, just came to see," the man had replied. "I had a son, once. And this, well … it reminded me. Terrible thing."

"I'm sorry. What happened to your son?"

"I lost him."

It was him, Aidan was sure of it.

"He was up at the graves the other evening," Aidan told the others.

"Probably remembered digging there as a student," Lisa said.

"No," Aidan said. "Hang on, the name Jones. The skeleton was called Jones." Aidan pulled out his phone and keyed in Eden's number. "Hi, Eden, does the name Dean Jones mean anything to you? *What?*" He ended the call and faced the team, who all leaned forwards as if waiting for a great pronouncement. "Dean Jones is the murdered boy's father."

CHAPTER TWENTY-EIGHT

The crime scene had little scrote written all over it. No finesse — a shattered pane in the back door showed how he'd gained entry. Evidently cut his hand reaching in to open the door, too, as there were bloody finger marks all over the door frame, and drips of blood that led a tell-tale path through the house from the kitchen up the stairs into the spare bedroom. He was smart enough not to leave prints though: the finger marks were large and blurry, showing he had at least half a brain cell and had remembered to wear gloves.

Eden was forced to wait outside while the police conducted a search, and took the opportunity to make friends with Forensics. A bit of a tale about scenes she'd attended when she worked in Customs did it. The story of the smuggled tank of exotic fish that had been fed on their journey by a notorious gang member's sworn enemy. Forensics loved it and, recognising a soul mate, matched her story with one of his own that included a stuffed gorilla and a kilo of heroin. Forensics was muffled in a white plastic suit with the hood pulled up, and most of his face was concealed behind a pair of large black framed spectacles. Behind the spectacles, two blue eyes twinkled with merriment.

"And the SIO sees the gorilla and shouts, and this is in front of all the press and gawpers you understand, he shouts, 'Who sent for the Home Secretary?'" Forensics concluded his story with a growly chuckle.

Eden joined him and picked her moment. "Any chance of catching him?" she twitched her head at the open front door, where uniformed cops were dancing round each other as they bustled in and out.

"Snowball's in hell with forensics," he said. "Most likely get cleared up with other offences taken into consideration. You know the drill. Bloody statistics."

"What about the blood? DNA?"

He snorted. "We'll collect it, obviously, but who's going to pay for the sequencing? Especially as it doesn't seem like anything was pinched." He sucked in a breath through his nose. "Old biddy was lucky. He could have been a vicious bastard and this a murder scene."

The old biddy in question was perched on the garden wall, a pink cardigan swaddled around her and her hands tucked into her armpits. Eden sat down beside her. "You OK?"

"It's just the shock and thinking what if he'd attacked me," Susan Wakefield said, shivering.

"Can you tell me what happened? Slowly, from the beginning."

Susan visibly straightened. "I decided to go into town about five o'clock. There's a restaurant that does early bird specials for seniors and I just fancied a treat. There's a bus leaves about a quarter past. Anyway, I'd only got as far as the end of the road when I realised I hadn't got my bus pass, so I went home to fetch it. I thought if I hurried I'd still have time to get the bus." She rubbed a tear away with the heel of her hand. "I let myself in and went upstairs to get my pass. I keep it in my bedside drawer, I don't know why, that's just where I put it. When I went upstairs I saw the spare room door was standing ajar. I always close it. I pushed the door open and suddenly someone shoved me, hard, and I hit my head on the wall, and I heard someone tearing down the stairs and out the back."

"And then?"

"I went round the rest of the house, to see what he'd done, and that's when I saw the back door all smashed and the blood, and I called the police."

"How long were you out of the house for?"

"Just minutes. Like I said, I only got to the end of the road."

"Can you describe him?"

"I told the policeman."

"Tell me."

Susan pulled a tissue from her pocket and wiped her nose.

Eden put her arm round her shoulders and gave her a little squeeze. "You're doing great, Susan. I'm sorry to ask you all these things. Especially as you've already told the police."

"I didn't really get a look at him," Susan said. She closed her eyes to aid her memory. "It's more of an impression. Tall and slim. What my mum used to call a streak of water. Grey jeans and a black hoody with the hood up over his face."

"Did you see his face?"

"No, it was all too quick."

"And which rooms do you think he went in?"

"The kitchen, because of the door. And the spare room because that's where he attacked me. But nothing was moved in the sitting room or in my room. I'll have to check properly though."

"Was he carrying anything?"

"I don't think so. Do you think I stopped him stealing from me?"

"Probably. Have you seen anyone hanging around lately?"

"No, but next door's dog's been barking a lot during the day. Do you think that was him? Casing the joint?"

Eden hid a smile at the phrasing. "Could be," she said. "Then again, it could just be bad luck. Most burglars are opportunists, and yours didn't seem too bright."

And yet he seemed to know where he was going. According to Forensics, the blood spatters led straight up the stairs, the burglar didn't stop to check for valuables in either the kitchen or sitting room. Nor did he try the main bedroom, so he wasn't after jewellery. So what was he hoping to find in the spare bedroom?

"We'll check what's missing once you're allowed back inside," Eden said. "Can you think of anything he might have been after?"

"Only the usual things, TV and DVD player, but they're old. I don't have any antiques apart from a few silver thimbles I collected. They're in the sitting room. Apart from my wedding ring and my pearl necklace, I don't have any jewellery," Susan said. "All I've got is my little bits of tat, and Philip's things."

Eventually the police allowed Susan back inside the house to check what had been stolen. She ran from cupboard to sideboard, yelping when she saw everything was in place. In her bedroom, she yanked open a small carved jewellery box on her dressing table, sighing with relief as she pulled out a pearl necklace. "He didn't get this." She clutched it to her breast. "This was stolen before, and I never thought I'd get it back. Thank goodness it's still safe."

Eden mooched into the spare room. There was a smear of blood on the chest of drawers and on the single wardrobe. Slipping on latex gloves, she opened the door. The wardrobe was of white melamine and had faded, peeling Batman stickers on the doors. It contained an old fur coat and a box full of jigsaws. There was blood on the box and on the cartons inside. Someone had had a good rummage in there. The chest of drawers was in matching melamine and held ancient tablecloths and a collection of old photo albums, all of it stirred up.

She stood and surveyed the room. Why did the intruder head to this room? What did he think was of value in here? It was obviously a spare room: a single bed with a blue duvet cover, the chest of drawers and matching wardrobe, no books, tissues, make-up or knickknacks to indicate someone lived in it, only an old china name plate screwed to the door. *Philip's Room.* As she looked at it, ice trailed down her spine. This burglary was not opportunistic. It was planned, and for a very definite purpose.

"Mind if I take a look?" she asked.

"There's nothing in here," Susan said. "Just some of Philip's old stuff I can't get rid of." She half-smiled at her sentimentality. "You'd think it'd get easier as the years went by, but it doesn't, it's harder. It'll only get thrown out when I die, I expect."

Eden tried to picture the room as a twelve year old boy would. Bed: even if he made it himself, chances were Susan changed the sheets. Wardrobe and chest of drawers: too obvious, unless there were hidden cavities. She started with the chest of drawers, removing each drawer and running her fingers over it, turning it over, then placing it on the bed. She hunkered down on the floor and examined every inch of the frame. Nothing. She repeated the exercise with the wardrobe, removing and checking everything until it was stripped down, then examining the bare bones. Again, nothing. She tried heaving the wardrobe out from the wall. It was phenomenally awkward and snagged on the carpet, but she shifted it a few inches, enough to peer behind and see nothing was taped to the back.

Panting with exertion, she sank onto the bed to get her breath back, and her eye caught the carpet under the window. It wasn't flush with the skirting board and a few long fraying strands poked out. Peeling it back, she found a loose piece of floorboard. Hope rising, she took out her penknife and prised up the board. Underneath she uncovered dust and a few old screws. She put her hand in the hole and groped around, and gained the trophy of a hand blackened with a century's worth of dust and muck.

Sitting back on her haunches, she scanned the room again. All that was left was a tiny fireplace with a narrow tiled surround and a mantelpiece above, the sort of thing that was only lit when the bedroom's occupant was sick, and in recent years was filled with decorative pinecones and paper fans. The fireplace in Philip's room held only the metal grate. She felt up the chimney stack, her hand coming away blacker than ever. Nothing concealed up there. But when she pulled out the metal ash pan beneath the grate, she came up trumps.

A videotape.

She ran to the bathroom to soap her hands before she touched it, careful to do several scrubbings before drying her hands on Susan's immaculate embroidered towels. Back in Philip's room, she prised the tape from the ash pan. The tape was encased in a cardboard sleeve; the label along the spine of the tape had 'World Cup Final 1981' written in an atrocious hand.

"Susan," Eden called. Susan bustled back into the room. Her eyes were red, and Eden suspected she'd been weeping in her room from the shock of the burglary. "Didn't you tell me you didn't have a video recorder when Philip was alive?"

"No, not back then. Not many people had videos."

"And Philip wasn't in to football, was he? So what do you make of this?" Eden handed over the videotape. "Ever seen it before?"

Susan turned the tape over and over in her hands as if it would suddenly start speaking and reveal hidden intelligence. "I've never seen this before." She looked at it again. "That's Philip's writing, though. Terrible it was, because he was left handed." She gave it back to Eden. "A football tape, it's not important, is it?"

"Actually, I think it might be," Eden said, wondering who else suspected the tape was hidden there, and how they knew.

CHAPTER TWENTY-NINE

"Who did you tip off?" Eden demanded, the moment the call connected.

"Who is this?" The friendly Geordie tones didn't fool her for a second.

"Eden Grey. Tell me, Bernard, who did you tell about my investigation?"

"You know who I told." His voice sharpened. "And I don't appreciate your accusations."

"Cut it out. You found out that your old mates the cops were bent as a nine bob note and you didn't like it all coming out into the open." She wasn't going to play his silly-bastard games. "So I'm asking you again, who did you tip off?"

"What's happened?"

"My client has been burgled."

"Burglary's not uncommon."

"The thief was evidently watching the house and was in there the moment it was empty."

"That's what burglars do, unfortunately."

"And the thief went straight to one particular room in the house, ignoring electrical equipment, jewellery and silver."

"Which room?"

"A room that evidently once belonged to a young boy." Eden rubbed her fingers against her temples, her head throbbing. "So, tell me, Bernard, which one of your bent cops arranged this?"

She heard him clicking his pen over and over again. When he spoke he was evidently trying to control his temper. "Now listen here, Eden. I didn't tip anyone off. But I started asking questions and it's spooked someone."

"Who? And why?"

"I don't like this any more than you," Bernard said, his voice growling with anger. "But give me the benefit of the doubt and a couple of days and I'll turn over some stones and see what crawls out."

Eden's office was in a block behind the High Street. She was on the upper level; directly underneath was an electronics repair shop. The shop was long closed for the day, but Eden detected a light glowing from the workroom at the back, and banged on the door until Kaz unchained the door with a sniff and a curt, "Keep your hair on."

Kaz was wearing red dungarees and her hair, which hung in dreadlocks that she proudly asserted hadn't been washed for over ten years, was tied up in a bronze and turquoise scarf.

"Do you have an old video recorder connected to a TV?" Eden asked.

"Watching reruns of the 'Good Life'?"

"It's for a case I'm working."

"Huh." Kaz masticated gum and studied Eden through kohl-laden eyes. "Tell you what, as we're closed and I'm bored, I'll help you out, on condition you pop to the offy and get us some of them fruit ciders."

"Done." There was a pub only yards away and in minutes she was back with her bribe.

Kaz was poking around in the workroom, shuffling about mixing decks and antiquated tellies to make space for a portable all in one unit of TV and video recorder.

"It is VHS, I take it?" she said. "Cause I've got a Betamax but it's behind a load of crap and'll be a bastard to dig out."

Eden checked the tape. "It's VHS." Turning it in her hands she noticed that the tab had been removed. "Kaz, doesn't this mean you can't tape over it?"

Kaz took it from her. "Yeah. Helpful if you have a dad like mine, kept recording David Attenborough over *Top of the Pops*. Bastard, rest his soul." She glanced at the label on the spine and let out a snort. "What's on this, then? Not the World Cup, that's for sure. Let's see." Kaz used the edge of the table to crack the top off one of the cider bottles and took a slug. Eden helped herself to another, and watched as the tiny TV warmed up. Kaz inserted the tape and pressed play. After a blizzard of lines and static, the video started. Shapes emerged from the gloom; masked figures loomed; a white face glowed spookily; a boy was led out.

"What's this bollocks?" Kaz asked. "Am Dram?"

"No, I've got a horrible feeling it's for real," Eden said. She jabbed the pause button and the figures on the screen jerked a St Vitus' dance. "I think it's going to be nasty."

"I've seen horror movies before," Kaz said. "All the Nightmares, Chainsaw, I know what you done in the summer, all that."

Eden ejected the tape. "If this is what I think, it's going to make that stuff look like Postman Pat. Can I borrow the TV? Just overnight. I'll bring it back first thing tomorrow. Promise."

Kaz drained her cider. "You'd better."

They switched off the TV unit and Eden lugged it out to her car, wedging it carefully behind the passenger seat so it wouldn't slip around. At her flat, she eased it out and lumped it upstairs, grateful for the lift, but it was with trepidation that she plugged in the TV unit and restarted the video.

For the first few minutes, the film was almost comical. Men in robes and masks, flouncing about and chanting. But then a boy was led out, pale and trembling, swaddled in a cloak that juddered with each heartbeat. He was laid out on a table tricked out with candles and cloths to resemble an altar, and trussed. It could have been a hokey student pastiche of an old horror film, if it wasn't for what happened next.

Another boy stepped forwards and killed the boy on the table.

Though the film was shot at night, and was amateurish in quality, she could easily make out the faces of the two boys involved. They were Adam Jones and Philip Wakefield.

PART SIX: 1981

CHAPTER THIRTY

Adam's relieved when the school holidays dawn, bringing with them not only six weeks of freedom but the chance to catch up on some sleep. Two nights a week up at the Devil's Chimney are leaving their mark. Even his mum comments on the dark circles under his eyes.

"You need some fresh air," she pronounces one morning as he yawns his way through breakfast. "You're looking peaky."

Maybe if they let him lie in in the mornings, instead of Dennis bouncing into the room at seven and yelling that they were missing the best part of the day. That morning he'd actually dragged the bedclothes off Adam and thrown water over him to make him get up. The man was a Nazi.

"Why don't you go and see Philip?"

"Could do."

"Or Lance." She pauses. "They haven't been over here for ages. Why don't you invite them over?"

So she can put out bowls of Twiglets and jelly? Not likely. "I'm going to see Tommo later."

She frowns. "You're seeing a lot of him lately."

"He's my friend. I can see my friends, can't I?"

"Don't you take that tone with your mother!" Dennis snaps. "Far too much lip from you these days."

"Oh drop dead!" Adam mutters under his breath. Bloody Dennis bossing him around like he's his real dad. Sometimes he closes his eyes and wishes and wishes with all his might that Dennis and Gregory are in a car accident, mangled to pieces, and things can get back to how they were when it was just him and Mum. If he wishes hard enough, he can bring it about for sure.

"Have you had a falling out?" His mum isn't going to let it drop.

"Philip's friends with Fat Simon now." And Lance? He wasn't sure about Lance; he'd been giving him some funny looks for a while, and every time he asked if he wanted to play football suddenly Lance was busy. His latest excuse was he had to go and see his grandma.

"You can be friends with Simon, too, can't you?"

She has no idea. He glares at her until she gets the message then gets down from the table.

"Oi!" Dennis bellows. "You ask before you leave the table."

"Please can I leave the table?" Adam shouts from the hallway, then sprints up to his bedroom. Below, Dennis's voice rumbles on, complaining about him. Hoping to get rid of him so they can be a cosy nest of Taylors without a nasty Jones messing up their happy family.

He's next at the Devil's Chimney in three days' time, and already he's anticipating the rub of notes in his palm. He has over a hundred pounds stashed away already, the roll growing fatter and fatter each week. He's spent some of it on weed, a little pinch of it for him to smoke in secret. And he's got Ray to buy him a bottle of vodka. A slug from the bottle every now and then helps him along. He sneaks upstairs for a swig whenever he needs cheering up. Magic potion.

But before then, he has a mission to accomplish. Last time, at the Devil's Chimney, Ray had pulled him aside and had a word.

"Wondered if you could do me a favour, Adam," he said, his breath pungent with cigarettes, close to Adam's face. "We need a few more people to help us make the films." Ray twitched his head at the robed, masked men. "Keep it interesting. Keep people buying new material. Get what I'm saying?"

Adam knew exactly what he was saying. More money for the actors. For him.

"This lot," another twitch of the head towards the masked men, "think I'm not doing enough to get people interested, but I can't just walk up to strangers in the street and ask them if they want to be in a film, can I?"

"Why not? Everyone wants to be famous."

"But they might not understand what we're doing up here," Ray said, his eyes narrowing. "If you told your Mum what you were doing, would she be OK with it?"

"Nah, she'd go mental."

"Exactly. So we need the right people. People who understand." Ray fixed him with a look. "You're a bright lad, Adam. You must know people."

Adam started to shake his head. This was his thing, him and Tommo. He didn't want other people muscling in, being part of the gang, sharing the money.

Ray sniffed and wiped his hand over his mouth. "There'd be a finder's fee for you, of course."

"What's a finder's fee?"

"Twenty-five pounds. For you, for every person you get to help us make a film."

Adam's mouth dropped open. Twenty-five pounds!

"And each time they make a film, I'll give you a bit of the wacky backy. How's that sound?"

It sounded ace, but who would he ask about being in the films?

"Any of your friends you could ask?" Ray was saying. "Got to be people you trust, cause this is secret. Any friends who might like a few quid?"

So now he's on a mission. He daren't let Ray down, not after everything he's done for him. And besides, if he gets twenty-five pounds for each person he brings along, that roll of cash will be so fat he'll have to spread it to the other shoe in the cupboard. And he'll buy himself the best remote controlled car he can, and won't let Gregory near it. Serve him right, little bastard.

First stop is Lance. Lance is always up for a laugh. He finds him in the arcade playing the penny slots and saunters over.

"All right, Lance?"

Lance's eyes narrow. "What do you want?"

"That's no way to greet a friend."

"You're my friend, are you?" Lance says. He slides a stick of Juicy Fruit out of the packet and folds it into his mouth. "How is Tommo?"

"We've been doing a project," Adam says, "and I wondered if you'd like to be in on it?"

"I'm not a bum boy."

"What?"

"I've heard what you're up to, Adam." Lance snaps his chewing gum. "No one's bumming me, not even for a million pounds."

Adam flashes cold. "What you talking about?"

"You and Tommo being rent boys. Being paid for dirty things up Leckhampton Hill."

"What do you know about it?"

Lance rolls his eyes and makes the 'how thick are you' face. "*Everyone* knows what you're up to, Adam." He scoops his winnings out of the cup. "See you, rent boy."

Adam watches him walk away, his mind whirring. He thinks of the films, of the men who sidle up to him after he's been on the table, the things they ask to do with him and to him, how much they pay him for it. Who told on him? Fear trickles through his veins. What if his mum finds out?

And what is he going to do about finding someone else to join in the films? If Lance thinks he's a rent boy, then other people probably think that, too. Who does he know who won't have heard or understood the rumours?

Philip is at home, painted pieces of a battleship spread over a sheet of newspaper on the kitchen table.

"Why don't you paint it when you've made it?" Adam asks, slipping into a seat opposite Philip.

"It doesn't look as good." Philip dips his brush into the small pot of grey enamel. "It's tidier this way."

Like anyone cares how tidy it looks. The fun bit is snapping all the pieces off the plastic grids and gluing it together. Painting's just the fiddly bit at the end. His pilots all have orange splodgy faces; Philip's look as though he's painted them pore at a time with a single hair.

Adam rests his forearms on the table. "Want to know a secret?" Philip frowns and glances up from the battleship. Adam lowers his voice. Philip's mum is in the front room, watching the racing on TV, but she keeps popping through to check whether they need orange squash or biscuits, and to prod at a banana cake in the oven. Making sure they're not telling dirty stories. "I've been in a film."

Philip scoffs. "Right."

"I have!" Adam scuffs his chair round closer to Philip. "And you could be in one, too."

Philip's eyes narrow. "What film?"

"A sort of horror film. You know like the ones we saw at Ray's?"

"Who would want us in a film? We're only kids."

"Extras!" Adam snatches the paintbrush out of Philip's hand. "All the films have them. People in the background, walking down the street, pretending to be soldiers, that kind of thing."

"What do you have to do?"

Adam shrugs. "Put on a funny cloak and lie on a table and keep still."

"Doesn't sound that interesting."

"The money is." The word hangs in the air.

"What money?"

"Oh, didn't I say?" Adam says, airily. "I get paid each time. Ten pounds."

"Ten pounds for lying on a table!" Philip's voice rises to a squeak and Adam shushes him. Last thing he needs is Philip's mum bustling in, just when he knows Philip is about to agree, and that remote controlled car is a big step closer to being his.

"Exactly! They've got money, these film makers." Adam studies Philip out of the side of his eyes. "What do you think?"

"I'll have to ask."

"No! It's all secret."

"Why?"

Adam sighs and shakes his head Ray like does when someone's being dense. "So no one makes the same film first, stupid! It's commercial practice." Another of Ray's sayings; he prays he's got it right. Philip's clever and likely knows about such things and will call him on it if he's got it wrong.

Philip tugs his lip. "I suppose that makes sense. What do I have to do?"

"First, keep quiet about it. No blabbing to your mummy or Fat Simon."

Philip bristles. "I wouldn't tell Simon."

"Good, because he's not part of our gang and never will be." Keeping his voice low, he tells Philip when and where to meet him.

CHAPTER THIRTY-ONE

It's a vicious night, cold, with scudding clouds and skirls of rain. Philip is in his school anorak with a fur lined hood, waiting at the corner of Bath Road, peeking anxiously up and down the street for Adam. The shops are all closed, but with that blank, watchful air as if the mannequins are peering out of the windows and taking note.

"You get away all right?" Ray asks when they bundle into his car.

"I think so," Philip says. His face is white and Adam thinks he's going to be sick. "Where are we going? Why do we have to meet at night?"

"It's a horror film, isn't it?" Ray says. "They're always filmed at night. Makes them scarier."

Philip snaps the seat belt round him, stares out of the window and chews his lips. Adam nudges his elbow. "Easiest tenner you'll ever make," he says.

He runs his tongue over his teeth. His braces are consigned to their plastic case and his mouth feels strangely empty, as though there's a lot more space in there. He likes it, calculating the earliest date he can be without the braces forever. At least ten months. His heart sinks.

Ray jolts along the farm track and pulls up where the wall is all tumbled down. They climb out of the car into a slicing wind that snatches the car door from his hand. Philip chatters away, his voice loud and carrying on the night air. Adam prods him in the ribs, whispering "Shh!" just as Ray turns and hisses, "Shut your cake hole!"

Philip looks offended and buttons it, and they walk in silence to the clearing where Ray hands them their costumes.

"I don't want to take my clothes off," Philip says. "It's pouring."

"Have a swig of this, Philip, it'll keep the rain out." Ray hands him a bottle. Philip studies it suspiciously.

"No thanks."

"Have a puff of this, then." Ray blows out a trail of smoke, the sweet scent hanging in the wet air.

"I don't smoke. I don't want to do this. Take me home."

"Don't be daft, Philip. There's nothing to it. And how long would it take you to earn ten quid on your paper round, eh?" Adam says, seeing his twenty-five pounds keeper's fee slipping away.

"I don't know." He's starting to sound like Gregory. Adam grinds his teeth and shoves the bottle into his hands. "Drink this and cheer up."

Philip takes a tentative sip and tries to hand the bottle back. Adam pushes it into his chest. "More," he orders, and Philip takes another few swigs until a bit goes down the wrong way and he chokes.

"Now this," Adam says, putting the spliff to Philip's lips. "Take it slow. It's nice."

He presses harder until Philip's lips open to receive the spliff. He puffs on it, his face screwed up, then he inhales again. A few moments later, his face relaxes and a lazy smile spreads his lips.

"Ready to be famous, then?" he asks, and Philip undresses, folding his clothes into a neat pile with his coat on top to protect them from the rain, and dons the long white cloak.

Ray materialises out of the gloom, carrying a bundle of dark material. "Change of plan for tonight. We're going to mix things up."

"What's up?"

"Nothing's up, just want a bit of variety. Variety's the spice of life, eh, lads?"

Philip stares at his bare feet. He could hare off at any moment. Goodbye remote controlled car.

"Sounds great, Ray. What's the plan?" Adam says, with bright enthusiasm that doesn't even fool himself.

"You get this on, Adam," Ray says, handing him a bundle of cloth. "Philip'll be on the table, and you'll be the … er … high priest, if you get my drift."

Adam's eyes meet Ray's. "You mean you want me to do the thing … with the…"

"That's right. You get changed and I'll fetch your props. Back in a tick."

Adam scurries out of his clothes and into the long, black robe, his mind whirring. What was it that the high priest did when he was on the table? His memory's hazy, recalling the initial fear and struggling for breath, the blackness, and then the rush when the night air sucked into his lungs again.

Ray returns and plants a meaty hand on Philip's shoulder. "Time for you to star, champ," he says, leading him away, Adam trailing behind, waiting for his cue.

He lurks in the trees to the side and watches Philip climb onto the table. He slips and Ray hoists him up, orders him to lie still. Philip struggles and cries when Ray fastens the ropes round his wrists and ankles. He can't hear what Ray says to Philip, but Philip shuts up and seems to curl into himself. When Ray comes back to Adam, he has the devil's mask in his hands and slips it over his head. Everything's muffled in there and he can barely see through the eye holes: he has to twist his whole body to take in the scene before him, the men in their gowns and masks, and Philip, shuddering, lying on the table.

The car headlights blaze and he marches forwards, head erect, as the chanting increases. Philip screams when the devil's mask appears, then falls silent and closes his eyes. Adam reaches out his hand in a peremptory gesture, and the plastic bag is placed in it. Slowly he slides it over Philip's head. Philip flinches at the touch of the plastic bag, thrashing about as it travels further over his face, encasing him. Adam twists the neck of the bag tightly shut. Through the slits in the mask he sees Philip's eyes wide open under the plastic, his nose squashed to one side. The bag sucks in and out, welding itself tighter to Philip's skin with each breath. He twists the bag harder and the chanting increases. Now for the next bit. He hesitates, takes a deep breath, then forces his hand down on Philip's mouth.

Philip bucks against the ropes, surprisingly strong, and Adam fights to keep the bag in place and his hand over Philip's nose and mouth. Beneath him, Philip is an eel, an unbroken horse, a furious tiger. He kicks and twists, and Adam presses down with all his weight onto Philip's mouth. His arms ache with the effort, it's taking forever, but eventually Philip's limbs go floppy and he's motionless on the table. Adam steps back, breathing hard, the smell of the rubber mask making him gag.

The chanting rises to screaming pitch. *Sacrifice him. Sacrifice him.* It sends a chill down his spine. It's only acting, he reminds himself. The chant changes. *Raise the Devil. Raise the Devil.*

Out of the corner of his eye, he catches Ray making frantic slashing movements with his hands. Adam shakes his head, not understanding, then Ray points to Philip, jabbing furiously.

Adam glances down. Philip is still limp on the table. With horror he understands Ray's signals and tears the plastic bag away from Philip's face. Philip doesn't move. Adam pinches him and whispers, "You can get up now, it's all over."

Nothing.

He hauls off the devil's mask to see Philip's face properly. It's flooded with blood, the lips blue and bruised and a dark trickle down his mouth where his teeth have nipped. Adam's blood turns to ice. The chanting stutters to a halt.

"Shit!" mutters one of the men. "He struggled too much. Little sod."

Another man elbows Adam aside, presses his fingers to Philip's neck and shakes his head.

"Do something!" Adam cries. The man tears off his mask and starts thumping Philip's chest and blowing into his mouth. Another comes to help him. Adam retreats to the trees, his eyes fixed on Philip's body, his mind numb. It isn't acting. Philip's dead. He's really dead.

It seems like hours that they punch his chest and breathe into his mouth, until at last Philip groans and is sick over himself. The men haul him up and stand clear as he spews over and over again.

Philip whimpers and wipes his hand across his mouth. He stares at the men with huge, terrified eyes, then jumps from the table and stumbles over to Adam.

"I want to go home," he says, his voice scratchy. "Take me home now."

"Get your clothes on," Adam says, sick with fear and relief. "We'll go."

He scrambles into his clothes, his fingers fumbling and his heart banging. Beside him, Philip flings on his clothes, sobbing loudly. As soon as he's dressed, Philip runs. Adam has barely got his toes into his shoes before he's after him, slipping on the muddy footpath. He catches up with Philip and grabs his hand. Philip screams.

"It's only me. You're all right."

Philip turns away, coughing horribly. "They tried to kill me."

"It was an accident."

"They tried to kill me." Philip hurtles off again down the track.

"Wait!" Adam sprints after him. "Ray will take us home."

"I'd rather walk." Adam watches him go, hears his sobs echoing away down the hill, and his skin crawls with fear. Philip could have died, and he would have murdered him.

He trudges back to the clearing where Ray is waiting for him.

"Where is he?"

"Gone home. Says he'd rather walk."

"Walking is one thing, talking is another," Ray says. "You better make sure he doesn't tell anyone." Silence swells between them, and Adam understands the threat. In case he hasn't got it, Ray continues, "Because you were the one who hurt him, Adam. You'd be the one the police came after, and you'd be the one with a lot of explaining to do."

"I'll make sure he doesn't tell," Adam says.

PART SEVEN: 2016

CHAPTER THIRTY-TWO

Kate thumped the cushion and scrunched it up under her head. The house was full of people. Her dad was in the spare bedroom repairing a broken wardrobe door. Her mother was in the kitchen with Patty, the police liaison woman, still wearing the same black skirt and grey jumper she'd been in all week. She'd been hanging around like a ghoul ever since it happened, sneaking out into the hall to take muttered calls on her mobile, and stretching her face into a patient mask every time she looked at Kate. Gareth was slumped on the settee, staring at the TV screen. A daytime show was playing, a basic general knowledge quiz made overcomplicated by the need to collect tokens, double your money at random points and with a joker card that could be played to outwit the competition. Outside, journalists filmed the tide of flowers and teddies that swept up the front wall, and questioned the mawkish neighbours who Kate had never met, but who stopped to leave cellophane wrapped flowers and tell the TV cameras how shocked they were.

They were all slowly driving her mad.

A smell of frying onions wafted down the hallway. Mum cooking another stew. In the past few days she'd stirred pot after pot, putting down plates of food in front of people who quite simply didn't want to eat. The freezer was stuffed. The fridge bulged with unwanted leftovers. And now she was cooking again.

Kate eased herself up on her elbow. Gareth's eyes never left the TV screen. The sound of hammering drifted down from upstairs. She unfolded herself from the settee and slowly climbed the stairs and slipped into the bathroom, sliding the lock stealthily so none of them downstairs could register it. The first time she'd shot the bolt since Jessica died, there had been a stampede on the stairs and people shouting through the door to please to come out now and what was she up to in there. But how could she shower and use the toilet with the door unbolted and the house teeming with strangers? So she perfected art of the silent slide.

The shower was gloriously cool on her skin. She wept under the water, letting the sound of the spray cover her weeping, relishing the water drumming on her scalp. When she stepped out, she felt purged. Her face was a mess: the skin peeling round her nose and her cheeks scrubbed raw with salt tears. Foundation stung too much, but she dusted on a little powder to cover the worst bits and carefully painted her eyelids. No point brushing on mascara, she'd be crying again soon, but the eyeshadow saved her face from the mad woman ravages she'd been cultivating for days.

She put on clean underwear and selected trousers and a blouse from her wardrobe. Dressed, with her hair dried, and with powder on her cheeks, she could pass as normal. She tilted the mirror so she could only see a small portion of herself at a time, afraid of glimpsing Jessica hovering behind her, waxy and white. Square at a time, she looked herself over. She'd do. Time to get out of this asylum.

She marched downstairs and grabbed her coat from the hook. She couldn't face the phalanx of reporters out the front, so she went to the back door.

"Going for a walk? I'll come with you," Mum said, switching off the gas under the latest casserole.

"No, stay here."

"I'll come, then," Patty said, brightening. No doubt she wanted a break from hearing about Mum's varicose veins.

"No," Kate said, as firmly as she could without spilling over into hysterical. "I want some time on my own."

Mum put down the wooden spatula. "Where are you going?"

"Just for a walk."

"You really shouldn't go on your own, you know," Patty said.

"Why?"

"It's just not a good idea right now."

"I'm fine," Kate said. "I just want a walk. On my own. I won't be long."

"At least tell us where you're going."

"Just round the park and back." Kate opened the back door and stepped out before they could question her further. She walked purposely down the path, knowing they were watching her, and went through the gate. It opened onto a path that led along the backs of the houses and came out at the end of the street, far enough away from her home for her not to be spotted by the journalists and gawpers. She turned left and hurried away.

No one noticed her when she entered the park. For days she'd wondered if there was a gigantic sign hovering above her head: *grieving mother. The one whose daughter was killed in that tear gas attack.* But no heads turned towards her. It was a chill day and Hatherley Park was quiet. A toddler and his mother were by the pond, chucking bread at a bunch of decidedly disinterested ducks, and a woman in running gear pounded the path on a circuit of the park. None of them gave her a second glance. Kate went round the far side of the pond and over to the little, scummy pond, and peered in. It was clogged with weeds, crisp packets and the little straws from cartons of fruit juice. Jessica had loved this pond.

She made a circuit of the park, then set out to do another. She didn't want to go home, to the quiet chaos and restrained grief. Here she was no one; here no one was pressing food and tea and questions on her. She tipped back her head and looked at the sky. It was white as bone. There was a man on one of the benches, looking out over the grass. As she drew level, he said, "Hello again."

Kate stopped and looked at him properly. It was John, the man who'd come to see her a few days ago.

"How are you?" he said, using a normal tone, not the ultra-careful, saccharine-worried tone everyone else was adopting when they spoke to her these days.

Without thinking, she took a seat next to him on the bench, her hands still in her jacket pockets. "I'm ... here," she said.

He smiled at her. "You're looking better. Brave face on it."

"It's a disguise so they'll leave me alone for a minute," she said.

"Clever," he said. "We all need space to be ourselves."

"What are you doing here?"

"I wanted some peace."

"Sorry, I'll go."

"No, stay," he said. "I meant some peace from clients and the phone ringing. You know what it's like."

"I used to," Kate said. "I used to have a very busy job."

"You miss it." It wasn't a question. She nodded. Sometimes she missed it very much, making decisions, feeling you were doing something that mattered. Not that being a mum wasn't important, just that no one else seemed to value it very much. Didn't see that it was work, too. Except now she wasn't even a mum.

"And what are you up to?"

"Just needed some time to myself. They're all driving me mad."

"So you're bunking off?" John said and she giggled despite herself, he made it sound so adventurous and a little bit naughty.

"I gave them the slip," she said.

"Good for you. You're a strong woman, you don't need other people telling you what to do." He looked at her out of the corners of his eyes and lowered his voice to ask, "Fancy an ice-cream? I won't tell if you don't."

"I haven't brought my purse."

"My treat."

They stood and walked together to the park's exit. An ice-cream van loitered there hopefully, the man at the counter brightening as they approached. John paid for their ice-creams and they took them back into the park to eat them.

"Jessica loved ice-cream," Kate said. A wave of grief was building, she could feel its power. John silently took her ice-cream as the wave crashed over her. She covered her face with her hands and howled. When the grief ebbed, and she'd scrubbed her face, he silently handed the ice-cream back. "Thanks," she said. "Sorry about that."

"Never apologise for loving your daughter," he said. "It hurts because you loved her so much and she's been taken away."

"When I wake up, I feel normal, except there's a little nagging voice saying I should be worrying about something," Kate said, "and then I remember, and it's like losing her all over again." John gave her a gentle smile: he was listening, at last someone was listening to her. "When I cry at home, they just want me to stop. They say, 'That's it, have a good cry', and then try to distract me."

"People find grief frightening," John said. "It's a powerful emotion, like love, or hate, or anger. People are afraid of that power. They're not strong like you."

"Sometimes I'm afraid of it," Kate said. "Afraid I might do something terrible."

"Like what?"

"Revenge," she said, simply. "I've been thinking about the woman, the one in the message."

"Eden Grey?"

"Yes. She went to see my cousin."

He stilled. "Why was that?"

"He said she was asking questions about my dad. And I'm worried."

"Tell me what's worrying you."

"When I was a baby, my dad was accused of a terrible crime, but the police couldn't prove it and we thought it had all gone away. Then when I was ten, it all started up again. They said he'd done awful things, put him in prison, and there was a trial."

"It sounds terrible," he said.

"He lost his job, because he was in prison, and we had to move house because everyone was saying he'd done this terrible thing. Killed a boy. And then it came to trial and he was found innocent, but it still didn't go away. Every one said the trial didn't prove anything. Just because they couldn't prove he did it didn't mean he didn't do it. But he didn't kill him! He swore he didn't!"

"That sounds very frightening."

"It was, and now it's starting again. She — this Eden woman — is digging around, stirring it all up. My dad!" She broke down and sobbed.

"It's not fair, Kate," he said. "You've lost Jessica and now she's trying to take your father away."

"There's nothing I can do to stop her."

"I wouldn't say that. I can help you stop this Eden Grey from hurting your family."

"How?"

"Let me come up with a plan."

CHAPTER THIRTY-THREE

Who invented spreadsheets, Eden wondered, cursing both the inventor and the bright spark who'd recommended she keep her accounts on one. She'd spent two hours checking off her bank records against her accounts, and still the bloody thing wouldn't balance. When her mobile rang she answered with a prayer of thanks for the interruption. Any more of these numbers and she'd induce a migraine.

"Eden? It's Mulligan. Free to talk?" Bernard never quite shook off his intelligence background.

"Free to speak, Bernard," she said. "Go ahead. What have you got for me?"

"I'm a bit stymied, actually." His Geordie burr rasped with frustration. "I've been hunting down a tame scrote who doesn't exist."

Interesting phrasing, she thought. "Which tame scrote?"

"Yours. Or the one you think did over your client's house."

"Susan Wakefield's?"

"That's the jobby."

"It looked like an inside job to me. Our would-be burglar went straight to the spare room, which had nothing in it but the dead boy's name on the door," Eden said. "Turned out there was key evidence hidden there."

"Nothing worse than a bent copper," Bernard said, "and I'd be the first to bang him up and lose the key, but I can't find a connection."

"There's police corruption all over this case," she argued. "Someone nobbled the coroner. You told me yourself that the case files went missing."

"Not went missing. Were destroyed by floods."

"My arse," she said. "You're seriously telling me this burglary isn't connected?"

"I've got no proof," Bernard said. "I've run checks on all the officers who were involved in the Philip Wakefield and Adam Jones cases and none of them have come up dodgy apart from Derek Godwinson, late of this parish."

"They could be under the radar," Eden said. "Who had scrote informants who could be persuaded to do a job on the QT?"

"As far as I can make out, all the informants are properly handled and accounted for," Bernard said. "That doesn't mean there isn't the odd unofficial scrote on the payroll, so I did a bit of old boy schmoosing to see what the dirt was around the stations."

"And?"

"Bugger all."

"So the burglary is just a burglary?"

"Looks like it."

She bit her lip. "Bernard, I'm sorry for the way I spoke to you yesterday. I thought —"

"I know what you thought," he said. "They caught your nemesis yet?"

"No."

"Don't forget, Eden. Fear fatigue is dangerous territory."

"Thanks, Bernard." She ended the call and bounced the phone against her palm. This burglary didn't feel right. She'd stake money on the thief going in for one purpose only: to steal the film that showed what was going on up at the Devil's Chimney. Now Adam Jones's body had been found, and there was a fresh enquiry into his death, finding and destroying that film must be a priority for them. But who paid the thief to do the job?

Two cups of coffee, one slice of Bakewell tart, and ten minutes' meditation and she was no closer to an answer. Her dining table was spread with papers: her timeline of the case, her interview notes, the printouts of the newspaper reports of Ray's trial, the coroner's report on Philip's death, and photographs of everyone involved.

Eden leaned over the table, shuffling pieces of paper around, trying to make them fit into a pattern. There was something missing here. She was looking at it all and not seeing what was in front of her.

The doorbell buzzing made her jump. She went to the intercom, her heart banging, instantly wary. "Hello?"

"Sanctuary! Give me sanctuary!" It was Judy. Eden kicked herself: she'd forgotten she'd invited Judy round for a girls' evening. She pressed the door release to let Judy in, and stood in the open door of her flat while Judy toiled up the stairs.

"Nearly here!" Judy puffed, as she reached the top. "Blimey, I'm unfit." She spotted Eden and smiled, her whole body seeming to relax into the smile. She wrapped Eden in a big hug, and kissed her cheek with a smacking sound, the sort of kiss she bestowed on her children. "Hey gorgeous! Ready to party!"

"Always," Eden said. "Come on in."

Judy stepped into her flat and went through to the kitchen, plonking a supermarket carrier bag on the worktop. She sniffed ostentatiously. "Can't tell what you're making for dinner," she said, pointedly. "Salad?"

"Ah," Eden said. "I'm really sorry, Judy…"

"I knew it!" Judy danced around the kitchen, her arms in the air, chanting, "I win! I win!"

When she came to a standstill, Eden gave her a 'what the hell?' gesture.

"Marcus owes me a fiver," Judy crowed. "I told him that you'd be so caught up in your case that you'd forget I was coming over and there'd be no dinner ready. He said you wouldn't so we put money on it, and I won!"

"Obviously I'm thrilled that the fact you're going to starve is a source of such joy and jubilation for you," Eden said.

"I'm not going to starve," Judy said. "And neither, my little private eye matey, are you. It's not just booze in the bag."

Eden peeked into the bags Judy had dumped in the kitchen and squealed. "Marks and Spencer's? Wow, Judy, you get a pay rise?"

"I don't normally get to eat naughty instant food, so I thought we may as well go top of the range."

Eden was pulling out cartons of ready meals. Lamb shanks with honey roast vegetables; chilli and wild rice; buttery mashed potatoes; beef wellington; duck a l'orange; medleys of prepared vegetables. "We'll never get through all this, Judy."

"Thought I'd top up your freezer for you," Judy said. "I don't want you starving. I know you forget to eat when you're working. Besides, I don't think it's fair your bum is smaller than mine — I'm trying to even things up."

Eden hugged her, hiding her face so Judy wouldn't see the tears in her eyes. "Thank you. You're the best, Judy."

"True. Right, how do you switch on your oven?" Judy bustled about, taking control, setting the oven to heat up and foraging in Eden's cupboards for plates and glasses. Eden popped the wine in the fridge to chill and carved the cheesecake into generous slices, leaving it out to thaw to room temperature.

"I'm afraid we'll have to be slobs tonight," she said. "Do you mind?"

Judy tipped back her head and bellowed a laugh. "Have you seen my house? This is an oasis of calm and tranquillity compared to the bomb site I lovingly call home."

"You won't think that when you see my table."

Judy stood with her hands on her hips and surveyed the mounds of paper, notes and sticky fixers. "Homework project? When do you make it all into a papier-mâché volcano?"

"I wish," Eden said. "This is as far as I've got on my case."

"This is the one you told me about?" Judy said, peering at pieces of paper, keeping her hands firmly to herself.

Eden could tell she was itching to pick things up. "You can look at it, but please don't rearrange things. Aidan does that — it drives me nuts."

"What's this?" Judy twisted round the video tape to read the label. "Dreadful writing. Left handed? The left handers in my class always have atrocious writing."

"Yes," Eden said. "YES!" She dived at the table and snatched up the coroner's report on Philip's death. Stapled to it was the pathologist's report. "Thanks, Judy."

"You're welcome. What did I do, exactly?"

"Look at this." Eden thrust the papers at her. "Philip had cuts across his left wrist, most of them shallow and then a deeper one. The experts concluded that he tried to slit his wrist, found it too difficult, and so hanged himself instead. But the cuts are on the wrong wrist! Philip was left handed, that means he would have cut his right wrist."

"So?"

220

"He didn't make those cuts, someone else did." Eden cast her eye over the paper trail. "Fancy giving me a hand?"

"Thought you'd never ask."

They put the meals in the oven and set to work, going over each piece of evidence together, querying it, and marking where there was corroboration. Judy drew it all into a giant mind map, linking evidence and witnesses and placing question marks next to items that hadn't been confirmed.

"Here's something," Judy said, brandishing a piece of paper. "Philip couldn't tie his shoelaces. Who can tie a noose but not shoelaces?"

"His teacher mentioned the same thing," Eden said. "And someone else told me Philip couldn't tie knots."

Trouble was, people who are determined to do away with themselves can be very resourceful: the fact he couldn't tie his shoelaces in itself didn't challenge the suicide verdict. But now they knew that he hadn't tried to slit his wrists, all the evidence relating to the suicide was questionable: the bruises on his neck, the scratches on his throat, the fact the rope gave way and he was found on the ground.

Eden studied Judy's mind map for a long time, and at last a pattern took shape. "We've been looking at the wrong murder," she said.

CHAPTER THIRTY-FOUR

Aidan smoothed his hair back and pressed the buzzer for Eden's flat. He felt ridiculously nervous about seeing her. Things were tense between them, and he had that vertiginous sense that they were on the point of either settling down forever, or breaking up. When Eden's voice sounded, telling him to come up, his stomach fluttered and he was glad of the flight of stairs in which to calm himself.

She was smiling as she opened the door. A good sign, and she kissed him and hung up his coat properly instead of slinging it over the back of a chair. He followed her into the kitchen and watched her spooning coffee into a cafetière. She was making rocket fuel, just the way he liked it. Seemed they were both on their best behaviour.

"What did you get up to last night?" he asked.

"Judy came over with enough ready meals to feed an army."

"How was she?"

"In fine form," Eden said. "She helped me with my case." He felt her eyes on him and a moment's intuition warned him he wouldn't like what was coming next. "She's been so good to me, I wanted to tell her who I really am. My cover here is well and truly blown. It was supposed to give me a new life free from Hammond. Well, that hasn't happened." She barked a short, mirthless laugh and his heart dropped like a stone. "So why am I still here, living as Eden Grey, and away from my family and friends?"

"You've got friends here," he said, hopelessly. "People who care about you." *Like me, but you won't let me in.*

"I don't have to choose," Eden said, reaching across the kitchen counter to take his hand and rubbing her thumb over his knuckles. "I would love see my parents. Tell them I'm OK, explain what happened."

"Do you want to?"

"Of course I do! I can't bear to think about them grieving," Eden said.

"Then go!" Aidan said, snatching his hand back. "I'll drive you. Come on, what are you waiting for?"

"Don't you see, with Hammond out to get me, I can't show up and say, 'Ta da! I'm not dead', when there's a risk he might kill me. I can't die twice. It would destroy them."

Aidan pulled her close, kissing her temple. There was nothing he could say, nothing he could do. For a mad moment a line from a play tolled over and over in his mind. *It's a game that must be played to the finish.* It made him shudder.

They remained like this for a long time, each of them wrapped up in their own private miseries. Eventually he cleared his throat, desperate to change the atmosphere between them. "I brought you a present."

She lifted her head. There were tear tracks down her cheeks. He wiped them away with his thumb. "Pastries?"

"No, it's about your case. Well, not your case, mine, I suppose, but you said you thought the two were linked."

Eden brightened. It always amazed him how thinking about crime could perk her up from even the deepest depression. "Philip Wakefield and Adam Jones? What have you found?"

He pulled a sheaf of papers out of the inside pocket of his jacket. "It bothered me about that fake Iron Age grave," he said. "It was too good. Only someone who knew about Iron Age graves could have made it. And the fact that it was so close to the real Iron Age graves suggested that someone knew they were there, so me and the team did some detective work."

"And you found something?"

"There was an archaeological dig up there in the 1970s," Aidan said, spreading the papers he'd brought over Eden's dining table. She dragged out a chair and sat down, suddenly eager as a robin watching a gardener. He selected a sheet of paper and slid it across to her. "These were the people involved with that dig."

Eden cast her eye down the list. "Dean Jones? That's Adam Jones's father." She glanced up at him. "He was on the early dig up there?"

Aidan nodded. "And on the dig the following year when they found the graves but didn't have time to excavate them."

"We know that the Conservation office was told, so that they could protect them." Eden said. She drummed her fingers on the table. "So now we have two people close to Adam Jones who also knew about the Iron Age graves: his father, and his step-brother."

"The step-brother was the one who called us in to excavate, and who seems to have deliberately sited the new path so it went through the graves," Aidan said. He saw the light brighten in her eyes while she worked through the implications. He decided to add to them. "You know I mentioned there was a gawper up there the other day?"

"Someone up at the dig?"

"Well, he was Dean Jones."

"Really? How do you know?"

"Recognised him in this picture. He's aged well." Aidan placed the photo of the 1977 archaeological team in front of her and jabbed his finger at the picture of Dean Jones.

"I suppose he came back here when they told him Adam had been found," Eden said.

"I asked him if he knew the boy who'd been buried there," Aidan said, "and he said 'not really'."

"That's true enough," Eden said. "He left when Adam was five and was so out of touch he bought him a Mickey Mouse watch for his twelfth birthday."

Aidan's head snapped up. "I found a Mickey Mouse watch in the grave. Is it the same one?"

Suddenly Eden lunged across the table. "Someone mentioned it in an interview. Let me find it." She was flicking through a sheaf of papers, skimming them at speed. "Here it is. Greg mentioned it. Said it wasn't fair because he wanted a watch like that at the time, but Adam got one and threw it away."

Excitement sent fire through his veins. "What happened to it?"

"Don't know."

"So how did it get in that grave?" Aidan asked.

"Was it actually on Adam's wrist?"

"No, tucked under one of the stones."

"So it might have been buried with the body, or added later?" Eden said.

"Why would anyone put it there later?"

"If they were trying to implicate someone else," Eden said. "Maybe someone was trying to frame Dean Jones. He had no reason to kill Adam."

"But who?"

Eden flicked through the pages of interview notes. "Dennis, for a start. From what I was told, there was no love lost between him and Adam. New marriage, wife's son resenting him. That's a motive for murder."

Eden refused to be cooped up and hide inside, and insisted they go out and get some fresh air. Aidan bit his tongue, knowing that nothing he said would divert her. This must be what it feels like having a loved one on death row, he thought. The awful, inescapable inevitability of it. Trying to forge a normal life while the impossible was happening.

They drove out to Bourton-on-the-Water and had lunch in a pub next to the stream. He barely registered what he ate, starting every time someone walked past their table, jumping when the door banged, and seeing hidden assassins lurking in every inglenook. Eden seemed unfazed, working her way through a plate of scampi and chips, and then dithering so much between treacle pudding and lemon torte that she ended up having both.

When Eden had scraped her dish clean and he'd paid the bill, they walked hand-in-hand through the throngs of old people on bus trips and Japanese tourists with cameras. Kids in bright red wellies paddled up and down the stream, prodding at a plastic duck with a shrimping net. The mother had a loud, braying voice, calling, "Araminta! Cyrus! Mind you don't slip!" just before one of them, inevitably, slipped and howled.

"You don't like children, do you?" Eden said, breaking into his thoughts.

"Not much," he said, without thinking. Not that he knew many, but those he saw in supermarkets and restaurants were loud, sticky and badly behaved. He thought of the pristine coolness of his flat and tried to imagine it cluttered with baby paraphernalia, and winced. He realised Eden was staring at him and tried to redeem himself. "They're a bit messy," he said, lamely.

She turned her face away and was inordinately interested in the plants in someone's front garden.

"Do you want children?" he said, adding, "At some point. Not now."

"Not anymore," she said.

Then it wasn't hopeless. He didn't like children and she didn't want any. Maybe they could make it work. If he could get over the danger she put herself in.

"The police will find Hammond sooner or later," he said. She shoved her hands in her pockets and didn't reply. "And then let's go away somewhere."

"Go away?"

"On holiday. We've never been on holiday."

"Where?"

"Anywhere you like."

She thought for a moment. "Somewhere warm where I can get a tan. With ruins for you to look at."

"Greece? Or Malta?" he said. "I've not been to Malta before."

"Neither have I," she said. She slipped her hand into his and squeezed it. "Malta it is."

The mood shifted and they strolled to the end of the village and back again, he wittering on about prehistoric sites and rotund stone goddesses, she asking questions and humouring him, and for a moment he saw a glimmer of hope that it would all be all right, eventually.

CHAPTER THIRTY-FIVE

Aidan had been awake for over an hour, exhausted yet unable to settle back into sleep. His feet hung over the end of Eden's mattress and he was afraid to fidget in case he woke her. The bottles on the top of her chest of drawers were an uneven number and no matter how much he juggled them about in his imagination, he couldn't get them into any sort of pattern. There was cramp in his calf now. He stretched his leg and tried to ease it, but it bit hard, forcing him to jump out of bed and hop around.

Eden stirred and propped herself up on one elbow.

"Sorry," he whispered. "I didn't want to wake you."

"S'alright," she said, running her hand through her hair. "I've been awake for ages. Fancy an early morning stroll?"

He massaged his calf. "Where?"

"Leckhampton Hill. I've been thinking about the case, and I'd like to go up there and look at the site. I'll treat you to breakfast afterwards."

"Give me five minutes to have a shower and get rid of my cramp."

It was just light when the car nosed into the carpark on Leckhampton Hill. They toiled up the path and along the ridge to the Devil's Chimney. Cheltenham lay glinting in the valley below. Beyond, the hills brooded, shrouded with a press of cloud. It was nippy up there, the wind whisking Eden's hair into a nest, and stinging his eyes.

They rounded the corner. A shred of blue and white police tape circled a tree trunk. As they approached the dig, he saw a foot poking out of the hole that had contained Adam Jones's

228

remains. He and Eden exchanged shocked looks, then ran towards the grave. A man lay unmoving at the bottom, face down in the soil. A bouquet of flowers was crushed underneath him.

Eden pressed her fingers into his neck. "He's alive!" she said. "Help me turn him over."

Together they hauled on his shoulders and belt and turned him onto his side.

"Simon!" Eden cried. She patted his face, trying to wake him. "Simon! Wake up."

Aidan pulled out his phone and rang for an ambulance. While he gave instructions to the dispatcher, the man groaned and his eyes flickered open.

"Simon, are you OK?" Eden said. "God, you're freezing." She tore off her coat and tucked it round him.

"Eden? Where am I?"

"At the Devil's Chimney."

Simon struggled to sit up. Aidan spoke into the phone, "He's come round but he doesn't look good." Eden was checking Simon over, looking in his eyes, feeling his arms and collar bone, and mouthed to him, 'head injury'. "He's got a head injury. No, I don't know how it happened, we've just found him."

He tugged off his coat and handed it to Eden. She threaded Simon's arms into the sleeves and buttoned it up, pressing close to him to keep him warm. Simon was shuddering, though whether with cold, shock or concussion, he couldn't tell.

The ambulance arrived and paramedics set about strapping Simon into a chair and lumping him back down the hill.

"I'll go with him in the ambulance," Eden said. "Meet you at the hospital."

He watched the ambulance lights recede and got in his car and switched on the radio. It was tuned to a classical music station and Faure's *Requiem* filled the car. He leaned back in his seat and closed his eyes, letting the music soothe him. So much for a quiet weekend.

CHAPTER THIRTY-SIX

"He's asking for you," the nurse said.

Eden unfolded herself from the waiting room chair and followed the nurse into a side room. Simon was sitting propped up against the pillows, his face deathly white and with a bandage swaddling his head. His fingers trembled as they plucked at the blue blanket stretched tight across the bed.

"How are you?" she asked.

"I've been better." Simon's voice came out croaky. He coughed and tried again. "Concussion, apparently. Got to keep quiet for a while."

"You're in good hands," she said. He waved at her to sit. The visitor's chair was padded and much easier on the posterior than the chairs in the waiting room, she was relieved to find. "Can you remember what happened?"

Simon tried to nod, and winced, his hand going up to his temple. "I wanted to see where Adam had been buried," he said. "I took him some flowers. I know he's not there, but it seemed right, somehow."

Simon and his flowers, single-handedly keeping florists in business. "When did you go?"

"Early evening. The sun was setting and there was no one else around. I liked the quiet: I could think about Adam and Philip."

"And then what?"

"A man came up and asked if I knew Adam. I said we were at school together. He said, 'Which one were you?' and I laughed and said, 'They called me Fat Simon. I've changed a bit since then.' And this look went across his face and he walked off."

"What sort of look?" Eden asked.

Simon thought for a moment. "Like he had IBS and his bowels were, you know."

"Can you describe him?"

"Sixties, black waterproof jacket, supermarket trainers."

"Have you ever seen him before?"

Simon made a minute movement with his head to indicate no.

"And then what?"

"I stayed there for a while." Simon blushed. "I was talking to him. Adam. Daft, I know. I was talking about when we were kids, and how he teased me, and then I told him I did what I could. You know, going to the police. And that I was sorry I hadn't tried harder." Simon reached for a plastic cup of water and took a sip. "Then something hit me on the back of the head and I fell forwards. I tried to get up, and I blacked out."

"Who hit you?"

"No idea. I just felt the blow and that was that."

"Did you hear anything?"

"Nothing. Too windy."

"Did you see anything afterwards? Shoes? A jacket?" Another negative. "Simon, can you think of any reason why someone would want to attack you?"

He plucked at the blanket, rolling a ball of fluff between his thumb and finger. "Was this a hate crime?"

Before Eden could answer, the nurse bustled in and shooed her out. "Mr Bird needs to get some rest," she said, in the bossiest voice Eden had ever heard. "You can come back at visiting time."

Aidan was waiting outside, his long overcoat wrapped around him even though the hospital was stifling. His hands were rammed in his pockets, which she recognised as anxiety caused by having nothing to read.

"Come on," she said. "He's going to be OK."

"Did he slip and fall?" Aidan asked.

"No," she said, "someone attacked him. But who, I have yet to work out." Privately her money was on Ray Thompson. This case of Adam Jones and Philip Wakefield always led back to Ray Thompson eventually.

As they left the hospital, they bumped into Greg Taylor dashing in. He was white and frantic, his eyes darting and wet with tears.

"He's fine." Eden detained him with a hand on his chest. "Take it easy, he's going to be OK."

"I've been worrying all night," Greg said. "When he didn't come home, I thought, I imagined the worst."

"He's fine, honestly."

Greg suddenly went greenish and turned away. "I think I'm going to be —" he said, and was copiously sick. Aidan skipped back out of the way, keeping his leather brogues well out of splashing distance. Eden rubbed Greg's back while he puked over and over until his insides were emptied out.

"It's shock," she said. "You'll feel better now."

Greg groaned and retched again, but brought nothing up. He fumbled in his pocket for a handkerchief and scrubbed at his mouth. "Sorry," he said.

"Let's get you cleaned up," said Eden. "They won't let you see him in this state."

They went back into the hospital, Aidan following a few steps behind, evidently wary in case Greg vomited without warning. Eden bundled Greg into a disabled toilet and went in with him to sponge flecks of vomit from his jacket and help him mop his face.

"How did you know about me and Simon?" Greg asked.

"I saw a photo of you in his wallet," she said. "How did you meet?"

"A school reunion. We got talking and realised we'd got something in common."

"You've both lost someone you love," she said. "Adam and Philip."

He gave her a surprised look. "It was a bond. And Simon remembered Adam. I could talk about him and Simon understood. He knew what it was like to lose someone and feel helpless about it."

"When did you become an item?"

"About six months ago."

"And that's when he started taking flowers to Philip Wakefield's grave."

Greg crumpled the paper towel and tossed it in the waste can. "Meeting me, talking about those days, brought it all up again. Simon felt guilty he didn't do more, but I keep telling him there's nothing more he could have done."

"He told you about going to the police?"

"And about the video tape," Greg said. "If only we still had that, we'd know what happened to Adam."

Eden held his jacket under the hand drier and blasted it with hot air. When it was dry, they came back out into the corridor. Aidan was pacing nearby. He marched up to Greg and demanded, "How did you know where Adam Jones was buried?"

Greg glanced from him to Eden. "I didn't, but then me and Simon started piecing it all together. He says he saw Adam running off saying he's going to the police, and Ray Thompson

234

after him. That's the last anyone saw of Adam. I always wondered if Adam was killed and buried up there, and then I came across the archaeological records at work." He glanced at Aidan. "When there was talk about a new path I thought it was a chance to get that area excavated properly."

He turned to go but Eden caught his sleeve. "Who knew what you two suspected?" she asked.

"No one," he said. He walked off a couple of paces and then turned. "Except I told my mum, obviously."

A thought occurred to her and she called him back. "You know you told me about the watch that Adam got for his birthday?"

"The one I wanted? Yes."

"You said he threw it away. What happened to it after that?"

Greg thought for a moment, stroking his miniature beard. "My dad picked it up."

"Dennis? You're sure?"

"I thought he might give it to me, but he didn't."

They watched him disappear down the corridor and slink into Simon's room to cries of welcome and relief.

"Great start to the week," Aidan said.

She threaded her arm through his. "But my case of the mystery flowers on the grave is solved." She sighed. "Case closed. Now I just need to work out who killed Philip, who killed Adam, and who attacked Simon."

CHAPTER THIRTY-SEVEN

Ian Cooper cut a fine figure on a horse: tall and erect, with soft hands holding the reins. He clucked gently to the horse as he took it round the indoor school, encouraging it to change up into a trot, down into a walk again. Eden leaned on the rail, mesmerised. It was ballet on horseback. When Ian let the reins go and allowed the horse to amble around, cooling off, she waved to him.

"Can't keep away?" he said, in his low Scots accent, dismounting. "More curry combing?"

"Happy to," Eden said. She opened the gate and he led the horse through. She followed them to the stables and watched him untack the horse and throw a blanket over its back. When he'd checked the hay and water, and closed the half-door of the stable, she told him what she'd really come for. "I think I know where to find the evidence that Raymond Thompson is a murderer."

"The CPS are already looking at the Adam Jones file," Ian said, striding across the yard with Eden scurrying after him. "It'll have to be good if they're to argue double jeopardy."

"Not Adam Jones. Philip Wakefield."

Ian halted and turned. "Philip Wakefield?"

"Adam's friend who supposedly committed suicide," Eden said. "I've been looking at all the evidence from the coroner's report, and comparing it to witness statements I've collected. There are contradictions that need explaining."

"You'd better tell me about it." Ian kicked open the door of his portacabin office. Inside it was warm and smelt pleasantly of hay and horses. His desk was against one wall, with a stack

236

of trays organising his invoices and paperwork. A giant diary was open at the day's date, the ribbon gnarled and frayed, the pages scrawled over, circled and marked with exclamations.

They sat down and Eden related what she'd discovered. "Philip Wakefield was left-handed and rubbish at tying knots. The cuts on his wrist, that everyone assumed were a pre-emptive suicide attempt, were on the wrong wrist. As a left-hander, they should have been on his right wrist, not the left. And how did he tie that noose?"

"The coroner's verdict was suicide," Ian said, leaning back in his chair with his hands linked behind his head.

"We both know the coroner was overly influenced by what he was told, and shortly after was diagnosed with dementia," Eden said. "Someone wanted it hushed up. No one examined the finger marks underneath the rope mark, or the scratches on Philip's neck."

"Quite common in hanging," Ian said. "They can't help clutching at the rope and scratching their own neck."

"But the bruises underneath the rope suggest someone tried to manually strangle Philip and then cover it up by hanging him and making it appear a suicide. What if the scratches were made by Philip trying to tear someone's hands from round his throat?"

Ian looked up at the ceiling. "I agree the evidence isn't tidy and more questions should have been asked at the time, but how this all points to Ray Thompson I don't know."

"When Ray Thompson was arrested, he had scratches on his hands and arms, and blood on his t-shirt. There was mud all over his car. What if that mud came from the wood where Philip's body was found?"

"It doesn't mean he killed him. And there's no motive."

"There is." Eden took a DVD from her bag. Half a dozen fruit ciders had persuaded Kaz to copy the video onto DVD for her. "Philip got involved, unwittingly, with some nasty stuff going on up at the Devil's Chimney. Stuff orchestrated and filmed by Ray Thompson. Philip and his friend stole the film. Here's a copy of it."

"Have you watched the film?"

"Yes, and I want you to watch it, too, and tell me if you recognise anyone in it."

Ian sighed deeply. "I thought I'd left all this behind when I left the force."

"There's something else."

"Go on."

"Is there any way you can get Ray Thompson's clothing DNA tested?"

"I did that years ago. It didn't match Adam Jones."

"I know. This time test it against Philip Wakefield's DNA."

Ian called Eden two hours later. She was in her office, still wrestling with her accounts, when the call came. A welcome distraction.

"I've watched the film," he said.

"That was quick."

"I was intrigued." There was a note of suppressed excitement in his voice. "I recognised some of the people in it. They take off their masks when they're trying to resuscitate Philip Wakefield. One of them was Raymond Thompson, no surprises there, but one of the others was none other than Derek Godwinson."

"Derek Godwinson?"

"Known to me as Guv. Inspector Godwinson."

"Jesus!" Eden breathed. "He was there? He was one of the masked men?"

"Yup. Makes sense now why he tried to stymie the case against Ray Thompson."

"And why he misled the coroner over Philip's death."

"Anyway," Ian said, briskly, "I've spoken to a colleague in the force. A good bloke, won't give us the run-around. He's agreed to watch the film and reopen the case into Philip Wakefield's death. And, he's agreed to get Ray Thompson's clothing retested for DNA, to see if it's Philip's blood on it. He's also going to see if the mud samples were kept, and if so, get them tested to see if they match the soil composition where Philip's body was found."

"That's wonderful. Thank you," Eden said. "Who's the helpful copper?"

"Says he knows you. Chap called Ritter."

Eden chuckled. "We've crossed paths a couple of times."

"He told me about the attempted burglary at Susan Wakefield's house," Ian said. "Think that was Ray Thompson, too?"

"Possibly," Eden said. "The burglary at the Wakefield's house after Philip died was orchestrated by Godwinson. Obviously he's not behind the recent burglary, but I suspect both were after the same thing: the film. The thing I don't understand is why now?"

"Mysterious indeed," Ian said. "I'll call you when I know about the soil and DNA. And Eden? Take care."

CHAPTER THIRTY-EIGHT

Aidan stayed over again at Eden's house, she suspected through a vain chivalry and urge to protect her rather than plain randiness. Still, it was nice to have him in bed beside her, even if he did freak out every time she turned over, and interrogate her every time she went to the bathroom.

Now he was knotting his tie at her dressing table mirror while she slicked on eye liner, the two of them jostling for space, elbows fencing. He finished the tie and checked his chin for stray shaving foam.

"Aren't you digging today?" she asked. Aidan was in what she thought of as his corporate archaeologist outfit of midnight blue suit, navy shirt and tie.

"Police won't let us up there. Again," he said. "It's a crime scene. Again. Since whatshisname got bashed."

"Those Iron Age graves are determined not to be excavated," she said, pumping the mascara wand.

"They've got to come out sooner or later, or they'll be buried under an all-weather path," he said, drily. He checked his watch. "I've got an early team meeting. Will you be OK if I leave you?"

"'Course I will."

"What are you up to today?"

"Accounts." She rolled her eyes. "And going to see Susan Wakefield, let her know who's been sending her dead son flowers."

"You'll be careful?"

"Yes." She kissed him. "I'll be so careful I'll be invisible. Now off you go, and say hi to the mob from me."

He gave her a last uncertain look then disappeared. She waited for a few seconds then drew the bolt across the door and double checked the door to her flat's balcony was secure. No point taking chances.

Just as she powered up her laptop, her mobile rang. It was Tony, who owned the sandwich shop just along from her office. He made a dangerously stacked bacon bap and never stinted with the sauce.

"Eden? Are you along the way?" 'Along the way' was Tony code for 'are you in your office?'

"No, I'm at home."

Tony swore. "Then I think you're being burgled. I'll call the cops."

"Thanks, Tony. I'll be right there."

She snatched up her car keys and tore across town, only slowing as she approached her office. She cased the carpark and parallel street in case it was a trap. Nothing suspicious. She eased herself from the car and padded up the metal stairs to the walkway that led to her office. There came the sound of filing cabinet drawers being dragged out and slammed shut. Her back pressed to the wall, she crept along until she could peer through the crack in the door. Whoever was in there hadn't slammed the door shut and it had popped open an inch. Just enough to see. She held her breath, her nerves straining, dreading seeing Hammond. When the intruder turned, she almost laughed with relief.

She ran on the balls of her toes back to her car, selected a CD case at random, and slotted it into the back of her jeans. Then she sprinted back to her office, flinging the door back so hard it rebounded, and shouting, "Looking for this?"

She tweaked the CD case out and held it up. The thief started and turned, then lunged at her.

He caught her off-balance and she tumbled backwards, righting herself with an awkward twist that wrenched her back before she hit the floor. She ploughed into him, aiming for his middle, flinging her arms round him in a rugby tackle. He staggered backwards and fell, and she dropped on top of him, winding both of them. His hands grabbed for the CD case. She punched him, twice, in the side of the head and his grip loosened, then he surged with effort and tipped her off him. His teeth sank into her hand and she released the CD. He scrambled to his feet and made to run off, but she grabbed at his ankles, tripping him. As he fell, a frying pan came down hard on his head.

"Good shot, Tony," Eden said, struggling to her feet. Her back hurt, and that was a nasty bite on her hand. Fuck it, she'd have to get a tetanus jab now.

"You OK, Eden?" Tony said.

"I'll live."

The figure on the floor stirred and tried to sit up. He was white haired and in his sixties. He protested when she snatched the CD case from him. She dangled it in front of his eyes to show him it was a dance music compilation. "Not what you thought, eh, Dean?"

He groaned and crumpled in on himself.

"You thought this was a copy of the tape that Philip and Simon took from up at the Devil's Chimney the night Adam died. You think that tape contains evidence that incriminates you. That's why you're desperate to get hold of it, including breaking in to Susan Wakefield's house and trying to kill Simon. You thought he might start talking to the police and this time they'd listen." Her legs wobbled as she stood. God, her back was killing her.

"I didn't!"

242

"A wooden framed car was seen outside Adam's school. That was your Morris, wasn't it, and you tried to force Adam into the car with you. He didn't want to know you, he threw away the gift you gave him, so you murdered him, didn't you?"

"No!"

"You lied about seeing Adam with his friends that night at the Devil's Chimney. I know they weren't there. Why lie about something like that unless it's to give yourself an alibi? To show you weren't the last person to see Adam alive?"

"I would never … he's my son!"

"Then why go to all this effort to try and get the film? Everyone knows you were up there looking for Adam, so what if you're on the tape? But you're not afraid the tape shows you looking for him, are you, Dean? You're afraid the tape shows you killing him."

"I was trying to save him!"

A police siren sounded and boots pounded up the metal stairs and along the walkway. Two burly coppers dragged Dean to his feet and snapped on handcuffs. Just as Eden was trying to explain what was going on, another copper appeared. Ritter.

"Right," he said. "You're coming with me."

"What have I done?"

"Nothing," he said. "We need a statement covering everything you know about Adam Jones and Philip Wakefield." He looked pointedly at the state of her office. "And then you can come and see what Forensics have found."

"The bloodstains?" she asked.

"The bloodstains."

He hooked his hand under her arm as if she was under arrest too and escorted her out to a waiting unmarked car. Dean was being loaded into the back of a squad car, the police officer pushing his head down to avoid banging it on the door. Ritter didn't do that to her, she was pleased to note, but he courteously opened the passenger door and waited until she was settled inside before getting into the driver's seat. The squad carrying Dean zipped away.

"Want to tell me what's going on?" Ritter said.

"That's Dean Jones. He's worried about what's on that tape, the one I gave to Ian Cooper."

"But he's not on it."

"He doesn't know that," Eden said. "Which means something happened up there that he'll kill to conceal." She shot him a wicked glance. "Over to you."

Ritter started the engine and they pulled away at a sedate pace. "I'm going to get the doc to give you the once over." He looked down at her hand. "Don't want you getting rabies."

The doc was a pleasant woman in her thirties, with a long black ponytail. When she was told that Eden wasn't a crim, but something of a hero, she clucked around her and made such a fuss of her Eden expected to be given a red lolly for being a brave girl. Dr Anand cleaned and dressed the bite on Eden's hand, and gave her a tetanus shot.

"That's you all patched up." Dr Anand patted her arm. Eden tried to jump down from the bed, and the pain in her back made her cry out.

"Sorry!" Eden said. "I hurt my back tackling that chap."

"Let me see." Dr Anand hoiked up Eden's top and examined her back, pressing the muscles and asking, "Does that hurt?" She stilled for a moment and Eden realised she was taking in the scars on her body. "Been in the wars?" she asked.

"Someone tried to kill me," Eden said, quietly, wishing her mind didn't echo with the words *and is still out there waiting to have another go.*

Dr Anand snapped off her latex gloves. "You've pulled a muscle. Keep moving around, but gently for the first few days. And put some cold freeze on it. Here." She went to a cupboard and took down a can, shook it, and squirted Eden's skin with an icy jet. "That'll reduce the inflammation."

"Thank you." Eden tucked in her top and stood straight. Her back felt better already.

"Careful not to overdo it," Dr Anand said, as if she'd read Eden's mind.

Ritter was lurking in the corridor outside when she came out. "Sorted?" he said.

"Fine," Eden said.

He led them into an interview room and took a statement from her about discovering Dean Jones ransacking her office.

"How did you know it was Dean Jones?" he asked.

"I've seen photos of him," Eden said. "Quite old ones, admittedly, from when he was a student and of him with his son. He hasn't changed much. I think if you show his photo to Simon Bird, he'll identify the man who spoke to him shortly before he was attacked."

"You think this is all about the tape?"

"It's the only thing that links me, Susan Wakefield, and Simon Bird."

"But how did Dean Jones know about it?"

"Through Greg Taylor, Simon's partner. Greg told his mum — step-mum — about it, and I think she mentioned the film to Dean when the new enquiry was opened into Adam's death." Eden smoothed down the edge of the band aid on her hand. "Plus, Dean helped out on archaeological digs at the Devil's Chimney when he was a student. He knew about those Iron Age graves."

Ritter twizzled his pen around his knuckles like a cheerleader practising her baton skills.

"Your turn," Eden said. "You've got something to tell me about bloodstains."

"Much as it pains me to say this," Ritter gave a wolfish smile, "you were right. We retested the clothing Ray Thompson was wearing when he was arrested, and the blood matches Philip Wakefield. Amazingly we'd also kept the soil samples, and they show spores and pollen from the woods where Philip's body was found."

"So it could have been murder."

"He's certainly got some explaining to do," Ritter said. "Not just about Philip's death, but all the shenanigans that are on that tape." He fell silent for a second, then said, "I shall enjoy arresting him." He picked up his folder of papers and rose from the table.

"Can I come?" Eden asked.

Ritter's shoulders sagged. "Only if you stay in the car."

Eden gave him a Boy Scout salute. "Aye, aye, Captain."

CHAPTER THIRTY-NINE

Aidan lined up his pens, their tips touching the edge of the desk, rearranging them in ascending order of size. Having sorted them, he placed them, one by one, to the right of the blotter on his desk, from the long slim fountain pen down to the stubby pencil. He sat back and looked at them, his mind scratching. It still wasn't right. Something didn't fit. He stood and looked at them from above. It was the pencil. It was considerably shorter than the pen it sat next to, breaking the smooth line of descent. He snatched up the pencil and checked the line of pens again. That was better. He slung the pencil into the bin and went to fetch a new one from the stationery cupboard.

Trev and Mandy were bickering gently across their desks when he went in. They both looked up eagerly.

"Boss, any news on —?" Trev began.

"No," he said shortly.

"Only asking."

Aidan puffed out his cheeks. "I'll ring the police in a minute." Now that man had been assaulted the area was, once again, a crime scene. They'd be lucky to get those graves excavated by Christmas at this rate. He looked around the office. There were piles of paper stacked on every desk. Not neat piles, either; tottering piles that could sway and collapse at any moment.

Lisa wafted into the office. She'd taken an extra week's leave to help them excavate the Iron Age graves, assuming they were ever allowed near them. As she sailed into the office, she caught one of the stacks of paper with the handbag swinging from the crook of her arm. Paper slewed across the floor.

"Sorry!" Lisa said, bending to scoop up the papers. Mandy joined her, the two of them scrunching and muddling the papers as they heaved them up any old how and dumped them on the desk. It was intolerable.

"Right!" he said. "While we're waiting to go and finish off that dig, we're going to sort this office out. I want everything sorted, shredded if it's no longer needed, and filed properly if we need to keep it." He waved his hand round the room. "No more heaps of paper, no more maps rolled up in the corner, no more mess. I want everything cleared."

Trev muttered something that sounded like 'Gestapo HQ', which he ignored. Mandy, bless her, grabbed a heap of papers and started sorting. Trev grumbled as he lifted a tray towards him and tossed a half-eaten biscuit into the bin. Aidan grabbed a new pencil from the cupboard and retreated to his office and closed the door. At least in there everything was ordered and clean and clear of clutter.

He jiggled his computer mouse and the screen bloomed into life. There was a document already open: budget forecasts for the projects the Cultural Heritage Unit had underway, and those where they'd applied for funding. Normally he loved the challenge of balancing the budget and working out where they could secure additional funding, but today all he saw was columns of numbers that just didn't fit into any sort of pattern. Why were there so many sevens? And a horrible lot of prime numbers. They were the worst, like a thorn under the skin, constantly irritating.

Lisa opened the door and came in, quietly placing a glass of water and two painkillers on his desk. Without saying a word, she crossed to the window and closed the blinds. Positioning herself behind his chair, she said, "I'm going to touch you now, just a shoulder massage, so brace. Ready."

He braced himself in the way he'd learned to do years ago when he realised that people hugging him and kissing his cheek was supposed to be a sign of affection, and that he offended them when he stiffened and tried to avoid it. When relatives approached, he now mentally reminded himself, "It's OK. They're going to hug you. Try to relax, it'll be all right."

He repeated this to himself now. *Relax, it's only Lisa, it'll be all right.* Even so, he couldn't help flinching when her hands landed on his shoulders.

"Sorry," he said, realising his fingernails were digging into his palms. Slowly he relaxed his fists.

"Just breathe, Aidan, it'll be fine," Lisa said. He dropped his shoulders, feeling her fingers working into the muscles.

"What's all this about?" he asked. "The tablets, the blinds, the massage."

"You've got a migraine coming," Lisa said. "Haven't you?"

"Uh-huh." He'd woken feeling exhausted and his vision was wobbling, and he kept on thinking about the word 'wheelbarrow' for no reason he could fathom. When he went into the coffee shop to grab an espresso, he felt the ground plunging away from his feet, and had the sensation that everyone around him was a ghost from Victorian times.

"Let's see if we can nip it in the bud," Lisa said. Her fingers dug into the muscles round his shoulder blades. "Nasty knot here."

"Careful, that's my sword arm," he said, the words coming out without him realising. He was spinning back in time; he wasn't here; he was someone else.

"I quite fancy you as a knight in shining armour," Lisa said. How many of his migraines had she seen over the years? When they were postgrads together he'd had them regularly. She was used to him talking nonsense, his words scrambled and his brain desperately trying to fit the world into an orderly pattern. "You could spear my garter on your lance." She paused and giggled. "That sounds rude."

He leaned away from her to get the painkillers, and slugged back the whole glass of water in one. "Thanks."

"I think you should go home," Lisa said. "That computer screen isn't going to help, and there's nothing that can't wait until tomorrow."

"I don't want to leave Mandy and Trev."

"In case they get the go ahead to finish the dig?" Lisa tutted. "They've been archaeologists longer than you have, they'll manage a few hours without you. Anyway, have you seen yourself lately? You look like Lizzie Hexam should be fishing you out of the Thames."

"That bad?"

She swung his chair round and faced him. "Let me take you home, Aidan. You'll feel better if you get some sleep."

He gave in. The headache was starting now and he knew he didn't have long before it crushed him utterly. He watched as Lisa saved the documents on his computer and closed it down, then allowed himself to be led out of the office and to his car. Lisa held her hand out for his keys, and he meekly surrendered them. It was odd, sitting in the passenger seat of his own car, but his vision was jumping now and there was no way Lisa would let him drive.

His flat was in an imposing Regency building, one of a sweep of elegant buildings of amber stone with delicate ironwork balconies. He made it up the stairs and into his flat, then collapsed full length on the settee. The cushion squishing beneath his head was so comforting he groaned. Lisa went into his kitchen and he heard her opening and closing the fridge door. She returned with a pint glass of sparkling water.

"This'll help," she said. "Come on, into bed with you, young man."

He stripped off his trousers, shirt and socks and climbed into bed in his boxers. Lisa hung up his clothes without a word. His mind smoothed for a second: thank God she knew the clothes had to be hung correctly, that he felt too sick to do it himself, but that the knowledge they were in a heap on the floor would haunt him and deny him any sleep.

"Can I get you anything else?" she asked.

"Curtains," he muttered. The pillow and sheets were deliciously cool on his skin. The room went dim and the door closed quietly.

He slept.

Aidan awoke a couple of hours later and found Lisa had placed a bucket beside the bed in case he needed to be sick. He half-smiled, turned over, and slept again, more easily now. The headache was receding.

When he awoke again, he found Lisa lying on top of the bed next to him, reading one of his books. "Hello, sleepyhead," she said. "How are you feeling?"

"Better. What are you doing?"

She tilted the book at him. "Reading *Sense and Sensibility*. The more I think about it, the more I'm convinced Jane Austen got it wrong. I bet five years after the happy ever afters, Marianne has run off with Willoughby."

He struggled to sit up. "What time is it?"

"After four. Your phone's been bleeping like mad."

"Let me see."

She fetched it and handed it over. There was a string of text messages from Eden.

Just arrested Dean Jones.

Found him breaking into my office. Bit of a punch up. I'm OK — just a bit battered.

Seen doc at cop station — I'm fine. Hurt back a bit.

So much for her being careful and keeping a low profile. She'd promised him to take care, and here she was bragging about being in a punch up, whatever the hell that meant, and charging off to arrest people. He groaned aloud. She had absolutely no sense of self preservation. What the hell was she thinking of? The woman had a death wish.

"OK?" Lisa asked.

"Eden, looking for trouble again," he said.

"She all right?"

"Yes, she's fine." He switched off the phone and tossed it into a drawer. He didn't want to know any more. If she wanted to live on the edge, thumbing her nose at danger, that was up to her. What he knew now, knew absolutely, was he couldn't take the worry any more. "I think I know why I got a migraine."

"Fancy a cup of tea?"

"Please. There's some peppermint stuff." Lisa raised an eyebrow. "I can't stand the taste of milk when I'm like this."

"Thank goodness for that," she said, "I thought for a moment there you'd turned into a hippy."

She returned with a cup of peppermint for him, and what she called 'normal person's tea' for herself, and resumed her place on the bed beside him. She stretched out her legs and wiggled her toes. Her toenails were painted fuchsia, little buds on the ends on her feet.

"Thanks for looking after me today," he said.

She turned to face him. "I care about you, you prat. Now drink your tea and go back to sleep. I'll make you something to eat later if you think you can manage it."

He flipped the pillow over to the cool side and settled back to sleep. It was a gentle sleep this time, the pain draining away and letting him rest. He swam out of sleep an hour later and found Lisa dozing, the book folded up on the bed beside her. He slid across the bed and wrapped his arms round her waist, spooning her from behind. She shifted and settled, draping her arm over the top of his and threading their fingers together.

"When are you going to Devon?" he asked.

"Thursday evening."

"And there's a Napoleonic fort nearby?"

"Two, in fact."

"Can I come?"

"Sure," she said.

CHAPTER FORTY

Eden recognised the turnoff to Abbeymead from when she came to interview Dave Thompson, but after the third mini roundabout she was well and truly lost in the maze of curving streets and identical cul-de-sacs, and marvelled that Ritter seemed to know where he was going. They'd put her in the back of Ritter's car, to keep her out of trouble; another detective occupied the passenger seat, and a second car followed them with two uniforms in it.

"He doesn't live in Cheltenham anymore?" Eden said.

"He moved after the trial," Ritter said. "Being acquitted isn't the same as being found innocent."

Ritter pulled up outside an anonymous semi. It had a square metre of AstroTurf and an overgrown laurel hedge. Most of the front was taken up with driveway, which was crowded with cars. The pavement outside the house was crammed with cars, too, including Dave Thompson's Clean 'N' Shine car.

"Looks like we're going to spoil the party," Ritter said. The detective next to him muttered something that sounded like, "Remember what the family's been through lately, Guv," then they got out of the car, cautioned Eden to stay put, and waited until the other cops joined him so they could march, in a phalanx, up to the door. Ritter gave the knocker three sharp raps. Eden wound down the window, saw the front door open, and a man appear on the doorstep. He was a gnome of a man, round shouldered and grey, in blue jeans and a cardigan that had come off worst in a fight with the washing machine.

"Ray Thompson," Ritter said, flashing his warrant card. The man lifted his hands in protest, then suddenly slammed the door in their faces.

Ritter stood back while a beefy detective wielded an enforcer and broke down the door. Three punishing blows later and the door was hanging open. The men charged inside, shouting, shoving people aside. There was the pounding of feet on the stairs, then Ritter shouting, "He's out the back. After him!"

Eden opened the car door and ran round the side of the houses, hunting for an alleyway. There was a cluster of wheelie bins on the pavement. She headed towards them and found a short passageway leading between the houses and round to the back gardens. She sprinted down the passage, scouting out the gardens, looking for movement or the tell-tale closing of a shed door. Nothing. Rounding the corner she saw Ray Thompson running towards her. Behind him came the two uniforms, fists and knees pumping. As Ray made to shove past her, she stuck out her leg, tripping him. He staggered and fell against the fence, shouting, "Out the way, bitch!"

"I don't think so," Eden said, dodging in front of him, weaving from side to side, delaying him enough for one of the cops to grab him.

"Nice work, Eden," said Ritter, materialising behind her.

"Who the fuck are you?" Thompson spat.

"She's been helping us with our enquiries." The cuffs snapped onto Ray's wrists. "Raymond Thompson, I'm arresting you for the murder of —"

"Murder!" Thompson cried. "You tried that before and couldn't prove anything."

"— of Philip Wakefield," Ritter said, with heavy emphasis, and proceeded with the arrest.

When they dragged Thompson back down the alleyway and out to the pavement, there was a cluster of people on the square of lawn plus a number of neighbours who'd come out for a gawp. Eden recognised Dave Thompson. He gaped at her as she walked past: evidently he recognised her, too. A woman in her sixties, Ray's wife she guessed, was shouting about her rights and Ray's rights, and protesting about the state of the front door.

The police ignored it all and stowed Ray in the back of the police car. Ritter went over to the screaming woman and said, "Shut up and go back inside or I'll arrest you for a breach of the peace." There was muttering and defiant swearing, and as the police cars pulled away, they were still outside, shouting and gesticulating.

"What did I tell you about staying put?" Ritter said, as he drove off.

"Old habits," Eden said, rubbing her back. "When we get back to the station, can I see Doctor Anand again?"

CHAPTER FORTY-ONE

The cat occupied the chair in the window again. Evidently zonked by its heavy sleeping duties, it didn't bother to open its eyes when Eden stroked it. Susan Wakefield hovered uncertainly by the gas fire, her arms folded across her chest, bracing herself for bad news.

"You've solved it, haven't you?" she said, her voice wavering.

"It's not what you think," Eden said, anxious to put the woman out of her misery. Years fearing that her son killed someone and then hanged himself, what torture that must have been. "Sit down, because this is going to be hard." She sat next to Susan on the settee, her body twisted towards her, and took Susan's hands. "Philip didn't kill Adam."

Susan let go of her breath in a whoosh and she bent forward, crying, "Thank God!"

"You were told a lie," Eden said. "Not intentionally, but someone said they'd seen Adam and his friends at the Devil's Chimney the night Adam disappeared. Adam's mother assumed it was Philip he was with, as you'd called her and said Philip was missing, but actually Philip was with Simon. They left the Devil's Chimney together and came home, and when they left, as far as they knew, Adam was still alive."

"Then why did he lie to me?" Susan wailed. "If he hadn't lied, I wouldn't have thought he had something to hide."

Eden took a deep breath. This was not going to be pleasant. "Philip knew that Adam had got caught up in some nasty stuff. He knew, because Adam tried to get him involved, too. What happened to Philip freaked him out. I imagine it was a mixture of shame, disgust and fear that stopped him telling you what went on up there."

"Did they hurt him?"

"Yes."

"Was it … child abuse?"

"Yes. He wasn't raped, but it was abuse."

Susan doubled over, her arms clutched around her stomach as though she'd been kicked. Her mouth opened in a long, silent scream. Eden put her arms around her and held her.

"Philip was very brave," Eden said, when the shock ebbed into weeping. "He wanted to protect Adam, so he and Simon went up there to get the evidence they needed to tell the police. The burglaries were people trying to steal that evidence."

"Why did he kill himself?" Tears slicked her face and fell unchecked onto her hands.

"He didn't," Eden said. "The police arrested Ray Thompson earlier today and charged him with Philip's murder."

"Murder?" Susan's face twitched with terror.

"I'm sorry." Eden held her while she wept, great shuddering sobs that rocked her body.

"And what about the flowers?"

"They were from Simon Bird, Philip's friend," Eden said. "He tried several times to tell the police what he and Philip saw. He's never forgotten Philip — still has his photo in his wallet. I think he still loves him."

CHAPTER FORTY-TWO

Kate had been in her parents' bedroom when the police arrived and dragged her father, Raymond Thompson, away. She couldn't go through the same nightmare all over again. The police all over the house with their cameras and plastic evidence bags, all of them being questioned, the sly looks from the neighbours and the people who used to be friends crossing the road and ducking into shops to avoid them. The bullying at school. *Your dad's a murderer.* Moving house. Changing schools. Trying to get away from the stain that never quite washed clean, despite her dad being found innocent.

But he had been arrested for a different murder this time. Not Adam Jones, but Philip Wakefield. It was all a horrible nightmare. And that Eden Grey woman had been with the police.

This woman had ruined her whole life. A vision of Jessica in her new party frock swum in front of her eyes, winding her. She'd never see her again. Never watch her twirl in front of the mirror, clumping round in Kate's shoes, pretending to be grown up. Never watch her with her first boyfriend, or graduating, or getting married. Everything she'd anticipated and looked forward to from the moment she knew she was pregnant, swept away by this woman.

Kate had the business card in her hand. Name, email, phone number, office address on thick, creamy card. Her fingers clenched around it, then she silently slid it into her pocket. John was right: the woman was evil.

The voice spoke as soon as Kate picked up the telephone. She arranged to meet him in the park.

Slipping away was easy. They were all used to it, now, letting her go off on her own for an hour here and there to clear her head and cry in private, so she simply had to announce she was going to the park for some fresh air. Now her dad had been arrested, Patty no longer came round to the house. Not that Kate would have let her in, anyway. Spy. Only Gareth and her mother to monitor what she was doing, and Gareth barely registered her existence these days.

John was in the park, sitting on a bench tucked in one of the corners, wearing a long black overcoat. Kate sat down next to him.

"It's happened," she said, without preamble. "They've arrested my dad. Eden Grey was actually there with them when they took him."

"Where is he now?"

"In custody." She blew out her breath on the word, imagining him in a dirty cell, his food slopped onto a plastic tray. It wasn't fair. She thought they'd left all this behind long ago.

"I can't imagine how difficult it was when you were a child," John said. "When your father was on trial."

"We were all on trial," she said. "Me, Mum and Dad. Everyone knew, everyone thought he was guilty. You know, the old 'no smoke without fire'."

"Cruel."

"It was," she agreed. "The kids at school, they called me names, spat at me a few times. I had to sit on my own because no one wanted to be near me. Murderer's daughter. That's what they said." Her voice broke. "And they're saying it again now."

He turned to face her, his eyes burning. "It's not right, is it?"

"I hate them all. Hate them!" She punched her fists into her thigh. "I could kill them for this. Starting it up all over again, and when Jessica has just ... and not even buried yet!" Her voice rose to a wail and ended in a sob.

Silently he handed her a handkerchief and waited until she was calmer, then said, "Would you be up to doing a bit of acting, Kate?"

"Acting?"

"Yes, pretending to be someone else."

"Why?"

He flicked a particle of fluff from his knee. As always, his suit was immaculate. *He* was immaculate; sympathetic; perfect. "I've had an idea for how Eden Grey can be made to pay. For what she did to Jessica and to your dad. It's quite simple, and I think you'll enjoy it." His eyes flickered with humour for a moment.

"What do you mean?"

"You do want revenge, don't you, Kate?"

"Yes, of course." Anger shoved the pain away. Some nights she could barely sleep for thinking up ways she wanted to hurt Eden Grey for what she'd done to Jessica. And now she'd persuaded the police to arrest her father. How many more people she loved was this woman going to snatch from her? "What do I have to do?"

"It's very easy, and I know you'll be brilliant. I know how strong and determined you are."

That was true. She was strong. She looked after Gareth and Jessica and looked after the house, day after day, never complaining. You had to be strong to do that.

He was speaking again. She dragged back her attention. "She's a private investigator. I want you to ring her up and pretend to be a client. Meet her and tell her your story, and then I want you to drive her somewhere. Tell her you need to show her something to do with the case." He reached into his inside jacket pocket and pulled out a slim envelope. "It's all here. You just need to play the part."

"I'll have to ask Gareth for the car."

"No need. I've hired one. It's parked around the corner, and here are the keys." Again his hand dipped into his pocket and out came a key fob emblazoned with the name of a car hire company. "We're going to get in that car now, and I'm going to show you where I want you to bring her. Is that all right, Kate?"

"Yes, yes, that's fine."

"I'll be waiting there for you, when the time comes."

"How will I know when it's time?"

"I'll ring you. Don't worry, it'll all be fine."

They left the park and walked to one of the side streets, a quiet road of nineteen-thirties detached houses with porthole windows in the porch and landing. The car was a black Honda, spacious inside but not flashy. "You don't want to stand out," John said.

They got in the car, Kate in the passenger seat. She dug her sunglasses out of her bag and put them on: all those days cooped up inside crying and her eyes stung in the light. He was a good driver, not like Gareth, she couldn't help comparing his smooth, sensitive hands on the steering wheel to Gareth's sausagey paws. Surgeon's hands, she thought, idly, recalling the cool touch on her feet.

He drove them out into the countryside and to a rendezvous point he'd chosen. "See how beautiful it is," he said, waving his hand at the vast dome of sky overhead. "And very quiet. No one will be here, just you and me. Taking care of a little business." He glanced at her. "Doing this for Jessica and for your dad."

"For Jessica and Dad," she echoed. She paused, then asked, "What are you going to do?"

"I'm going to show her she can't go around hurting people," he said.

"You're not going to … harm her, are you?"

He braked sharply. "You really think that of me?"

"No, no, sorry."

He turned the car round and returned to the same quiet side street. "We'll leave it here — don't want your neighbours gossiping," he said, with that gentle smile that let her know everything was going to be fine. Her hand was on the door when he said, mildly, "Oh, I got you something else. Probably won't need it, but better safe than sorry."

He flipped up the lid on the central console. Inside was a gun. "Just in case she needs persuading," he said.

PART SEVEN: 1981

CHAPTER FORTY-THREE

The TV is on loud in the room below. Adam can make out a steady chuntering and bursts of canned laughter but can't tell what his Mum and Dennis are watching. He eases himself up on his elbow and peers across the room to Gregory's bed. A humped shape beneath the covers lets out a gentle snore. Adam lifts his covers and glides out of bed. His pyjamas are over the top of his t-shirt and jeans. He shucks them off quickly and stuffs them in his bed, then drags one of his pillows under the blankets. If you don't look too closely, it could be his sleeping form. Good enough to fool Gregory if he wakes in the night, anyway.

He creeps over to the bedroom door and presses his ear to it. The TV noise continues, and above it his mum's voice, and Dennis's answering rumble. He cracks open the door and tiptoes down the landing. He's part-way down the stairs when he remembers he hasn't pocketed his key. Swivelling on his heel, he heads back up the stairs and towards his bedroom. A snore from Gregory. Adam steals to his chest of drawers and tugs open the top drawer, wincing as the wood scrapes. He fumbles inside and takes out a balled sock where he's concealed a copy of the key. As he palms it, a voice speaks. He jumps and stubs his toe.

"What are you doing?"

"Nothing. Go back to sleep."

The figure in the bed rouses itself. "What are you doing?"

"Shhh!"

"Why?" Gregory's voice is high and carrying. Any more from him and Mum will be up the stairs and demanding to know why they're both still awake and talking. His stomach crunches at the thought. He's already late meeting Ray.

"Shh! Go back to sleep."

"I want to know what you're doing," Gregory says in his most self-important voice. "Why aren't you in your pyjamas?"

"I'm going out," Adam hisses.

"Are you running away?" There's a pause, and Adam knows that Gregory is calculating if he'll get Adam's bike if he disappears, and his football albums.

"No, I'm just going out, that's all."

"Can I come?"

"No!"

"I'm going to tell Mum." Gregory flips back his covers.

"Get back into bed."

"Tell me where you're going and what you're doing and I *might* keep quiet."

Adam runs his hands through his hair in despair. At this rate Ray would have given him up and gone without him.

"All right!" he says. "I'm meeting some friends up at the Devil's Chimney."

"Why?"

"What?"

"Why are you going up there in the middle of the night?"

"It's a sort of adventure."

"What sort of adventure?"

Adam pinches Gregory's shoulder and forces him back into his bed, then tucks the covers round him tightly, pinioning his arms inside. "It's with Tommo's uncle. We're making a film."

"A film at night?"

"Yes. Now go to sleep."

Adam heads back to the door. Just as he's about to open it, Gregory's voice comes again in the darkness. "It'll cost you."

Adam turns. "What?"

"I'll keep quiet if you pay me."

Devious little sod. "How much?"

"Ten pounds."

There's no time to argue, and the longer they talk, the more danger there is of Mum hearing and coming to investigate. "Close your eyes," he says.

Gregory plants his hands over his eyes and Adam goes to his wardrobe. In the bottom is a pair of shoes, the roll of money shoved tight into the toe. He eases it out, thumbs a tenner off the top, and stows the wedge of money back in his shoe. When he turns back, Gregory is staring at him, his eyes bright. He'll have to find a new hiding place or Gregory's sticky little mitts will be all over his roll of cash, borrowing a fiver here, a tenner there, all the time threatening to tell Mum he has a stash of secret money. There's no time to find a place now, not with Gregory agog with interest. He'll do it later, when the little twerp's out of the way.

He walks over to Gregory's bed and slaps the tenner — hard — onto his forehead. "The money for your silence," he says, trying to sound like a gangster. Gregory only giggles. He fights the urge to grab the pillow and force it down on his face, stop him whining and telling and giggling once and for all. "Now go to sleep," he says, and slinks out of the house.

Ray's already at the corner when he sprints up, flustered and out of breath.

"Where the hell have you been?"

"It was hard to get away," Adam says, sliding into the passenger seat. His bum barely connects with the cracked black vinyl before Ray accelerates away and he's flung to the side, narrowly avoiding the gear stick.

"I hope you weren't seen," Ray says, darkly.

"I wasn't."

"Glad to hear it, because I have to tell you, Adam, that was a right balls up you made the other night."

Adam crawls with shame. Philip. He could have killed him. He *did* kill him; it was only the other men who brought him back to life. He didn't know what to do.

"That happens again, you'll be the one on the table," Ray continues, "and I tell you, Adam, I won't be taking the bag away. You understand me?"

He understands all right. He's playing the Devil again tonight, and for days his mind has been on a constant loop, what he has to do, what he must remember so he never, *never* messes it up again.

"Who's on the table?" he asks, running his tongue over his braces. His mouth feels thick and dry. He can taste his own breath.

"Some kid I found at the bus station," Ray says. "Didn't dare go home. Said his mam drinks and his old man does dirty things to him. Says he'd rather take his chances on the street."

Ray powers up the hill and along the track, and suddenly cackles with laughter, as though a stray thought amuses him. He flashes a wicked smile at Adam and says, "Least if you kill this one no one will miss him."

Adam's stomach churns. It's all going wrong tonight. Late out, forgetting the key, Gregory threatening to tell, having to reveal his secret stash of money, Ray in a temper because of Philip. A deep sense of foreboding haunts him. Can he get out of it for once? Say he feels sick, needs to go home. Would they let him go?

As they trudge along the path, Ray catches his arm and yanks it behind his back, twisting it until his shoulder burns. "Remember what I said, Adam. You mess this up, you won't mess up again."

CHAPTER FORTY-FOUR

It wasn't right. Dean drained his pint and thumped it down on the bar. Adam was his son, not just hers; he had every right to see him. And all he got from Barbara was, "You want to see your son, you have to pay for your son," as though she hated the lad and counted every penny. He'd paid what he could. God knows he paid for everything when they were first married and Adam came along, while she was at home, keeping house she called it, and he was at the fire station.

Until it all came crashing down. The fall, the damage to his back and leg that meant he could never work as a fireman again, the honourable discharge. But what do you do when you're used to running into danger every day, being a hero, being the man running into the burning building as everyone else is running out? Slogging day after day on the production line at an engineering firm wasn't it, that's for sure.

He signalled the waitress for another pint and sluiced the warm liquid to the back of his throat. They had some pints in the fire service, that's for sure. Hashing over the day, awarding prizes for tosser of the day. Never hero of the day, that would never do. They were all heroes, but sometimes they could be tossers, too. He smiled at the memory. He won tosser of the day on several occasions. Standing on the hose; getting his braces caught in his locker; stupid stuff that didn't matter but which fostered friendships.

How could she marry that Dennis? Did she know what sort of man he was? He wasn't sure which was worse, that she knew and didn't care, or that she was so stupid she didn't even realise what she'd shackled herself to. Except it wasn't just her, was it? She'd taken Adam, his son, to live with that pervert, too.

He drained the pint and set it down, shaking his head at the barmaid who raised an eyebrow to ask if he wanted another. He slid from the barstool and headed for the door, the gust of wind shocking him as he stepped outside and reigniting his anger.

He was sorted now. The years of study all behind him. He was earning, not a fortune, but proper money. He could afford the price she demanded to see his own son. And by God he was going to see him. A new job in Birmingham, close enough to keep an eye on the boy, far enough away that he wasn't always bumping into Barbara and that Dennis. He'd deliberately chosen a flat with two bedrooms so Adam could come and stay. He'd spent all last weekend repapering the second bedroom and screwing the bed together.

His car was parked at the end of the street. A green, wooden framed Morris Traveller. An antique, but he loved her. He unlocked the door and climbed in, started the engine, and pulled away. He was going to see his son, and no one was going to stop him.

The lights were still on downstairs, the light creeping round the edges of the curtains and glowing in the central V where the curtains didn't meet. A bluey, TV glow; and if he strained his ears he could make out canned laughter. Still up, and watching TV. Well, they could let him in, let him see Adam. He pressed his finger to the doorbell and leaned his whole weight on it, only releasing it when he saw the hall light snap on in the tiny pane in the front door, and heard a voice calling, "All right, all right!"

"Hello, Dennis," Dean said, planting one foot over the doorstep. "Adam in?"

"What time do you call this?"

Dean glanced at his watch. "Ten thirty. What time do you call it?"

"I call it a bloody cheek." Barbara appeared in the hallway. "What do you want, Dean?"

"I want to see Adam."

"Not at this time of night you're not."

"Just for a few minutes. I've come here specially."

"Then you've had a wasted journey." When had she got so hard? Was she always so slatternly, in her pale blue nylon housecoat and the discontented lines framing her mouth. "You should have phoned and made an appointment."

"I don't need an appointment to see my own son." Dean shoved past Dennis and headed for the stairs. "Don't bother to show me up. I'll find him."

"Here! You can't just march in here…" Barbara shouted, but he was already bounding up the stairs, calling, "Adam! It's me. Dad."

At the top of the stairs was a bathroom, then along the landing were two further doors. Dean opened them in turn; the first room reeked of Barbara's perfume; the second was in darkness, but the light from the landing revealed two occupied single beds.

"Adam?" He lowered his voice a little. No point scaring the little guy out of his wits. "Adam, it's me, Dad."

A figure in the far bed stirred and a sleepy voice said, "Who is it? What's the matter?"

"Adam?"

"I'm Gregory."

Footsteps pounded along the landing. "Get out, now!"

"Just a minute. Please!" He crossed to the other bed and placed his hand on the recumbent form's shoulder. "Adam? Adam!"

No response. He gave the shoulder a little shake. When there was no response at all, he drew back the covers. "Come on, sleepyhead, it's your dad."

He sat back on his heels, and behind him, someone clicked the light switch, revealing the pillows wedged in the bed. There was a stunned silence for a moment, then Barbara said, "Where is he?"

"He's gone out," Gregory said, in a small voice.

They all rounded on him. "What's that?"

"He told me not to tell."

Barbara seized Gregory's shoulders. "That doesn't matter, tell me where he's gone. Has he run away?"

Gregory shook his head. "He's gone out with Tommo's uncle. They're making a film."

"Stop telling stories, Gregory!" Barbara said. "I've told you before. Now where is Adam?"

Gregory started to cry. "I'm not lying!" he wailed. "He's gone out with Ray to make a film. Up at the Devil's Chimney."

Dean went cold. "Ray Thompson?"

"Uh-huh." More snivelling and nose blowing on the corner of the sheet. "He sneaks out all the time, when you're in bed tickling."

Dean stood. "I'll go and find him."

"I'll come with you," Barbara said.

"No, you stay here." He couldn't have her there. He recalled finding a packet of photos, secreted by Ray in the toilets at the engineering works. Photos of men doing stuff to kids. He'd returned the photos to their hiding place, and lo and behold Dennis came in and went straight to them. And that wasn't all:

he'd heard things about Ray. Not nice things, and a finger of dread stroked his spine as he thought of Adam caught up with a man like that. He looked meaningfully at Dennis. His son lived with one pervert and sneaked out at night to meet another. What the hell was going on here?

Dennis hovered by the door. "Perhaps I should go with you."

No. "I'll be all right. I'll fetch him home." Dean hurtled back down the stairs and out into the chill night air. Fear propelled him, as much as he dreaded what he might find. And once he found Adam, he was taking him away to come and live with him where he'd be safe. Barbara could squawk all she liked.

The road was clear and he powered up the hill, turning into the carpark half-way up Leckhampton Hill. There were a few cars there, tucked nose in. He parked as far away from them as possible.

He charged up the path and along to the Devil's Chimney. Half-way there, a figure came crashing down the path towards him. Adam. His head was down and he was running for his life, his breath in ragged gasps and tears flying from his eyes. Dean sagged with relief that he was alive, and spread his arms to catch his son; to save him.

Adam's head jerked up as he collided with Dean. He let out a scream and pushed him away, hurtling down the path. "Adam!" Dean sprinted after him, caught him, and swung him round. "Son, son, it's me. You're safe."

The boy sagged in his arms. "Dad?"

"Let me take you home."

"No! I don't want to!"

"What's happened?"

But Adam kicked him and ran away, and Dean belted after him. The path twisted and the bowl of the quarry yawned steeply just inches away. He grabbed Adam's jumper. He swung round, aiming a punch. Instinctively, Dean punched back. His fist connected with Adam's jaw. The boy teetered on the edge for a terrifying moment, then he lost his footing and fell, over the lip and down into the quarry, bouncing on a rock part way down then dropping to the bottom.

Dean gaped into the void, his mind numb, then scrambled along the path, down into the quarry, and back along to where Adam fell. His body was crumpled at the bottom, seeming much younger than his twelve years. His spine and neck were impossibly angled, his hand stretched out as though pleading. Dean dropped to his knees beside him, trying desperately to make the spine and neck straight again. Adam's head lolled against his chest.

Panic overwhelmed him. He'd killed him. He'd hit his son and killed him. He'd lose his job. He'd go to prison. He couldn't go to prison. No one must ever know. It wasn't his fault, he just reacted; anyone would react the same if someone punched them, wouldn't they? What should he do? He could leave Adam here, go back and say he couldn't find him, but he jibbed at the thought of leaving him exposed to the night air, exposed to whoever came along.

He raised Adam and hoisted him over his shoulder, then lifted him into the back of his car and covered him with a blanket. Then he went back to Barbara's house.

"Where is he, then?"

"He's with his friends, refuses to come home," Dean said.

Her eyes narrowed. "What are they doing?"

Dean shrugged. "I begged him to come home, but he wouldn't. Sorry, Barb."

"What am I going to do with him?"

He rubbed his eyes. "Wait until tomorrow, then speak to him. He's not a bad lad, he'll listen." He turned away, then called over his shoulder, "Sorry I barged in. Just wanted to see him, that's all."

"That's all right," she said. He could hear the tears in her voice, worried about Adam. Guilt scoured him. "Call tomorrow and we'll arrange for you to see him at the weekend."

That finished him. "Thanks," he said, his words muffled. "See you."

He heard the door close behind him and he started to shake. Adam was dead, curled in the back of his car. What the hell was he going to do with him?

He waited until the early hours, calculating that whatever Ray and his cronies were up to, they'd be gone by then, then drove back to the Devil's Chimney. The track was still there, the one they'd used when he came up here on digs when he was at university and they all camped in the farmer's field. He bumped his car along it, his lights dimmed, and stopped near the Iron Age Hill Fort. He'd excavated that, he thought, only a few years ago but it felt like a lifetime. It was fun, that dig, lots of Iron Age stuff up; Iron Age burials. He couldn't leave Adam alone and exposed, but he could bury him respectfully.

Scraping the hole was hard, but he persevered until the grave was deep enough to protect it from dogs and foxes. A tumble down dry stone wall provided the lining; nice, amber Cotswold stones, a ring of them standing sentry around the grave. He eased Adam's body into it, folding him into a foetal position on his side. On his own wrist was the Mickey Mouse watch he'd bought Adam for his birthday. He'd worn it ever since, hoping for a chance to give it to him, to explain everything. Too late. With a surge of shame he recalled the look on Dennis

Taylor's face as he'd handed the watch back to him. *Your son doesn't want this.*

There was already a watch on Adam's wrist, and he baulked at the thought of removing it from his son's body. Instead, he bent into the grave and removed one of the stones lining the sides, and tucked the Mickey Mouse watch deep beneath it, then replaced the stone on top. Adam would have something from him to accompany him into the afterlife. He gazed at Adam's furled body for a long moment, imprinting every detail onto his memory, then shovelled in the soil, covering his face, concealing his body. When he'd finished, he stood back and looked at it. The ring of stones poking their tips out of the soil, just like the Iron Age cist burials nearby. No one would ever know.

CHAPTER FORTY-FIVE

Philip was hunched up next to a mean camp fire that spat and hissed as raindrops fell into it. Ray hid behind a tree and watched him for a long time, as Philip prodded at the fire with a skinny stick, breaking off now and then to wipe tears from his cheeks. The boy still had bruises around his mouth and his eyes were bloodied with pin pricks. Ray's guts churned to water when he thought how the boy got them, remembering that heart-stopping moment when the boy refused to come back to life. Stupid little bastard; Ray almost died himself, terrified they'd never get him breathing again.

He knew he'd be here. Knew he'd be hiding out like a frightened rabbit in its burrow. He stepped forwards and a twig snapped, and Philip's head shot up, his face taut with fear. Ray started whistling as he approached, the Laurel and Hardy theme tune.

"You heard about Adam?" Ray said, coming over and sitting next to him. Philip cringed away. "Silly boy's run away. Gone to London no doubt, gone to make his fortune."

"No he hasn't."

"You know where he is, then?"

The words were so quiet Ray had to crane forwards to hear. "He's dead."

"Don't be silly! Of course he's not dead."

"He is, and I know who killed him."

A cold knife sliced through Ray. "What do you mean?"

"I was there. I saw."

"You saw someone kill Adam?"

Philip wedged the stick against the side of his shoe and worked away at the sole. Ray grabbed the stick from him. "What did you see, Philip?"

Philip's face twisted. "I saw him running away, and you running after him, shouting, saying you were going to kill him. And now he's missing."

So that's what the boy thought. It was so ridiculous Ray almost burst out laughing. "Philip, people threaten to kill people all the time. It doesn't mean they really are going to kill them." No answer. "I bet you've said to your friends, 'Stop that or I'll kill you'. Haven't you, eh? And you didn't kill them, did you? I was mad at Adam, that's all."

"Mad at him because he wouldn't do the thing again." Philip couldn't meet his eyes, couldn't look him in the face, just gestured at the marks around his mouth.

"That was all just a bit of fun that got out of hand, that's all."

"He killed me, because you told him to!"

"That wasn't meant to happen." Ray dug in his pockets and pulled out a packet of cigarettes and lit one. He blew a smoke ring. Normally the boys loved to see that, begging to be shown how, but Philip just wafted the smoke away like a prissy queen. "You haven't told anyone, have you?"

Philip shrugged. "What if I have."

The bravado didn't fool Ray for a second. "Because if you do, you'll get into a lot of trouble. Not from me, but from the authorities. Police and the social."

"How could I get in trouble? I didn't do anything wrong!"

Ray sucked hard on his cigarette, and pretended to be weighing his words. "But you did, didn't you, Philip? You took money to do what you did. You agreed to it, and you drank alcohol and took drugs. The police put boys in Borstal for that.

And when you come out, you won't go home, you'll be put in care. That's what happens to boys like you."

"I didn't do anything wrong!" Philip was on his feet, his fists clenched at his sides. "I can prove it!"

"It'll be your word against a lot of grown-ups."

"I've got the film." Philip covered his mouth with his hands, as if he wished he could shovel the words back in again, unsaid.

Ray slowly got to his feet. "You've got what?"

"Nothing."

"Which film?"

"Nothing. I didn't say anything."

"Tell me what you meant." Ray's hands were on Philip's shoulders, shaking him. "Tell me what you meant." The boy's head snapped back and forth; his eyes were wide with terror.

"I stole the film," Philip gasped, eventually.

"Where is it?"

Philip shook his head and suddenly was off, sprinting through the woods. Ray hurtled after him, tripping on tree roots and stumbling over logs, churning up the scent of wild garlic and decay. Philip was fast, but Ray was determined. He launched himself at Philip and tackled him to the ground, pinning him down with his whole weight as Philip tried to fight him off. He clawed at Ray's face and hands as he struggled to hold him still, then Ray's hands were round Philip's throat.

"Tell me where you put that film. Tell me!"

Philip lashed and scratched, his fingers tearing at Ray's hands on his neck. His eyes bulged, black with fear. His legs kicked and bucked, his spine arching. Then suddenly he was still and limp. Ray let go and Philip's head lolled sideways, his tongue poking out, bleeding.

"Philip! Philip!" He shook him. The head rolled in the leaf litter. Ray bent to Philip's face, trying to quiet his breathing so that he could hear. Nothing. Digging his fingers into Philip's neck he felt for a pulse. Nothing. *Shit.*

He had to act fast and get out of there before some nature freak wandered by and wanted to know why there was a dead boy underneath him. Hooking his hands under Philip's armpits, he hefted him up onto his shoulders, and carried him in a fireman's lift back to the camp. There was a rope in the den, left there from when they dragged the wood back to make the shelter. He unwound it now and fastened a noose and tugged it over Philip's head.

As he looked round for a suitable branch to lynch him from, his eye fell on Philip's penknife, half-hidden in the mulch by the campfire. Belt and braces, make sure no one was in any doubt what happened here. Ray took the knife and drew it across Philip's left wrist. Three shallow cuts, one deeper one. That'll do. Now for the final act.

There was a tree nearby that looked climbable. Lots of branches leading like a ladder up the trunk. He tossed the end of the rope over a branch about ten feet up, made a noose on one end, and hauled Philip up by the neck. It was too hard to hold the boy suspended and tie the end of the rope to the branch, so he let Philip swing for a few minutes then let go. Philip plummeted into the leaf litter, face down. Stupid bastard never was any good at tying knots.

Poor Philip. Worried about his friend Adam. Terrified because he thought he was gay. It was too much for him and he killed himself.

Ray collected the cigarette end and put it in his pocket, and scrubbed the ash into the dirt. Swishing a fallen branch over his footprints, he obliterated any sign he'd been there. All that was left was Philip's footprints, his sweater balled on the floor, and Philip himself, swinging from the tree, dead.

Ray walked backwards to the track, sweeping away his footprints as he went. When he got in the car, his hands were shaking so much he could barely start the engine. He eased the car down the track, taking it steady through the muddy patches. His wheels spun in a dip, slurry spraying. His heart banged painfully. He couldn't get stuck here, he had to get away. Eventually the wheels gained traction and he jerked forwards, but he held his breath until the track met the road and he was on firm ground again.

PART EIGHT: 2016

CHAPTER FORTY-SIX

Everything was ready. Kate needed to look the part to play the part, so for the first time in days she showered thoroughly, rather than the cat's lick she'd been making do with, and even smeared on some of her body conditioner. Her old work suit was hanging at the back of the wardrobe. She'd changed shape after having Jessica, and wondered if she'd fit in it, gazing at it doubtfully when she pulled it out. The trousers were a little tight, but she could suck her tummy in. She was doing this for Jessica, she chided herself, she could put up with a pinching waistband. The jacket didn't suit her anymore, but she had a plain cream one that went with the trousers, and a silk sleeveless top in burnt orange to wear underneath. With her hair covered by a blonde bob wig, and makeup covering the worst of her dark circles and tear-ravaged face, she was ready to act the part.

Only when she'd constructed her shell did she feel ready to make the call. Her fingers were shaking and she misdialled, hung up, and dialled again.

"Hello, Eden Grey."

"Hello, Miss Grey, I'm Tara Frere." She'd almost blurted out her real name, only remembering the made-up name at the last minute. She pinched herself; must stay alert.

"How can I help you?"

"I've got a problem that needs a private investigator."

"Can you tell me a bit more?"

"I think it might be industrial espionage."

"Really?" Kate heard the quickening of interest in Eden's voice. John'd told her she'd like that, that missing puppies and cheating husbands were too parochial for Eden. "She thinks she's above all that," he'd said.

"I wondered if you were free today, for me to tell you a little more?" Kate said.

"Today? That's a bit tricky."

Playing hard to get. Pretending she was full up with clients and work, and so if she saw you, you should recognise it as a favour. The illusion of scarcity. Two could play at that game. "I'll ring someone else if you don't have availability," she said, "only someone recommended I try you first."

"I could see you in about half an hour, if you can get here, then?"

"Let me see." Kate pretended to be consulting a diary. "Yes, yes, I can do that. Half an hour?"

Eden Grey gave her directions that she didn't bother to note down: she'd already been to scout out Eden's office. It was a nasty, poky one room affair off the end of the High Street, with a pub in front and a carpark behind. The sort of grubby place she'd expected. Now all she needed to do was persuade Eden to come with her.

Eden's office was better inside than the outside led her to expect. She glanced at the carpet and pale walls, at the light coloured desk and comfortable clients' chairs with a pinch of resentment. This wasn't the seedy hole she'd imagined. It was bright and efficient looking. Eden herself was younger than she anticipated: in her mid-thirties, stylishly dressed and slender. She made a pot of coffee and ushered Kate into a chair, then took her seat behind the desk and cracked open a notebook.

"You intrigued me when you said industrial espionage," Eden said, with a frankness that floored her. "Can you tell me what's been going on?"

"I own a riverside inn," Kate said. "Lovely location, very peaceful; I've been running it as a wedding venue for just over a year. We've got gorgeous gardens for photographs, and the wedding party can literally have the run of the place. It's been doing very well indeed."

"I sense a but," Eden said.

"There have been some problems over the past couple of months. Someone stealing from the guests. Wallets, jewellery, watches, phones, that sort of thing."

"Police involved?"

"I've called them, but they were pretty useless, frankly. And I don't want to make a big fuss about it. I don't want my reputation to be the wedding venue where you lose your wallet."

"And what makes you think it's industrial espionage?"

"I hire in staff for the weddings, and on a couple of occasions I'm sure I've counted one more member of staff than I should have." Kate slid the cup of coffee away from her; the smell was making her feel sick. She should have had something to eat before she came out, but she was too nervous. "I think the extras were from a rival firm, coming in to steal and ruin my reputation."

"Any firm in particular?"

Kate twisted her wedding ring round on her finger. "I had a bit of a run-in with someone just before all this started." She waited until Eden's pen stopped moving and announced, "Can you come in, under cover, and see what's going on?"

Eden tapped the end of her pen against her cheek. "The chances are it's nothing more sinister than a gang of thieves who've spotted an easy opportunity, but I can take a look and advise you on your security."

"That's what I was hoping."

"Have you got a list of all the staff who've worked for you?"

"Yes, I've put all the details in a spreadsheet." Kate hunted around in her bag, hoping it looked convincing. "Drat! I think I've left it in the car." She glanced up at Eden. "I don't suppose you could come and take a look now? Just a preliminary?"

Eden hesitated. "I've got an appointment this afternoon. I must be back for that."

"It's not far. It will take less than an hour to go and come back." Kate played her last card. "Only no one will be there today as we're having a room repainted. It's all back to normal tomorrow. If you're going to go undercover we can't risk any of the staff seeing you."

"OK," Eden said. "Actually, a drive out to the river sounds quite nice."

Eden closed her laptop and picked up her handbag, and the two women went out of the office. Kate surveyed the carpark while Eden locked up, noting where there were people getting into cars, and where there was an old man fumbling with change at the ticket machine.

"I'll get that list for you," Kate said, and trotted off at speed before Eden could say she'd grab it later. Just as she'd hoped, Eden followed her. Kate opened the back seat of the car and pretended to dig through a briefcase. She'd rehearsed this bit over and over in her mind. Now she prayed it worked. "Jump in the front, Eden," she said, as gaily as she could.

"I've got my own car, I can follow you," Eden said.

"If you come with me, I can tell you more about what's been happening."

"I'd prefer to make my own way," Eden said. "Anyway, you'd have to drive me back to Cheltenham. No point making the journey twice."

"I don't mind." The gaiety was starting to wear thin, now. A frown flickered across Eden's face and she started to back away.

"I'll just hop in my car. Meet you at the exit," she said.

Kate plunged her hand into her bag and pulled out the gun. "Don't scream. Now get in the car."

Eden's hands crept up into the 'surrender' position. "What's going on?" she said, quietly.

"Get in the car."

"I don't think so."

The old man was ambling back to his car, a ticket clutched in his fingers. There was no time. Kate raised the gun and smashed it into Eden's face. She caught her as she fell, and bundled her into the back seat, slamming the door shut. Kate scrambled into the driver's seat and jabbed the button to activate the child proof locks. Then she started the engine and drove out of the carpark. Behind her, Eden wasn't moving.

"There, that wasn't so bad, was it?" Kate muttered to herself, as she nosed the car through the traffic and out of town.

CHAPTER FORTY-SEVEN

Eden jolted into consciousness. What the fuck just happened? There was salt tang of blood in her mouth, and her head was about to explode. She eased herself up, groaning at the machete slam into the back of her skull. Her vision was spotted with black holes and she breathed deeply until it cleared. When it felt as though her head was back in its right place on her neck, she pressed her hands on the seat and slowly inched herself into a sitting position.

Her gaze met the back of Tara's head. She was staring straight ahead, gripping the steering wheel so tightly her knuckles looked as though they were carved on a thirteenth century tomb. From the clench in her jaw she was bricking it. Great. Just what she needed, an antsy nutter with a gun.

Slowly, her hand crept to the door and tugged the door handle. Locked. One by one she weighed her options. She'd dropped her handbag in the carpark when she was struck — her phone was in it, so sending a text was out. She could launch herself at Tara and try to wrest control of the car. Not possible now, with cars passing at speed, all she'd do is kill them both. She could strangle her from behind and hope she took her foot off the accelerator, the car drifting slowly to a stand-still. Also dangerous and there was no guarantee Tara wouldn't just stamp on the pedal. Third option, she could talk herself out of it.

"Tara, where are we going?" she asked. Tara jumped and half-turned in her seat. An amateur: there was hope she could negotiate her way out.

"You're awake."

"Yes. Tara, where are we going?"

"I told you. I want you to look at my pub."

"Usually my clients make an appointment. They don't kidnap me."

No reply.

"Tara?"

"Look, stop calling me Tara, OK?" A dark flush spread up her neck.

"Why? Why, Tara?"

"Because that's not my bloody name!"

"What is your name?"

A derisory snort. "Like you care."

"I do care. Tell me who you are and what it is you want," Eden said. "I'm sure we can sort it out."

"My name is Kate Smithson."

"OK, Kate, what is it you want?"

"You don't know who I am, do you?"

"Why don't you tell me."

"You kill my daughter and you don't even remember my name."

Panic surged through her. Kate was too erratic, too emotional. She could get them both killed if she didn't calm down. She needed to take this nice and slow. "I'm sorry, Kate, tell me about your daughter."

"Jessica. She was called Jessica."

Oh shit. Now she knew who Kate was. "It was horrible," Eden said. "Truly terrible. But I didn't have anything to do with it."

"Yes, you did. You were the one the man named. You were the one he wanted."

"He's a very dangerous man, Kate, and he's very angry because I got him put in prison. And it's awful that Jessica died, but you have to understand that it's his fault. He did it."

A sob from the front and the car wobbled across the central line and back again. A car passing in the other direction hooted and flashed its lights.

"What is it you want, Kate?"

"You're going to pay for Jessica."

"What are you going to do, Kate? Kill me? That won't bring Jessica back."

"I'll feel better." The car swerved again as she scrubbed her hand across her face.

"You've got a husband, haven't you? What will he think when he hears what you've done?" Eden said.

"He doesn't care."

"And what about Jessica? Is this what she'd want her mummy to do?"

"She's not here anymore!"

Eden noticed that Kate's voice had weakened. Doubt was creeping in. She curled her fingers into her palms, pressing her nails into the skin to keep herself alert. Keep her talking, help her to think about what she's doing, get her on your side.

"You don't want to go to prison, Kate. It's horrible in there. We can sort this out. Don't make this any worse than it is, it's not too late to go back."

"Shut up!" Kate screamed. "Shut up! Shut up! He said you'd try to talk me out of it."

"Who?"

"John. He understands."

Eden turned to ice. "John? John who?"

"I don't know ... I can't remember..."

"What does he look like, Kate?"

"What do you care?"

Eden persisted. "Tall? Good looking? Smart? Fair haired?" Please God this wasn't happening.

"That's him. He understands. He told me all about you. What to say, what to do, and he was right!" A triumphant note had insinuated itself into Kate's voice and Eden knew to drop it for now. She sank back in the seat and started to hum 'If you're happy and you know it'. Then 'The Wheels on the Bus', 'Twinkle Twinkle Little Star', 'Away in a Manger'. One of these must hit home. One of them had to remind Kate of the little girl she'd lost, and catapult her from rage into grief.

"Stop singing!" The crack was back in her voice. Eden lowered the volume and carried on humming. "Please!"

"Where are we going?"

"To the pub. I've already told you."

"Will John be there?"

"Yes, he says he's looking forward to it."

I bet he is, Eden thought, grimly. They were heading down quiet country lanes now, no other cars around. The road suddenly became bumpy and potholed, a single lane track, the hedges pressing forwards on each side and stroking the car's flanks. Over the tips of the hedges she could make out brown corrugated fields. It was some time since they'd passed a house. Kate took a left turning, and now the road followed the line of the river.

Ahead loomed the outline of a pub and her heart rose for a second, plummeting when she clocked the buddleia sprouting from the guttering and the sheets of steel mesh screwed over the windows. A weathered 'For Sale' sign hung crookedly from a stanchion. Surrounding the pub was a scabby moat of concrete that had once been the carpark. Now it was crazed and veined with weeds.

As the car approached, a man stepped out from the shade in the lee of the pub. Eden's stomach clenched. Hammond. He was watching the car and smiling.

Suddenly, she launched herself at Kate, bringing her fists down on her head. Kate slumped sideways, her foot jammed on the accelerator. Eden jabbed at the door release. She'd have to jump, but the car was going too fast. Hammond was directly ahead, in his immaculate suit and with that leer on his face.

Eden seized the steering wheel and pointed the car at Hammond. It hit him at speed. His body crunched on the bonnet and was tossed aside. She lunged for the door handle, as the car mounted the river bank, flew through the air, and plunged into the river.

CHAPTER FORTY-EIGHT

"Ready?"

Aidan glanced around his flat. The washing up was all done, dried, and put away. There was no laundry sweating in the basket, and no ironing in a heap on the spare bed. Everything was neat and in its place. He could go away and walk back in and not instantly be irritated by things pointing in the wrong direction, by mess, or by chores that had been left undone for days. "Ready," he said.

"Then let's go." Lisa waggled her car keys at him. She'd turned up half an hour before and had stood tutting in the doorway while he did his final checks and put his flat in order.

He picked up his weekend bag. It weighed a ton because he couldn't decide which books to take with him, and had ended up piling all of them in there: *Vanity Fair*, Horace's poems, a history of the Renaissance, a book about the Russian revolution, and the latest academic text on Iron Age archaeology. He grunted when he lifted the bag and Lisa raised an eyebrow.

"It's not a sitting by the pool and reading sort of break," she said. "It's a cliff top walks and hot chocolate type break."

"I know, I just don't like being without something to read," he said. And it had to be the right thing to read. At home he could just grab a volume from the shelf, but on holiday, he might have a yearning to read Latin poetry in translation, but then again might want to dive into some history. He suspected that the holiday cottage, if it contained any books, wouldn't have the sort of books he liked.

He locked up and followed Lisa down to her car. It was a Mazda MX5, petite and fast, like Lisa herself. Her case was already in the boot and he slotted his bag in on top, careful not to squash it in case he bent one of his books. Lisa was already strapped in and the engine running by the time he climbed in. He shoved his seat back as far as it would go, wondering if his long legs would have any sensation in them by the time they got to Devon. He was fastening his seat belt as Lisa pulled away.

"It's ages since I've been to Brixham," Lisa said. "There are lovely walks round the cliffs."

"Sounds wonderful," Aidan said. What were Mandy and Trev up to at this moment, he wondered? They were still waiting to get the OK to excavate the Iron Age graves, and he was anxious in case the police cleared the site while he was away. He didn't want Mandy and Trev up there on their own: he was the one who was called in to look at them, it should be him excavating. He'd call Mandy as soon as they got to the cottage, make sure everything was all going fine.

They cleared the M5 in good time and soon were in a line of traffic wending its way to Paignton, then followed the road to Brixham, passing signs for steam railways and Agatha Christie's house. The streets narrowed and then they were winding round the harbour and up a steep road. Lisa headed out along the coast road and pulled into the driveway of a stone cottage that looked out over the sea to Torquay.

"This is it," she said, killing the car's engine. She peered through the windscreen at the cottage. "Cute."

It was an attractive cottage with a cheerful red front door and window boxes crammed with spring bulbs. Lisa punched a code into a key box mounted on the wall, took out the key and let them in. The kitchen and sitting room were decorated in cream with fresh paintwork and crisp curtains. Aidan relaxed. He'd worried that it would be dingy and have that old bathwater smell of holiday cottages. Or that it would be an obvious romantic shag pad with silk sheets, satin curtains and a whirlpool bath for two.

"It's great," he said.

His phone started ringing when his hands were full with their luggage. By the time he'd lugged it inside, the phone had gone to voicemail. For a moment, he thought about ignoring it, then worried it was Trev or Mandy and a problem with the dig. He dumped the bags in the hall and listened to his voicemail. It was Trev. His heart jumped when he heard his voice.

"Aidan. It's Trev here. Call me back straight away. I'll keep trying you until I get you."

Shit. Something drastic must've happened. What could it be that would make Trev sound so serious? A complete skeleton but they managed to smash the skull? That could do it, though it wasn't unknown for bones to crumble as you levered them out. Or maybe the conservation people had sent in the bulldozers and the graves had been pulverised.

He dialled Trev's number and listened to it ringing. He didn't get a chance to speak before Trev piled in. "Aidan, thank goodness you've called me back. Listen, mate, there's all hell let loose here. You've got to come back."

"What it is? What's happened? Is it the skeletons?"

"What? Skeletons? No, it's Eden."

"What about Eden?"

"She's ... look, she was in a car that's gone into the river. It doesn't look good, mate. I'm sorry."

CHAPTER FORTY-NINE

Miranda Tyson flashed her ID and was buzzed into the building. "I'm here to see Detective Inspector Ritter," she said. "He said he'd meet me here."

She was shown into a soft interview room. It was carpeted in dark brown but the walls were cream. A couple of analgesic prints: a bowl of flowers, a Victorian cottage with smoke chuffing out of the chimney. Bucolic idealism; she bet the reality of life for the inhabitants of those dreamy cottages was much harsher. There was a table in the middle of the room, with four chairs with padded seats. Comfortable. Not like the cement floors and metal tables and chairs she was used to. And they certainly didn't have prints on the walls: nothing that could be used as a weapon by whatever little bastard you'd dragged in there.

She plonked her handbag on the table and paced the room until Ritter came in. His suit was crumpled and there were flecks of dandruff on his shoulders. He carried with him the smell of fresh smoke. Her nostrils twitched. She'd had a cigarette in the carpark before she came in and now she could do with another.

"Miranda Tyson?" Ritter said, briefly offering his hand. His was cold and clammy. He pulled out a chair and sat down, placing a cardboard folder on the table in front of him.

Miranda took a seat opposite. "How's it going?"

"Not well," Ritter said. He flipped open the folder and took out a photograph. "Can you tell me, do you know this man?"

Miranda picked up the photo. It was a full colour crime scene picture of a man lying dead on the ground. He had extensive injuries and a lake of blood around his head, but even so she recognised him. A mixture of revulsion and elation went through her. "This man is John Hammond. I led the team that put him away a few years ago."

"He escaped a couple of weeks ago, after tear gas was put in a children's attraction in Cheltenham and killed a girl," Ritter said. "We believe that he was behind it."

"Yes," Miranda said. "That's his way of doing business." She put the photo down.

After all this time, Hammond was dead. She wanted to jig around the room shouting, "Hallelujah!" and simultaneously wanted to fall to her knees and give thanks for her deliverance. Now he was dead, no one knew how she'd helped him, how she'd connived at his pursuit of Eden Grey.

"And you know this woman?" As if he'd read her thoughts, Ritter placed in front of her a photo of Eden. Not a very good photo, as Eden was turning away, not wanting to be photographed. Good girl, she'd absorbed every second of her training, every trick, every defence, everything that would keep her alive. Except.

"What happened?" Miranda asked.

"Do you know her?"

"I knew her as Jackie Black. She was a deep cover officer in my team. She lived with Hammond's gang for two years, was instrumental in getting him sent down." Miranda licked her lips. "But she was outed as an undercover officer and needed protection. Hammond's web is wide. So she was furnished with a new identity as Eden Grey, and she came here to make a new life."

Not that the new life lasted long. A worm of guilt crawled in her stomach.

"What happened?" Miranda asked again.

"As far as we can work out, the mother of the child that was killed in the tear gas attack kidnapped Eden. A witness saw something odd in a carpark near Eden's office. They didn't understand what they'd seen at the time, but came forward when we appealed for witnesses. CCTV in the vicinity backs up their story, and we found Eden's handbag in the carpark. This woman, Kate Smithson, then drove to a derelict pub by the river where John Hammond was waiting. We're not sure how Hammond knew Kate, but we have several incoming calls from different unknown and unregistered numbers to Kate's phone in the days before this happened."

"Cell tower analysis?"

"All the calls were made from different locations."

"That's Hammond," Miranda said. "He knows how to avoid leaving a pattern."

"We don't know quite what happened and why, but it seems the car went out of control, hit Hammond, killing him, and then plunged into the river," Ritter said. "We've retrieved the car, but it was empty."

"No one strapped in the driver's seat?"

"No. So they got out somehow, but…" He left the word hanging. "Last night a body was found further down the river. It was caught in the weeds."

"And you want me to identify it?"

"Please." Ritter coughed. "Eden Grey's boyfriend is also here. He wants to try and help, but frankly —"

"I understand." Miranda rose. "Let's get this over with."

Ritter scooped the photos back into the file and opened the door for her. Miranda stalked out, her head held high. Her pulse was fast, she could feel it thumping at the base of her throat. She always hated viewing the body. She'd seen plenty over the years, but it was always the same, her heart banging so hard she thought everyone could hear it.

There was a man waiting on a chair in the corridor. Ritter stopped in front of him. "Aidan Fox, this is Miranda Tyson. Miranda worked with Eden when she worked undercover." He gave Miranda a meaningful glance. "This is Eden's boyfriend."

She looked him over. A handsome bugger when he wasn't crucified by grief. Typical Eden, she always picked the lookers. This one was tall, dark haired, in a well-fitting suit. Clean shaven. She imaged him going through the motions of washing, dressing, shaving, clinging to the ritual of everyday just to keep himself from falling to pieces.

She held out her hand. "It's not over till it's over," she said. "Don't run towards trouble."

"That's the kind of thing Eden would say," he said.

"How are you bearing up?"

"The past few days ... waiting ... it's been a nightmare."

"I know," she said. "The not knowing is the worst bit."

"I keep on thinking, what if it's not her? And that feels good for a moment, like a scrap of hope, and then I think, if it's not her, where the hell is she? But then if it is her..." His voice trailed away. "If only I hadn't left," he said, almost to himself.

"None of this is anyone's fault, apart from that bastard Hammond," she said. She went to rub his back to comfort him but he flinched away.

A man in green scrubs came to get them. "Ready?"

She looked at Aidan. He was grey and shaking. He unfolded himself from the chair. "Ready," he said.

They were shown into a viewing room. She knew that was to protect them from the smell. A body that had been in the water for days was not pleasant. There was a window set into one wall of the small room, the curtains closed. Ritter hovered in one corner, determined not to influence them either way. Miranda and Aidan stood side by side at the window and she told the attendant they were ready. He opened the curtains and they saw a figure lying prone, a white sheet folded back from the face and a blanket protecting the rest of the body.

"Take your time and look carefully," the attendant said.

"It looks like her," Aidan said, "but I can't tell."

"Take your time," the attendant said again.

She stared and stared. Could it be her? The figure was the right height, the same age, the same dark hair. But the days in the water had been cruel. She'd seen worse, but the face was bloated, the features distorted.

Aidan smothered a sob. "I can't tell. It looks like her, but I can't tell." He turned to her, hopelessly.

She shook her head. "I can't say for definite," she said. "I'm sorry."

EPILOGUE

Dead again. This was becoming a habit. Eden had followed the reports of her disappearance and suspected death online in the local news, amused that her story was after the charity bike rides and late bin collections. She hadn't made the national news, but just to be safe she'd cropped her hair and dyed it mucky blonde.

So it was with a new identity she made her way through the lych-gate. A path led to the church door, deep grooves showing where pushchairs and wheelchairs had done battle with the gravel. The church itself was a chequerboard of flints, glinting in the sun. She left the path and headed for the verdant, cool churchyard. There were yews and holly dotted about, and lots of ramshackle headstones, cracked, broken and leaning. Some of the graves dipped in the middle; others were humped up and blanketed with daffodils. She walked past these old graves, past the church, to where a new field had been tacked on at the back. It was more regimented here: one side for buried cremations; an area set aside for dead children; then lines of graves and headstones.

The sun warmed her hair as she paced the lines of graves, reading the inscriptions. There didn't seem to be an order to the dates: burials from twenty years ago lay next to those from last year. She'd have to read them all to find the one she wanted. Behind her, the church bells started ringing, summoning worshippers to the Good Friday service.

Her grave was towards the back, in a line with only a handful of neighbours. She wondered if that was deliberate: separate in death as in life. The mound was grassed over, and there was a stark black granite headstone bearing her real name, with a container in front for flowers. There were some old stems in there: frazzled carnations. She wondered how long they'd been there, if they'd been placed to mark her birthday, or if they were evidence of ongoing grief.

She hunkered down at the grave and pulled out the stems, folding the slimy ends back onto the stalks. She stowed them in a compost bin to the side of the churchyard and returned to the grave. The grave looked more respectable somehow, tidier.

So this was where she was buried. It was odd, standing there, seeing her own memorial. What was under her feet? A weighted coffin, or a Jane Doe standing in for Sara White, undercover officer killed in the line of duty? Eden twisted her fingers together and fought tears. Tears that it was over at last. Hammond was dead and she could come out of the shadows, go back to her old life if she wished. Tears also for those left behind: Judy, Mandy, Trev and Aidan. Aidan. She wondered how he was coping. If Lisa was taking care of him. And she wept for her old self, knowing in her heart that Sara White was dead and could never be resurrected. Too much had happened, and she'd changed too much for that.

After a while she dried her eyes and thought about what to do next. The world was open to her, she could do anything, go anywhere, be anyone she wished. Yet what she really wanted was a cup of tea and a biscuit and her dad chuntering on about slugs on his allotment. As if she'd conjured him up, a figure came through the gate at the end of the field, and made its way slowly across the grass.

She knew that walk, the slightly bowed legs, the stoop. His hair was the same pepper and salt she remembered. And that jacket! He got it for his birthday years ago. Evidently it was still his favourite. He was looking away, embarrassed to be sharing the graveyard with another person; walking slowly and hoping the stranger would go and leave him in peace.

She waited until he was a few yards away before she turned to face him fully.

"Hello, Dad," she said softly, watching the disbelief chase across his face. He stumbled, and held out his arms. She ran to him, tears flying from her eyes. "I've come home."

A NOTE TO THE READER

Dear Reader,

Thank you for reading *Devil's Chimney*, the third Eden Grey conspiracy thriller. I do hope that you enjoyed Eden's latest adventure.

To a large extent, *Devil's Chimney* is about grief, and in the way that life does sometimes imitate art, I experienced the loss of several people close to me while I was writing it. This book is dedicated to the memory of Sheila Ferrari – a true inspiration not just to me, but also to the hundreds of people whose lives she touched.

Readers often ask me where I get the ideas for my novels, and for *Devil's Chimney*, historical child abuse allegations reported in the news stirred in me a memory from school. A policeman came in to speak to all of us, and all the teachers were sent out. He asked if anyone knew a boy who had been found dead in the woods on the outskirts of town, and he assured us that whatever we told him, we would not be in any trouble. I didn't know the boy, but some of my classmates did, and they whispered that the child was a 'rent boy', doing 'rude' things with men for money. Looking back on it, I was (and still am) horrified by the attitude of the time, which very much blamed the victim, and knew that I had to write about it.

Before any of my novels is sent out into the world, I pass it to a handful of trusted friends to read and critique, and so my thanks to Kelly, Sara Jane, and Clare for your feedback and suggestions regarding *Devil's Chimney*.

Reviews of novels and word of mouth recommendations are essential to novelists these days, so if you enjoyed reading

Devil's Chimney, I should be very grateful if you could spare a moment to write a review of it on **Amazon** or **Goodreads**. Word of mouth recommendations are also very important, so please tell your friends!

I always love hearing from readers. You can contact me **via my website**, where you'll find more information about what I'm writing and get a behind the scenes look at what it's like being a crime writer. If you'd prefer to email me directly, you'll find me at **info@kimfleet.com**. I always write back. I'm also on social media, and you can connect with me **on Twitter** and **Instagram**.

Thank you again for reading *Devil's Chimney*, and I hope we'll meet again.

With best wishes,

Kim Fleet

www.kimfleet.com

Sapere Books is an exciting new publisher of brilliant fiction and popular history.

To find out more about our latest releases and our monthly bargain books visit our website:
saperebooks.com

Printed in Great Britain
by Amazon

69455061R00182